Magic Seeds

A NOVEL BY

V. S. NAIPAUL

PICADOR

First published 2004 by Picador
an imprint of Pan Macmillan Ltd
Pan Macmillan, 20 New Wharf Road, London N1 9RR
Basingstoke and Oxford
Associated companies throughout the world
www.panmacmillan.com

ISBN 0 330 48520 2 HB
ISBN 0 330 48522 9 TPB

1 3 5 7 9 8 6 4 2

A CIP catalogue record for this book is available from the British Library.

Typeset by Intype Libra Ltd
Printed and bound in Great Britain by
Mackays of Chatham plc, Chatham, Kent

LATER – IN THE teak forest, in the first camp, when during his first night on sentry duty he had found himself for periods wishing only to cry, and when with the relief of dawn there had also come the amazing cry of a far-off peacock, the cry a peacock makes in the early morning after it has had its first drink of water at some forest pool: a raucous, tearing cry that should have spoken of a world refreshed and re-made but seemed after the long bad night to speak only of everything lost, man, bird, forest, world; and then, when that camp was a romantic memory, during the numbing guerrilla years, going on and on, in forest, village, small town, when to travel about in disguise had often appeared to be an end in itself and it was possible for much of the day to forget what the purpose of the disguise was, when he had felt himself decaying intellectually, felt bits of his personality breaking off; and then in the jail, with its blessed order, its fixed time-table, its protecting rules, the renewal it offered – later it was possible to work out the stages by which he had moved from what he would have considered the real world to all the subsequent areas of unreality: moving as it were from one sealed chamber of the spirit to another.

ONE

The Rose-Sellers

IT HAD BEGUN many years before, in Berlin. Another world. He was living there in a temporary, half-and-half way with his sister Sarojini. After Africa it had been a great refreshment, this new kind of protected life, being almost a tourist, without demands and without anxiety. It had to end, of course; and it began to end the day Sarojini said to him, 'You've been here for six months. I may not be able to get your visa renewed again. You know what that means. You may not be able to stay here. That's the way the world is made. You can't object to it. You've got to start thinking of moving on. Do you have any idea of where you can go? Is there anything you feel you want to do?'

Willie said, 'I know about the visa. I've been thinking about it.'

Sarojini said, 'I know your kind of thinking. It means putting something to the back of your mind.'

Willie said, 'I don't see what I can do. I don't know where I can go.'

'You've never felt there was anything for you to do. You've

never understood that men have to make the world for themselves.'

'You're right.'

'Don't talk to me like that. That's the way the oppressor class thinks. They've just got to sit tight, and the world will continue to be all right for them.'

Willie said, 'It doesn't help me when you twist things. You know very well what I mean. I feel a bad hand was dealt me. What could I have done in India? What could I have done in England in 1957 or 1958? Or in Africa?'

'Eighteen years in Africa. Your poor wife. She thought she was getting a man. She should have talked to me.'

Willie said, 'I was always someone on the outside. I still am. What can I do here in Berlin?'

'You were on the outside because you wanted to be. You've always preferred to hide. It's the colonial psychosis, the caste psychosis. You inherited it from your father. You were in Africa for eighteen years. There was a great guerrilla war there. Didn't you know?'

'It was always far away. It was a secret war, until the very end.'

'It was a glorious war. At least in the beginning. When you think about it, it can bring tears to the eyes. A poor and helpless people, slaves in their own land, starting from scratch in every way. What did you do? Did you seek them out? Did you join them? Did you help them? That was a big enough cause to anyone looking for a cause. But no. You stayed in your estate house with your lovely little half-white wife and pulled the pillow over your ears and hoped that no bad black freedom fighter was going to come in the night with a gun and heavy boots and frighten you.'

'It wasn't like that, Sarojini. In my heart of hearts I was always on the Africans' side, but I didn't have a war to go to.'

'If everybody had said that, there would never have been any revolution anywhere. We all have wars to go to.'

They were in a café in the Knesebeckstrasse. In the winter it had been warm and steamy and civilized with its student waiters and waitresses and welcoming to Willie. Now in late summer it was stale and oppressive, its rituals too well known, a reminder to Willie – in spite of what Sarojini said – of time passing fruitlessly by, calling up the mysterious sonnet they had had to learn by heart in the mission school. *And yet this time removed was summer's time . . .*

A young Tamil man came in selling long-stemmed red roses. Sarojini made a small gesture with her hand and began to look in her bag. The Tamil came and held the roses to them but his eyes made no contact with theirs. He claimed no kinship with them. He was self-possessed, the rose-seller, full of the idea of his own worth. Willie, not looking at the man's face, concentrating on his brown trousers (made by tailors far away) and the too-big gold-plated watch and wristlet (perhaps not really gold) on his hairy wrist, saw that in his own setting the rose-seller would have been someone of no account, someone unseeable. Here, in a setting which perhaps he understood as little as Willie did, a setting which perhaps he had not yet learned to see, he was like a man taken out of himself. He had become someone else.

Willie had met a man like that one day, some weeks before, when he had gone out on his own. He had stopped outside a

South Indian restaurant, without customers, with a few flies crawling on the plate-glass windows, above the potted plants and the display plates of rice and dosas, and with small amateurish-looking waiters (perhaps not really waiters, perhaps something else, perhaps electricians or accountants illegally arrived) lurking in the interior gloom against the cheap glitter of somebody's idea of oriental decoration. An Indian or Tamil man had come up to Willie then. Soft-bodied, but not fat, with a broad soft face, and with a flat grey cap marked with thin blue lines in a wide check pattern, like the 'Kangol' golfer's caps that Willie remembered seeing advertised on the back pages of the early Penguin books: perhaps the style had come to the man from those old advertisements.

The man began to talk to Willie about the great guerrilla war to come. Willie was interested, even friendly. He liked the soft, smiling face. He was held by the flat cap. He liked the conspiratorial talk, the idea it carried of a world about to be astonished. But when the man began to talk of the great need for money, when this talk became insistent, Willie became worried, then frightened, and he began to back away from the restaurant window with the trapped, drowsy flies. And even while the man still appeared to smile there came from his soft lips a long and harsh and profound religious curse delivered in Tamil, which Willie still half understood, at the end of which the man's smile had gone and his face below the blue-checked golf cap had twisted into a terrible hate.

It unsettled Willie, the sudden use of Tamil, the ancient religious curse into which the man had put all his religious faith, the deep and abrupt hate, like a knife thrust. Willie didn't tell Sarojini about the meeting with this man. This habit of keeping things to himself had been with him since childhood, at home and at school; it had developed during his time in London, and had become an absolute part of his nature during the eighteen years he had spent in Africa, when he had had to hide so many obvious things from himself. He allowed people to tell him things he knew very well, and he did so not out of deviousness, not out of any settled plan, but out of a wish not to offend, to let things run on smoothly.

Sarojini, now, lay the rose beside her plate. She followed the rose-seller with her eyes as he walked between the tables. When he went out again she said to Willie, 'I don't know what you feel about that man. But he is worth far more than you.'

Willie said, 'I'm sure.'

'Don't irritate me. That smart way of talking may work with outsiders. It doesn't work with me. Do you know why that man is worth more than you? He has found his war. He could have hidden from it. He could have said he had other things to do. He could have said he had a life to live. He could have said, "I'm in Berlin. It's cost me a lot to get here. All the false papers and visas and hiding. But now that's done. I've got away from home and all that I was. I will pretend to be part of this rich new place. I will watch television and get to know the foreign programmes and start to think that they are really mine. I will go to the KDW and eat at the restaurants. I will learn to drink whisky and wine, and soon I will be counting my money and driving my car and I will feel that I am like the people in the advertisements. I will find that, really, it wasn't hard at all to change worlds, and I will feel that that was the way it was meant to be for all of us." He could have thought in that false and shameful way. But he saw he had a war. Did you notice? He never looked at us. Of course he knew who we were. He knew we were close to him, but he looked down on us. He thought we were among the pretenders.'

Willie said, 'Perhaps he was ashamed, being a Tamil and selling roses to these people and being seen by us.'

'He didn't look ashamed. He had the look of a man with a cause, the look of a man apart. It's something you might have noticed in Africa, if you had learned to look. This man's selling roses here, but those roses are being turned to guns somewhere else far away. It's how revolutions are made. I've been to some of their camps. Wolf and I are working on a film about them. We'll soon be hearing a lot more about them. There is no more disciplined guerrilla army in the world. They are quite ferocious, quite ugly. And if you knew more about your own history you would understand what a miracle that is.'

* * *

ANOTHER DAY, in the zoo, in the terrible smell of captive and idle wild animals, she said, 'I have to talk to you about history. Otherwise you will think I am mad, like our mother's uncle. All the history you and people like you know about yourself comes from a British textbook written by a nineteenth-century English inspector of schools in India called Roper Lethbridge. Did you know that? It was the first big school history book in India and it was published in the 1880s by the British firm of Macmillan. That makes it just twenty years or so after the Mutiny, and of course it was an imperialist work and it was also meant to make money. But it was also a work of some learning in the British way and it was a success. In all the centuries before in India there had been nothing like it, no system of education like that, no training in that kind of history. Roper Lethbridge went into many editions and it gave us many of the ideas we still have about ourselves. One of the most important of those ideas was that in India there were servile races, people born to be slaves, and there were martial races. The martial races were fine, the servile races were not. You and I half belong to the servile races. I am sure you know that. I am sure you half accept that. That is why you have lived as you have lived. The Tamils selling roses in Berlin belong wholly to the servile races. That idea would have been impressed on them in all kinds of ways. And that British idea about the servile and the martial races of India is utterly wrong. The British East India Company army in the north of India was a Hindu army of the upper castes. This was the army that pushed the boundaries of the British Empire almost to Afghanistan. But after the great Mutiny of 1857 that Hindu army was degraded. Further military opportunities were denied them. So the warriors who had won the empire became servile in British propaganda, and the frontier people they had conquered just before the Mutiny became the martial ones. It is how imperialisms work. It is what happens to captive people. And since in India we have no idea of history we quickly forget our past and always believe what we are told. As for the Tamils in the south, they became dirt in the new British dispensation. They were dark and unwarlike, good only for labour. They were shipped off as serfs to the plantations in Malaya and Ceylon and elsewhere. Those Tamils selling roses in Berlin in order to buy guns have thrown off a great weight of history and propaganda. They have made themselves a truly martial people, and they have done so against the odds. You must respect them, Willie.'

And Willie listened in his blank way, in the bad smell of the unhappy animals in the zoo, and said nothing. Sarojini was his sister. No one in the world understood him so well. She understood every corner of his fantasies; she understood everything of his life in England and Africa, though for those twenty years they had met only once. He felt that, without words passing between them, she, who had developed in so many ways, might have understood even the physical details of such sexual life as he had had. Nothing was hidden from her; and even when she was at her most revolutionary and ordinary and hectoring, saying things she had said many times before, she could by an extra phrase here and there, calling up aspects of their special shared past, start touching things in him that he would have preferred to forget.

He said nothing when she spoke, but dismissed nothing that she said. Gradually in Berlin he noticed something about her which he had never noticed before. Though her talk never ceased to be about injustice and cruelty and the need for revolution, though she played easily with tableaux of blood and bones in five continents, she was strangely serene. She had lost the edginess and aggression which she had had in the early days of her life. She had been rotting in the family ashram, with nothing but piety and subservience to look forward to; and for many years after she had left, that dreadful ashram life, offering simple and needy people counterfeit cures for everything, was still close to her, as something to which she might have to return if things turned out badly with Wolf.

She didn't have that anxiety now. Just as she had learned how to dress for a cold climate, and had made herself attractive (the days of cardigan and woollen socks with a sari had been left far behind), so travel and study and the politics of revolution, and her easy half-and-half life with the undemanding photographer, appeared to have given her a complete intellectual system. Nothing surprised or wounded her now. Her world view was able to absorb everything: political murders in Guatemala, Islamic revolution in Iran, caste riots in India, and even the petty theft practised as a matter of shop-keeping habit or principle by the wine-shop man in Berlin when he delivered to the flat, two or three bottles always short or changed, the prices altered in complicated, baffling ways.

She would say, 'This is what happens in West Berlin. They are at the end of an air corridor, and everything runs on a subsidy. So their energy goes on this kind of petty theft. It is the great failing of the West. They will find out.'

Sarojini herself, through her photographer, lived on a subsidy from some West German government agency. So she knew what she was talking about; and she was easy.

She would say, when the new box of wine and beer came, 'Let's see what the scoundrel is getting up to this time.'

The Sarojini he had left behind at home twenty or more years before could never have done anything like this. And it was to this serenity of hers, this new elegance of language, that he found himself responding more and more in Berlin. He regarded his sister with wonder. It amazed and thrilled him that she was his sister. After six months with her – they had never been together so long as adults – the world began to change for him. Just as he felt she could enter all his emotions, and even his sexual needs, so he began to enter her way of looking. There was a logic and order in everything she said.

And he saw, what he felt now he had always understood deep

down but had never accepted, that there were the two worlds Sarojini spoke about. One world was ordered, settled, its wars fought. In this world without war or real danger people had been simplified. They looked at television and found their community; they ate and drank approved things; and they counted their money. In the other world people were more frantic. They were desperate to enter the simpler, ordered world. But while they stayed outside a hundred loyalties, the residue of old history tied them down; a hundred little wars filled them with hate and dissipated their energies. In the free and busy air of West Berlin everything looked easy. But not far away there was an artificial border, and beyond that border there was constriction, and another kind of person. Weeds and sometimes trees grew on the old ruins of big buildings; everywhere shrapnel and shell had dug into stone and stucco.

The two worlds co-existed. It was foolish to pretend otherwise. He was clear in his own mind now to which world he belonged. It had seemed natural to him twenty and more years ago, at home, to want to hide. Now all that had followed from that wish seemed to him shameful. His half-life in London; and then all his life in Africa, that life when he was permanently in semi-hiding, gauging his success by the fact that in his second-class, semi-Portuguese group he didn't particularly stand out, and was 'passing', all that life seemed shameful.

One day Sarojini brought a copy of the *Herald Tribune* to the flat. The paper was folded to show a particular story. She passed it to him and said, 'It's about the place you used to live.'

He said, 'Please don't show me. I've told you.'

'You must start looking.'

He took the paper and said to himself, speaking the name of

his wife, 'Ana, forgive me.' He hardly read the words of the story. He didn't need to. He lived it all in his mind. The civil war had become truly bloody. No movement of armies: only raiders from across the frontier coming to burn and kill and terrorise and then going back. There was a photograph of white concrete buildings with their roofs burnt off and with smoke marks outlining empty windows: the simple architecture of rural settler Africa already a ruin. He thought of the roads he knew, the blue rock cones, the little town on the coast. They had all pretended that the world had been made safe; but deep down they all knew that the war was coming, and that one day the roads would disappear.

One day, at the beginning of the insurgency, they had played this game at their Sunday lunch. Let us assume, they said, that we have cut off the world. Let us imagine what it would be like living here with nothing coming in. First, of course, the cars would go. Then there would be no medicines. Then there would be no cloth. There would be no light. So, at the lunch, with the boys in uniform, and the four-wheel drives in the sandy yard, they had played the game, imagining deprivation. And it had all come to pass.

Willie, full of shame in Berlin at the thought of his behaviour in Africa, thought, 'I mustn't hide any longer. Sarojini is right.'

But, following old habit, he didn't tell her what he was thinking.

* * *

THEY WERE WALKING one afternoon below the trees in one of the great shopping avenues. Willie stopped in front of the

Patrick Hellmann shop to look at the Armani clothes in the window. Twenty years before he had known nothing about clothes, had no eye for cloth or cut; now it was different.

Sarojini said, 'Who would you say is the most important person in the world?'

Willie said, 'Armani is pretty great, but I don't think you want me to say that. You want me to say something else?'

'Try.'

'Ronald Reagan.'

'I thought you would say that.'

Willie said, 'I said it to provoke you.'

'No, no. I think you really believe it. But I don't mean powerful. I mean important. Does the name Kandapalli Seetaramiah mean anything to you?'

'Is he the most important man?'

'An important man is not necessarily a powerful man. Lenin in 1915 or 1916 wasn't a powerful man. An important man in my book is someone who is going to bend the course of history. When, in a hundred years, the definitive history of twentieth-century revolution comes to be written, and various ethnocentric prejudices have disappeared, Kandapalli will be up there with Lenin and Mao. Of that I have no doubt. And you haven't even heard of him. I know.'

'Is he part of the Tamil movement?'

'He's not a Tamil. But Kandapalli and the Tamil movement are parts of the same regenerative process in our world. If only I could get you to believe in that process you will be a changed man.'

Willie said, 'I know nothing of French history apart from the storming of the Bastille. But I still have an idea of Napoleon. I am sure I'll understand about Kandapalli if you tell me.'

'I wonder. Kandapalli's towering importance as a revolutionary is that he did away with the Lin-Piao line.'

Willie said, 'You are going too fast for me.'

'You are being provocative. You are pretending. You must know about Lin-Piao. The whole world knows about Lin-Piao. He gave us the idea of liquidating the class enemy. It was simple and exciting in the beginning and it seemed the way ahead. In India we also liked it because it came from China and we thought it put us right up there with the Chinese. In fact it destroyed the revolution. The Lin-Piao line turned the revolution into middle-class theatre. Young middle-class exhibitionists in the towns putting on peasant clothes and staining their skin with walnut juice and going out to join the gangs and thinking that revolution meant killing policemen. The police had no trouble in wiping them out. People in that kind of movement always underestimate the police, I don't know why. I suppose it's because they think a little too highly of themselves.

'All of this happened while you were in Africa, where you were witnessing a real war. Afterwards here people would say that we had lost a whole generation of brilliant young revolutionaries and would never be able to replace them. I felt like that myself, and was cast down for many months. Intellectual advance is slow in India. I don't have to tell you that. The landless labourer moves to the town, and his son perhaps becomes a clerk. The clerk's son perhaps gets a higher education, and then his son becomes a doctor or a scientist. And so we grieved. It had taken generations to create that pool of revolutionary talent, and the police in a short time had destroyed the struggle and intellectual development of fifty or sixty years. It was terrible to think about.

'I will tell you what it felt like. Sometimes in a storm beautiful old trees are uprooted. You don't know what to do. The readiest emotion is anger. You start looking for an enemy. And then you very quickly understand that anger, comforting as it is, is useless, that there is nothing or no one to be angry against. You have to find other ways of dealing with your loss. I was in that empty, unhappy mood when I heard of Kandapalli. I don't actually think I had heard of him before. He proclaimed a new revolution. He said that the talk of the lost generation of brilliant revolutionaries was sentimental rubbish. They were not particularly brilliant or well-educated or revolutionary. If they were they would not have fallen for the foolish Lin-Piao line. No, Kandapalli said, all that had happened was that we had had the good fortune to lose a generation of half-educated, self-centred fools.

'This was wounding for me. Wolf and I had done a lot of work with the revolutionaries. We knew some of them personally. But the brutality of Kandapalli's words made me think of certain things I had noticed but put to one side. I thought of the man who had come to the hotel to see us. He was absurdly vain. He wanted us to know how well connected he was in the world outside. When we offered him a drink he asked, pointedly, for a treble of imported whisky. In those days imported whisky was three or four times the price of Indian. He was asking for something extremely expensive, and then with something like self-satisfaction he studied our faces to see how we were reacting. I thought he was contemptible, but we of course were trained to control our faces. And of course the treble whisky was too much for him.

'I thought of that and other things, and then, from being wounded by Kandapalli's words, I was dazzled by the brilliance and simplicity of his analysis. He proclaimed the death of the Lin-Piao line. Instead, he announced the Mass Line. Revolution was to come from below, from the village, from the people. There was to be no place in this movement for middle-class masqueraders. And – would you believe it? – out of the ruins of that earlier, false revolution he has already set going a true revolution. He has liberated large areas. He does not court publicity, unlike the earlier people.

'It was very hard for us to get to meet him. The couriers were suspicious. There was a relay of them. They wanted to have nothing to do with us. In the end we walked for many days in the forest. I thought we were going nowhere. But at last one afternoon, nearly time for us to camp for the night, we came to a small clearing in the forest. The sunlight fell beautifully on a long mud hut with a grass roof. In front there was a half-harvested mustard field. This was Kandapalli's headquarters. One of them. After all the drama, we found a simple man. He was short and dark. A primary school teacher, without qualifications. A man from Warangal. Nobody in a town would have noticed him. Warangal is one of the hottest places in India, and when he started talking about the poor his eyes filled with tears and he trembled.'

* * *

THIS WAS HOW, in the late summer in Berlin, a new kind of emotional life came to Willie.

Sarojini said, 'Every morning when you get up you must

think not only of yourself but of others. Think of something that's close to you here. Think of East Berlin, and the overgrown ruins, and the shell-marks from 1945 on the walls, and the people today all looking down as they walk. Think of where you've been in Africa. You might want to forget poor Ana, but think of the war there. It's going on now. Think of your house. Try to imagine Kandapalli in the forest. These are all real places with real people.'

Another day she said, 'I was awful to you twenty years ago. I rebuked you too much. I was foolish. I knew very little. I had read very little. I just knew our mother's story and I knew about our mother's radical uncle. I know now that you were no different from Mahatma Gandhi, and couldn't help being what you were.'

Willie said, 'Oh, goodness. Gandhi – that would never have occurred to me. He's too far away from me.'

'I thought it would surprise you. But it's true. When he was eighteen or nineteen Gandhi came to England to study law. In London he was like a sleepwalker. He had no means of understanding the great city. He hardly knew what he was looking at. He had no idea of the architecture or the museums, no idea of the great writers and politicians who were hidden in the city of the 1890s. I don't think he went to a play. All he could think of was his law studies and his vegetarian food and cutting his own hair. Just as Vishnu was floating on the primeval ocean of non-being, so Gandhi in London in 1890 was floating on an ocean of not-seeing and not-knowing. At the end of three years of this half-life or quarter-life he became dreadfully depressed. He felt he needed help. There was a Conservative member of parliament who had a reputation of being interested in Indians.

This was the only person Gandhi felt he could turn to. He wrote to him and went to see him. He tried to explain his depression, and after a short while the M.P. said, "I know what your problem is. You know nothing about India. You know nothing of the history of India." He recommended some imperialist histories. I am not sure that Gandhi read them. He wanted practical help. He didn't want to be told to read a history book. Don't you feel you can see yourself a little bit in that young Gandhi?'

Willie said, 'How do you know this about Gandhi and the M.P.? It was a long time ago. Who told you?'

'He wrote his autobiography in the 1920s. A remarkable book. Very simple, very fast, very honest. A book without boasting. A book so true that every young Indian or old Indian can see himself in its pages. There's no other book like it in India. It would be a modern Indian epic if people read it. But people don't. They feel they don't need to. They feel they know it all. They don't have to find out. It's the Indian way. I didn't even know about the autobiography. It was Wolf who first asked me whether I had read it. This was when he'd just come to the ashram at home. He was shocked when he found I didn't know about it. I have read it two or three times now. It's so easy to read, such a good story, that you read on and on, and then you find you haven't been paying proper attention to all the profound things he's been saying.'

Willie said, 'I feel you've been lucky in Wolf.'

'There's his other family. That's a great help. I don't have to be with him all the time. And he's a good teacher. I suppose that's one reason why we are still together. I am someone he can teach. He found out fairly soon that I had no feeling for historical time, that I couldn't tell the difference between a hundred years and a thousand years, or two hundred years or two thousand. I knew our mother and our mother's uncle and I had some idea of our father's family. Beyond that everything was a blur, a primeval ocean, in which figures like Buddha and Akbar and Queen Elizabeth and the Rani of Jhansi and Marie Antoinette and Sherlock Holmes floated about and crisscrossed. Wolf told me that the most important thing about a book was its date. No point in reading a book if you didn't know its date, didn't know how far away or how close it was to you. The date of a book fixed it in time, and when you got to know other books and events the dates began to give you a time scale. I can't tell you how liberating that has been for me. When I think of our history I no longer feel I am sinking in a timeless degradation. I see more clearly. I have an idea of the scale and sequence of things.'

* * *

HE FELL INTO old ways. Twenty-five years before, when London had been as formless and bewildering for him as (according to Sarojini) it had been for the mahatma in 1890, Willie had tried to read himself out of his bewilderment, running to the college library to look up the simplest things. So now, to match the breadth of Sarojini's knowledge, and with the hope of arriving at her serenity, he began to read. He used the British Council library. There one day – he wasn't looking for it – he found the mahatma's autobiography, in the English translation by the mahatma's secretary.

The sweet, simple narrative swept him along. He wished to go on and on, to swallow the book whole, short chapter after short chapter; but very soon he was nagged by many things, already only half remembered, already without clear sequence, that he had read with speed; and (as Sarojini had said) he had often to go back, to read the easy words more slowly, to take in the extraordinary things the writer had been saying in his very calm way. A book (especially in the beginning) about shame, ignorance, incompetence: a whole chain of memories that would have darkened or twisted another life: memories that Willie himself (or Willie's poor father, as Willie thought) would have wished to take to the grave, but which the courage of this simple confession, arrived at by heaven knows what painful ways, made harmless, almost part of folk memory, in which every man of the country might see himself.

Willie thought, 'I wish this healing book had come my way twenty-five years ago. I might have become another man. I would have aimed at another life. I wouldn't have lived that shabby life in Africa among strangers. I would have felt that I wasn't alone in the world, that a great man had been there before me. Instead, I was reading Hemingway, who was very far away from me, who had nothing to offer me, and doing my bogus stories. What darkness, what self-deception, what waste. But perhaps I wouldn't have known how to read the book then. Perhaps it would have said nothing to me. Perhaps I needed to live that life, in order to see it more clearly now. Perhaps things happen when they are meant to happen.'

He said to Sarojini, when they were talking about the book, 'This wasn't the mahatma we heard about at home. We were told he was a scoundrel and an actor, false to his fingertips.'

She said, 'For our mother's uncle he was a caste oppressor. That was all that they passed on to us. It was part of their private caste war, their own revolution. They couldn't think of anything bigger. No one felt they had to know more about the mahatma.'

Willie said, 'If he hadn't gone to South Africa, if he hadn't run into that other life, would he have done nothing? Would he have gone on in his old way?'

'It's more than likely. But read the relevant chapters again. You will find that everything is fairly laid out, and you will make up your own mind.'

'How South Africa shocked him. You can feel the shame, the bewilderment. He was in no way prepared for it. That terrible incident in the overnight train, and then the indentured Tamil labourer with the bloody head coming to him for justice.'

Sarojini said, 'Beaten up by the planter to whom he had been indentured. The transplanted serfs of the empire, with no rights at all. You could have done anything with them. The ancestors of our rose-sellers here in Berlin. They've travelled far in a hundred years. They can fight their own war now. That should make you feel good. We can't put ourselves in Gandhi's shoes. To be faced with the most casual kind of brutality and to have no power in one's hands. Most of us would have run away and hidden. Most of the Indians did, and they still do. But Gandhi, with his holy innocence, thought that there was something he could do. That was how he began his political life, with this need to act. "What can I do?" And that was how it was at the very end. Just before independence there were very bad communal riots in Bengal. He went there. Some people strewed broken bottles and glass over where he, the frail old mahatma, the man of peace, was to walk. He was by now swamped by his own religious search, but there was enough of the old lucidity left, and he was often during these days heard to say to himself, "What can I do? What can I do?"

'There wasn't always much he could do. It's easy to forget that. He wasn't always the semi-nude mahatma. The semi-religious way he started with in South Africa – the commune, the idea of bread labour, all the mixed ideas of Tolstoy and Ruskin – couldn't do anything in that situation. In his autobiography his account of his twenty years in South Africa is vivid and full of incident, full of things he is doing. You might think that something big is happening, something that is going to change South Africa, but a lot of the struggle he is describing is personal and religious, and if you step back just a little you will see that the mahatma's time in South Africa was a complete failure. He was forty-six when he gave up and went back to India. Five years older than you, Willie, and with nothing to show for twenty years of work. In India he was starting from scratch. He would have to think and think, then and later, about how as a stranger he was going to inject himself into a local situation, where there were already many better-educated leaders. It might seem today that things were already happening, and that as the mahatma all he had to do in 1915 was to let himself be carried to the crest. It wasn't like that. He made things happen. He created the wave. He was a mixture of thought and intuition. Thought, above all. He was a true revolutionary.'

And Willie said nothing.

She had taken him far away. She had given him the daily mental exercise of thinking himself back into more desperate places of the world he had seen or known. That had already become a habit of his mornings; and now, in an extension of this morning meditation, he found himself reconsidering his life in

India and London, reconsidering Africa and his marriage, acknowledging everything in a new way, hiding nothing, submerging all the pathos of his nondescript past in an ennobling new ideal.

For the first time in his life he began to experience a kind of true pride. He felt himself, so to speak, taking up space when he walked in the streets; and he wondered whether this was how other people felt all the time, without effort, all the secure people he had met in London and Africa. Gradually, with this pride, there came to him an unexpected joy, which was like further reward, the joy of knowing that he rejected everything he saw. Sarojini had told him that the people he saw lived for pleasure alone. They ate and watched television and counted their money; they had been reduced to a terrible simplicity. He saw the unnaturalness of this simplicity; at the same time he felt the excitement of the new movements of his heart and mind; and he felt above everything around him.

Five months before, in the lovely, shocking, refreshing winter, as a refugee from Africa, with no true place of his own to go back to, it had all seemed welcoming and blessed. The buildings hadn't changed; the people hadn't changed – all he could say was that he had learned to spot the harassed, heavy, middle-aged poor women from the east, two frontiers away. He remembered that time, that memory of his own happiness, very clearly. He didn't reject it. It told him how far he had come.

That happiness, existing not in the real Berlin but in a special bubble – Sarojini's apartment, Sarojini's money, Sarojini's conversation – couldn't have endured. Twenty years before he would have wanted to hold on to that good time, would have tried to do, in Berlin, the city at the end of a narrow air corridor, what he had later done in Africa. It would have ended worse than Africa. He might have become like the Indian he met one day, an educated man in his thirties, with gold-rimmed glasses, who had come with high hopes to Berlin and was now a shiny-faced, fawning tramp in ragged clothes, with no place to sleep, his mind no longer whole, his breath very bad, a broken arm in a sling black with grime, complaining of his torments at the hands of young thugs.

In those five months he had come far. There had never been a time like that for him, when he had been without immediate anxiety, when he had not to act with anyone, and when as in a fairy story he and his sister had become adults without suffering too much harm. He felt that everything he had thought and worked out in those five months was true. They issued out of a new serenity. Everything he had felt before, all the seemingly real longings that had taken him to Africa, were false. He felt no shame now; he could acknowledge everything; he saw that everything that had happened to him was a preparation for what was now to come.

TWO

Peacocks

THEY BEGAN TO wait for Kandapalli. But no word came from him. The summer began to fade.

Sarojini said, 'You mustn't be disheartened. This is just the first of many trials. It happens when you are doing something unusual, and Wolf says it wouldn't be as easy for you as it would be for a tribal on the spot. They would be worried by exotics like you. We ourselves had a lot of trouble with Kandapalli's people, and we were only making a film. If you were a tribal you would just have to go to someone in trousers – that's the way they think of people in authority: trousers-people – and say, "Dada, I want to join the movement". And the trousers-man would say, "What is the name of your village? What is your caste? What is the name of your father?" All the information needed would be in those simple replies, and it can be easily checked. They would need a little longer to work you out. We told them about our mother's uncle, and we told them about your African background. We stressed the radical side.'

Willie said, 'I would have liked to start without any stories. I would have liked to be myself. To make a clean start.'

She seemed not to hear. 'You will have to do a lot of walking. You should practise now. Wear canvas shoes. Toughen up the soles of your feet.'

He spent hours walking in the sandy forests of Berlin. He let the paths lead him on. One afternoon he came to a sun-struck clearing, and before he could fully take in where he was he found himself walking between scores of naked, staring men stretched out on the long grass, among the bicycles that had no doubt brought some of them there. The bicycles lay on their sides on the grass, and the twisted postures of men and machines seemed oddly expectant and alike.

When he told Sarojini of the unnerving little adventure she said, 'That's a homosexual area. It's well known. You should be careful. Otherwise you'll be getting into trouble long before you get to Kandapalli.'

The leaves on some trees were beginning to turn, and day by day the light was taking a yellower tone.

One day Sarojini said, 'At last. Wolf has had a letter from India from a man called Joseph. He's a university lecturer. You can tell by the name that he's a Christian. He's not underground. He's very much in the open, and he takes care to keep his nose clean. All these movements have people like that. Useful for us, useful for them, useful for the authorities. Joseph will see you, and if he likes you he will pass you on.'

* * *

AND SO, AFTER more than twenty years, Willie saw India again. He had left India with very little money, the gift of his father; and he was going back with very little money, the gift of his sister.

India began for him in the airport in Frankfurt, in the little pen where passengers for India were assembled. He studied the Indian passengers there – people he most likely wasn't going to see again after a few hours – more fearfully than he had studied the Tamils and other Indians in Berlin. He saw India in everything they wore and did. He was full of his mission, full of the revolution in his soul, and he felt a great distance from them. But detail by detail the India he was observing, in the airport pen, and then in the aircraft, the terrible India of Indian family life – the soft physiques, the way of eating, the ways of speech, the idea of the father, the idea of the mother, the crinkled, much-used plastic shop bags (sometimes with a long irrelevant printed name) – this India began to assault him, began to remind him of things he thought he had forgotten and put aside, things which his idea of his mission had obliterated; and the distance he felt from his fellow passengers diminished. After the long night, he felt something like panic at the thought of the India that was approaching, the India below the colour-destroying glare he could see from his window. He felt, 'I thought of the two worlds, and I had a very good idea of the world to which I belonged. But now, really, I wish I could go back a few hours and stand outside the Patrick Hellmann shop in Berlin, or go to the oyster and champagne bar in the KDW.'

It was early morning when they landed, and he was better able to control his emotions. The light was already stinging, heat was already rising from the tarmac. The small, shabby airport building was full of movement and echoing noise. The Indian passengers from the aeroplane were already different, already at home, already (with briefcases and cardigans and the plastic bags from shops in famous foreign cities) with an authority that separated them from lesser local folk. The black-bladed ceiling fans were busy; the metal rods or shanks that fixed them to the ceiling were furry with oil and sifted dust.

Willie thought, 'It's an airport. I must think of it like that. I must think of all that that means.'

The carpentry was not what Willie expected in an airport building. It was not much above the carpentry of the rough beach-side weekend restaurants Willie had known in Africa (where roughness would have been part of the style and atmosphere). The concrete walls were whitewashed in a rough-and-ready way, with paint splashed beyond concrete on glass and wood; and for many inches above the terrazzo floor the walls were grimy from broom and dirty washing-water. A blue plastic bucket and a short dirty broom made of the ribs of coconut branches stood against the wall; not far away a small, dark, squatting woman in a camouflage of dark clothes moved slowly on her haunches, cleaning, giving the floor a suggestion of thinly spread grime.

Willie thought, 'Twenty years ago I wouldn't have seen what I am seeing now. I am seeing what I see because I have made myself another person. I cannot make myself that old person again. But I must go back to that old way of seeing. Otherwise my cause is lost before I have begun. I have come from a world of waste and appearances. I saw quite clearly some time ago that it was a simple world, where people had been simplified. I must not go back on that vision. I must understand that now I am among people of more complicated beliefs and social ideas, and at the same time in a world stripped of all style and artifice. This is an airport. It works. It is full of technically accomplished people. That is what I must see.'

Joseph lived in a provincial city some hundreds of miles away.

It was necessary for Willie to take a train. To take a train it was necessary for him to take a taxi to the railway station; and then, having found at the booking office (cave-like, hidden away from the fierce light of day, with very dim fluorescent lighting) that the trains for the next few days were full, it was necessary for him either to stay in one of the railway station's accommodation rooms or to find a hotel. And soon India, with all its new definitions of things (taxi, hotel, railway station, waiting room, lavatory, restaurant), and all its new disciplines (squatting in the lavatory, eating only cooked food, avoiding water and soft fruit), engulfed him.

There is a kind of yoga in which the disciple is required to move very slowly, concentrating the while on what his mind is making his body do; until after months of practice (or, for the worldly and ungifted, perhaps years) the disciple feels each separate muscle move within himself, minutely obeying the impulses of his mind. For Willie, in those first days of return to India, the mechanics of day-to-day life had become a kind of yoga like that, a series of hurdles; every simple thing had to be re-thought, learned afresh.

(Yoga: shut away in his Indian hotel room, with the windows open to noise and smells, or in the street outside, Willie found himself, within his intense and fast-moving interior life, fixing intermittently on Africa, and remembering that near the end of the colonial time yoga had become something of a rage among middle-aged women, as though the simple shared recognition of spiritual and bodily perfection as an ideal was going to make their collapsing world more bearable.)

He had wondered for some time in Berlin about the books he should bring with him. His first idea was that after his long forest marches and in the silence of village huts he would need light reading. The reading habit had more or less left him in Africa, and all he could think of was *Three Men in a Boat*, which he had never finished, and a thriller of the 1930s by Freeman Wills Croft called *The Cask* or *The Cask Mystery*. He had happened on the Croft in a tattered paperback copy in somebody's house in Africa. He had lost the book (or it had been taken back) before he had read very far, and the very faint memory of the mystery (London, a floating cask in the river, calculations about tides and currents) had remained with him, like a kind of poetry. But it occurred to him, before he began looking for those books in Berlin, that he would come to the end of them very quickly. And there was this further complication: those books would, with his complicity, create pictures in his head of a world for which he had no further use. So in an insidious way they were corrupting, and not at all as harmless and 'light' as he thought.

He gave up the idea of books. But then one day, near the end of his walk, he had gone into an antique shop, attracted by its casual choked display of coloured glass and lamps and vases and other rich-looking and delicate things of the 1920s and 1930s which had somehow survived the war. There were books on one table, mainly paper-bound German books in the German black letter; but among them, and noticeable because of their faded cloth binding and English script, were English-language textbooks about algebra, advanced geometry, and mechanics and hydrostatics. These books had been printed in the 1920s, and the paper, from that earlier time of stringency, was cheap and grey; perhaps some student or teacher had brought these textbooks from England to Berlin. Willie had liked mathematics at school. He had liked the logic, the charm of solutions; and it occurred to him now that these were the books he would need in the forest. They would keep his mind alive; they would not repeat; they would move from lesson to lesson, stage to stage; they would offer no disturbing pictures of men and women in played-out, too-simple societies.

In his Indian hotel now, near the railway station, with a night and a day to spend before he could get on the train to Joseph's town, Willie took the books out from his little canvas suitcase, to get started on his new discipline. He began with the geometry book. The ceiling light was very dim. He could barely see the faint print on the old grey paper. His straining eyes began to ache. To deal with the problems he needed paper and a pen or pencil. He had none of those things. So there was nothing he could do. But he couldn't hide from himself the fact that the geometry book and the others were too hard for him. He had overestimated his powers; he needed to start at a lower level; and even then it was clear he would need a teacher and an encourager. He had been reading, or trying to read, in bed; there was no table in the little room. He put the books back in the canvas case.

He thought, 'I would have had to get rid of those books anyway. They would have given me away.'

This failure, so simple, so quick, so comprehensive, before he had got started, filled him with gloom, made it hard for him to stay in the little room with the blotched walls, and even harder for him to go out into the warm, buzzing city. The books had given him a kind of pride, a kind of protection. Now he was naked. He ground out the night, ticking off the quarter-hours, and he ground out the next day. And all the way in the train to Joseph's town his gloom grew; but all the time, through the night, through all the stops at squalling railway stations, the train was taking him on, whether he liked it or not, to what he had now committed himself to.

In the early morning, when the sun rose, the moving train cast a complete shadow from the top of the coaches to the wheels on the rails. He looked for his own shadow, and when he found it he played with it for a while, moving his head and hands and seeing the shadow answer. He thought, 'That's me.' It was oddly reassuring, seeing himself at this distance, possessed of life like everybody else.

* * *

THE TOWN IN which Joseph lived was big, but it was without a metropolitan feel. The road outside the station was a mess, with a lot of urgent shouting and excitement but very little movement. Everybody was in everybody else's way. Pedal rickshaws and scooter rickshaws and taxis competed for space with horse-drawn or mule-drawn carriages that tilted dangerously downwards at the back, seemingly about to throw out their heavy load of women and children. There were various hotel agents about, and Willie, choosing at random, allowed himself to be led by one of these men to the Hotel Riviera. They took a carriage. 'Modern, all modern,' the Riviera man said all the time, and then vanished as soon as he led Willie into the little lobby of the hotel, as though not wishing now to be held responsible for anything.

It was a small concrete building of two storeys in the bazaar area, and though of concrete it felt fragile. The room Willie was given was stale and stuffy, and when, with too firm a gesture, Willie tried to open the window, the catch, which was of a strangely soft metal, seemed to bend in his hand. Gently, then, not wishing to break anything, he eased the catch free, and opened the window. A room service menu standing upright on the small table promised food around the clock, with dishes 'from our baker's basket' and 'from the fisherman's net' and 'from the butcher's block'. Willie knew that it had no meaning, that it had all been copied from some foreign hotel, and was to be taken only as a gesture of goodwill, a wish to please, an aspect of being modern.

He thought he should telephone Joseph. But the red telephone beside the bed, in spite of the printed card that said 'Your friends and loved ones are just a few digits away', was a dummy. He went downstairs and (catching sight of the furtive hotel agent in an inner room) asked to use the desk telephone. The man at the desk was very friendly.

It might have been Joseph himself who answered, bright and clear and reassuring. It was the first clear communication Willie had had since he arrived, the first indication he had had of a kindred mind, and he found himself close to tears.

Joseph said he had classes that morning but would be free in the afternoon. They fixed a time for late afternoon, and Willie went back to his room. He was suddenly exhausted. He lay down in his clothes on the thin mattress of his iron bed and for the first time since Berlin and Frankfurt fell deeply asleep.

A sensation of heat and light wrenched him awake long before he was ready to get up. It was mid-afternoon, and the sun was making the open glass window glow. He ached in his eyes and head at being awakened too soon. He felt he had done himself some deep damage. But it was just an hour and a half before his meeting with Joseph, the only person he could hold on to; and he forced himself up from the bristly thin mattress on the iron bed.

The scooter-driver said, 'New area,' when Willie gave the address, and they drove – Willie still half in a daze, still with the ache of his sudden awakening – for fifteen or twenty or twenty-five minutes out of the town along main roads in the warm dust and fumes of noisy trucks and buses. They turned off into an unasphalted flinty road that made the little scooter bump up and down, and came finally to a development of concrete apartment blocks on bare, hummocked earth, as though the builders had forgotten or didn't care to clean up the ground after they had done their work. Many of the blocks were on concrete pillars, and the complicated number or address of each block had been daubed on its pillars in big, dripping numbers and letters.

The elevator shaft of Joseph's block, situated between pillars, didn't come all the way down to ground level. It stopped perhaps three feet short, resting on pounded earth as on some rock formation in a cave; and steps cut into this pounded earth led down from the shaft. It might have been done like that for the style of the thing, or to save money; or someone, the architect, the builder, or the shaft-manufacturer, might simply have mis-measured. But, Willie thought, it is an elevator shaft nonetheless: that is how the people living in this block would see it.

They would see themselves living in a new and rich area in a modern concrete block with an elevator.

He thought, 'I must remember not to mention it to Joseph. He may be a tough customer, not easy to talk to, but I must not make his block, the place where he lives, a topic of conversation. It's just the kind of thing that fatigue might make me do. I will have to be careful.'

The elevator had folding metal doors. They were black with grease and were very noisy opening and closing. Willie was used to rough building in his remote corner of Africa (where people in their heart of hearts had always known that one day they would have to pack up and leave); but he had seen nothing so unfinished-looking as what he saw when he got out at Joseph's floor. The building here seemed to have been abandoned at its first brutal stage, with nothing to soften the raw concrete, which was pegged along the top of the corridor walls with many cables, thick and thin and covered with old dust. And all the time, to the distress of Willie, there came the happy cries of children playing in the warm afternoon dust among the dirt-mounds in the yard, and the threatening shouts of women.

Joseph opened the door himself. He was a big man, as his voice and manner had suggested, and he was dressed in white or near-white, wearing something which might have been a tunic suit or pyjamas. He would have been about fifty.

He said to Willie, 'Do you like my university quarters?'

Willie didn't fall into the trap. He said, 'It's for you to tell me.'

They were in the sitting room. Through an open door at one corner Willie could see the kitchen, with a woman sitting on the terrazzo floor and kneading something in a basin. Two other doors led to inner rooms, bedrooms perhaps.

Willie also saw that there was in the sitting room a couch or narrow bed spread with bed clothes. Joseph lay down carefully on the couch, and Willie saw that Joseph was an invalid. Below the couch, and nearly all hidden by the bed clothes, could be seen the handle of a chamber pot, and just below Joseph's head was a tin cup, made perhaps from a condensed milk tin, with a welded tin handle – his spittoon.

Joseph, perhaps seeing the distress in Willie's face, stood up again and showed himself to Willie. He said, 'It isn't as bad as it looks. You see, I can stand up and move. But I can only move for about a hundred yards a day. That's not a lot. So I have to ration myself, even here, in my university quarters. Of course, with a car and a chair it is possible to have something like a normal life. But you have seen our lift. So when I am at home I am most disadvantaged. Every trip to the toilet takes up a precious part of my ration. When that is used up it's pure pain. Something about my spinal cord. I've had the trouble before, and they did something then. Now they tell me that it can be cured, but then I will have no sense of balance. Every day I measure one against the other. When I lie down I'm all right. They tell me that there are some people with this condition who are in pain when they lie down or sit still. They have to keep on the move. I can't imagine that one.'

Willie's ache began to come back. But he thought he should explain himself. Joseph made a gesture with both hands that told Willie he was to stop. And Willie stopped.

Joseph said, 'How do you think it compares with Africa? Here.'

Willie thought, and couldn't say. He said, 'I always had sympathy for Africans, but I saw them from the outside. I never really found out about them. Most of the time I saw Africa through the eyes of the colonists. They were the people I lived with. And then suddenly that life ended, Africa was all around us, and we all had to run.'

Joseph said, 'When I was in England I did a course in Primitive Government for my degree. Just after the war. The time of Kingsley Martin and the *New Statesman*, people like Joad and Laski. Of course, they wouldn't call it that now, Primitive Government. I loved it. The Kabakas, the Mugabes, the Omukamas, the various chiefs and kings. I loved the rituals, the religion, the sanctity of the drum. So many things I didn't know about. Not easy to remember. Like you, my attitude to Africa was the colonial one. But that's where we all have to begin. It was the colonialists who opened up Africa and told us about it. I thought of it as bush, common ground, open to anyone. It took me some time even to understand that when you entered somebody's territory in Africa you had to pay your dues, as you would anywhere else. Primitive, they say, but I think that's where the Africans have the edge on us. They know who they are. We don't. There's a lot of talk here about ancient culture and so on, but when you ask them they can't tell you what it means.'

Willie, heavy with sleep, considered the woman in the kitchen. He saw that she was not sitting flat on the terrazzo floor, as he had thought, but on a narrow and very low bench, perhaps about four inches high. With clothes and flesh she overhung her little bench, almost hiding it. Her head was covered, correctly, because Willie was a visitor; and she was kneading something in a blue-rimmed enamel bowl. But there was something in her back and posture that indicated she was listening to what was being said.

Joseph said, 'We are in one of the saddest places in the world here. Twenty times sadder than what you saw in Africa. In Africa the colonial past would have been there for you to see. Here you can't begin to understand the past, and when you get to know it you wish you didn't.'

Willie, fighting sleep, and the old ache of being awakened too soon, studied the back of the sitting woman and thought, 'But this was what Sarojini told me in Berlin. I have heard this before. I used to think that she was trying to motivate me. I respected her for that, but I only half believed the terrible things she was telling me. This must be the way they do it. The cause is good. I believe in it, but I mustn't let this man agitate me.'

And for a second or two he dozed off.

Joseph must have noticed, because when Willie came to again he thought Joseph, still standing beside his settee, had lost a little of his bounce and earlier style and was trying harder.

Joseph said, 'All the land of India is sacred. But here we are on especially sacred ground. We are on the site of the last great Indian kingdom, and it was the site of a catastrophe. Four hundred years ago the Muslim invaders ganged up on it and destroyed it. They spent weeks, possibly months, destroying it. They levelled the capital city. It was a rich and famous city, known to early European travellers. They killed the priests, the philosophers, the artisans, the architects, the scholars. They knew what they were doing. They were cutting off the head. The only people they left behind were the serfs in the villages, and they parcelled them out among themselves. This military defeat was terrible. You cannot understand the degree to which the victors won and the losers lost. Hitler would have called it a war of annihilation, a war without limits and restraints, and this one succeeded to a remarkable degree. There was no resistance. The serfs in the villages policed themselves. They were of various low castes, and there is no caste hatred greater than that of the low for the low, one sub-caste for another. Some ran before and after the horses of their lords. Some did the scavenging. Some did the gravedigging. Some offered their women. All of them referred to themselves as slaves. All of them were underfed. That was a matter of policy. It was said that if you fed a slave well he would want to bite you.'

Willie said, 'My sister told me that.'

Joseph said, 'Who is your sister?'

That took Willie aback. But then almost immediately he understood why Joseph couldn't pretend to know too much. He said, 'She does television in Berlin.'

'Oh. And they were taxed and taxed. There were forty kinds of taxes. After four hundred years of this kind of rule the people here would have grown to believe that this was their eternal condition. They were slaves. They were nothing. I am not going to mention any names. But this was the origin of our sacred Indian poverty, the poverty that India could offer the world. And there was something else. Thirty years after the destruction of the last Indian kingdom the conquerors built a big gate of victory. That gate of victory is now an Indian heritage site. The destroyed city has been forgotten. Defeat can be terrible. You would have thought that at independence all the lords of the conquered people would have been hanged with their families and their bodies left to turn to bones. That would have been a kind of redemption, the beginning of something new. But nothing like that happened. It was left to some very simple people to raise the standard of revolution.'

The door of the flat opened. A tall, dark man, almost as tall as Joseph, came in. He had the figure of a sportsman, broad shoulders, narrow waist, slender hips.

Joseph sat down on his settee. He said, 'The government thinks I am the cheerleader for the guerrillas. Well, I am that. I would love nothing better than to see a revolution sweeping everything away. The very thought of that makes my heart light.'

Sounds and smells of cooking came from the kitchen, worrying Willie with old taboos he thought he had abandoned. The woman's posture had subtly altered.

Joseph said, 'My son-in-law. He does research for a pharmaceutical company.'

The dark man with the sportsman's physique, the well-kept body, turned his face full to Willie for the first time. There was an odd twist of pleasure in the mouth: he clearly liked having his professional skills known right away to a stranger. But the eyes, flecked with red at the corners, were full of a contradictory rage and hatred.

He said, 'But as soon as they know you are an untouchable they don't want to have anything to do with you.'

There were quieter words he might have used, legal words, religious words, government-approved words. But the very anger, humiliation, pride, that had made him give his involuntary twisted smile when Joseph had introduced him correctly had also made him use the brutal, old-fashioned word. Not a word of self-pity so much as a kind of threat to the world outside.

Willie thought, 'That man has won his revolution, whatever he says. I had no idea they were fighting this war still. But how difficult he makes the whole thing. He wants it all ways. I don't think I'll be able to get on with him. I hope there are not too many of them like this.'

The dark man with his sportsman's presence swaggered – as it seemed to Willie – through one of the doorways at the end of the sitting room. Joseph was noticeably affected. He seemed momentarily to have lost his flow of words. Inside there was the sound of a lavatory flush. And Willie had some little conviction that in Joseph's little household, in the brutal concrete flat with the exposed cables, and Joseph's unseen daughter, the revolution had already done some kind of unacknowledged damage.

Joseph said, 'Yes, I would love nothing better than to see a revolution sweeping everything away.'

He stopped, as though having to feel for his place in a script. He took up the tin spittoon from below the settee. The handle, made from a strip of tin, was stylishly curved: craftsman's work. The edge of the strip had been bent back on itself and soldered, to lose its sharpness; and the thicker, slightly irregular edge shone from handling. He held the cup for a while, rubbing his thumb along the edge of the handle, still seeming to feel for his place in the script which his son-in-law's entry had disturbed.

At last he said, 'But at the same time I have no faith in the human material we have left, after the centuries of slavery. Look at this little cricket of a girl here. Our servant.'

Willie looked at the very small hunchbacked figure who had come out from the kitchen to the sitting room and was moving about on her haunches, inches at a time, using a small broom of some soft rushes, making very small gestures. Her clothes were dark and muddy-coloured; they were like a camouflage, concealing her colour, concealing her features, denying her a personality. She was like a smaller version of the cleaning woman Willie had seen days before at the airport.

Joseph said, 'She comes from a village. One of those villages I've been telling you about, where people ran barefooted before and after the horse of the foreign lord and no one was allowed to cover his thighs in the presence of the lord. She is fifteen or sixteen. No one knows. She doesn't know. Her village is full of people like her, very small, very thin. Cricket people, matchstick people. Their minds have gone after the centuries of malnourishment. Do you think you can make a revolution with her? It's what Kandapalli thinks, and I wish him well. But I don't somehow think it's what you were expecting after Africa and Berlin.'

Willie said, 'I wasn't expecting anything.'

'When people here talk of the guerrillas they are talking of people like her. It's not exciting. It's not Che Guevara and strong men in military fatigues. In every other flat or apartment in this area there is a helpless woman like this from a village, and they will tell you it's all right, the woman is going to fill out. The old lords have gone away. We are the new lords. People who don't know will look at her and speak of the cruelty of Indian caste. In fact we are looking at the cruelty of history. And the most terrible thing is it can't be avenged. The old lords oppressed and humiliated and injured for centuries. No one touched them. Now they've gone away. They've gone to the towns, they've gone to foreign countries. They've left these wretched people as their monument. This is what I meant when I said that you have no idea of the extent to which the victors won and the losers lost here. And it's all hidden. When you compare this with Africa you will have to say that Africa is all light and clarity.'

The smells of food became stronger, filling Willie with old taboos, and strengthening him in the idea of the unhappiness in the revolutionary's little flat, where a daughter had already been made a kind of sacrifice. He didn't want to be asked to stay. He made to get up.

Joseph said, 'You are staying at the Riviera. You might not think it's much of a hotel. But for people here it is high-class and international. None of the people you are interested in will want to come to see you there. They will be too noticeable. There is an Indian place called the Neo Anand Bhavan, the new abode of peace, after the Nehru family house. Over here everything's the neo this or the neo that. It's a style. It's the usual Indian thing, with the squat-toilet and the bath bucket. Stay there for a week. The people you are interested in will get to know you are there.'

Willie went down in the rackety old elevator. The light had changed. It had turned gold. Night was about to fall. Dust hung in the golden light. But heedless children still played and shouted among the dust hills in the yard, and the voices of contented women still scolded. Just a little while before it had all seemed raw and crowded and hopeless. Now, seeing it for the second time, it was as it were a tamed view, and this made him rejoice.

He thought, 'It was never going to be easy, what I am doing.'

* * *

THE ACHE OF broken sleep was still in his bones, still in his head. But the actual sleepiness had gone. He went walking in the bazaar, the lights coming on around him, looking for the cheapest and simplest and safest cooked food he could find. He was not really hungry now, but he wished to practise whenever he could what he thought of as the new yoga of his day-to-day living, in which every act and need was to be worked out again, reduced to what was most basic. He was amazed to find how far he had come, how adaptable he was. A year ago or less there were, after the splendours and excesses of the colonial time, the deprivations and camp-life, the siege conditions of Africa towards the end of the war. Just a few days before there was all the bustle and luxury of West Berlin. Just a few minutes before there was the comparative comfort and order of Joseph's kitchen. And now he was here, in the dim and varied lights of the bazaar, the smoky flambeau, the hurricane lamp, the pressure lamp, looking with excitement for what he might subsist on, wishing to take his needs down and ever further down. Soon, he knew, when he found himself in forest or countryside, this bazaar would appear an impossible luxury. There would be other foods, other austerities: he would be ready for them when they came. He was already in his own mind a kind of ascetic, almost a seeker. He had never known anything like it – Africa in the bad days had been the opposite of this, had been suffering alone – and it made him lightheaded.

He spent a penny or so on a dish of spicy chickpeas. It had been simmering for hours, and would have been safe. It was served to him in a leaf bowl, a bowl made of a dried leaf pinned together with pieces of twig. The spices burnt his tongue, but he ate with relish, surrendering to his new simplicity. He went back to the Riviera and the warmth in his stomach soon returned him to his interrupted sleep.

The next day he moved to the Neo Anand Bhavan, and after the exaltation of his night at the Riviera there followed the emptiest and most tormenting days Willie had ever known, days of waiting in an almost empty room with a strong sewer smell for unknown people to come and take him on to his destiny. The walls were a strange mottled colour, as though they had absorbed all kinds of vile liquids; below the coconut mat dust was at least a quarter of an inch thick; and the ceiling bulb gave hardly any light. He had thought in the beginning that he should always be there, in the room, waiting for the person who was going to come for him. It was only later that he thought that this person would have time on his hands and would be prepared to wait. So he prowled about the town, and found himself going with many other people to the railway station, for the excitement of the trains, the crowds, the harsh calls of hawkers and the cries of wounded or beaten dogs.

One evening on the station platform he found a little swivel stand of very old American paperbacks, discarded stock, dirt seeming to have worked itself into the shiny covers, rather like the ancient electronic goods that on occasion turned up in certain traders' shops in Africa, with the instructions leaflets yellow with age. He wanted nothing that would remind him of the world he had abjured. He rejected and rejected, and then at last he lighted on two books that seemed to meet his need. A book from the 1950s or 1960s about Harlem, *The Cool World*, a novel, told in the first person; and a book about the Incas of Peru, the *Royal Commentaries*, by a man partly of the Inca royal family. Willie could hardly believe his luck.

At the Neo Anand Bhavan they gave him a hurricane lantern to read by. He would have liked candles, for their old-fashioned romance; but they had no candles. And then, as before, when he had tried the mathematical books, he soon floundered. The *Royal Commentaries* required knowledge of a sort that Willie didn't have; it very quickly became abstract. And *The Cool World* was simply too far away, too American, too New York, too full of allusions he couldn't get.

Willie thought, 'I have to understand now that, in this venture, books are a cheat. I have to depend on my own resources.'

It didn't become easier for him at the Neo Anand Bhavan. He began then consciously to concentrate on the yoga of his hour-to-hour life, looking on each hour, each action, as challenging and important. No segment of time was to be wasted. Everything was to be part of his new discipline. And in this new discipline the idea of waiting on external events was to be banished.

He lived intensely; he became absorbed in himself. He found he had begun to deal with time.

And then one day the courier arrived. The courier was very young, almost a boy. He wore the local style of loincloth and long-tailed shirt.

He said to Willie, 'I will come for you in seven days. I have to look for some of the others.'

Willie said, 'What clothes should I wear?'

The courier didn't appear to understand. He said, 'What clothes do you have?' He might have been a college boy.

Willie spoke to him as though he was that. He said, 'What would be best for me? Should I wear canvas shoes, or should I be barefoot?'

'Please don't be barefoot. That will be asking for trouble.

There are scorpions and all kinds of dangerous things on the ground. The local people wear ox-hide slippers.'

'What about food? You must tell me what to do.'

'Get some *sattoo*. It's a kind of powdered roasted grain. You can buy it in the bazaar. It's actually like sand when it's dry. When you are hungry you mix it with a little water. Very little, just enough to soften it. It's very tasty, and it lasts. It's what people use when they travel. The other thing you might get is a local towel or shawl. Everyone here has a towel. It's about four or five feet long, with tasselled ends, and about two feet wide. You wear it around the neck or over a shoulder. The material is very thin and fine. You can dry yourself with it after a bath, and it dries very quickly, in about twenty minutes. I will come for you in seven days. In the meantime I will report that I have found you.'

Willie went to the bazaar to buy *sattoo*. It wasn't as easy as he thought. There were different kinds, made from different grains.

Willie, in his new mood, thought, 'What ritual, what beauty.'

Seven days later the college boy came back for him. The college boy said, 'Those other fellows made me waste a lot of time. They weren't really interested. They were just talking. One of them was an only son. He had a bigger loyalty to his family. The other one just loved the good life.'

They went in the evening to the railway station, and there they took a passenger train. A passenger train was a slow train, stopping at all the halts. At every halt there was commotion and racket and pushing and shoving and grating voices raised in complaint or protest or just raised for the formality of the thing. At every halt there was dust and the smell of old tobacco and old cloth and old sweat. The schoolboy slept through most of it. Willie thought in the beginning, 'I am going to have a shower at the end of this.' Then he thought that he wouldn't: that wish for hour-to-hour comfort and cleanliness belonged to another kind of life, another way of experiencing. Better to let the dust and dirt and smells settle on him.

They travelled all night, but the passenger train had actually covered very little ground; and then in the bright light of morning the schoolboy left Willie, saying, 'Someone will come for you here.'

Behind the screen doors and the thick walls the waiting room was dark. People, wrapped up from head to toe in blankets and dirty grey sheets, were sleeping on benches and the floor. At four o'clock that afternoon Willie's second courier came, a tall, thin, dark man in a local loincloth of a gingham pattern, and they began walking.

After an hour Willie thought, 'I no longer know where I am. I don't think I will be able to pick my way back. I am in their hands now.'

They were now far from the railway town, far from the town. They were deep in the country, and it was getting dark. They came to a village. Even in the dark Willie could see the trimmed eaves of the thatched roof of the important family of the village. The village was a huddle of houses and huts, back to back and side to side, with narrow angular lanes. They walked past all the good houses and stopped at the edge, at an open thatched hut. The owner was an outcast, and very dark. One of the cricket people Joseph had talked about, created by centuries of slavery and abuse and bad food. Willie did not think him especially friendly. The thatch of his hut was rough, untrimmed. The hut was about ten feet by ten feet. Half of it was living space and washing-up space; the other half, with a kind of loft, was sleeping space, for calves and hens as well as people.

Willie thought, 'It's pure nature now. Everything I have to do I will do in the bush.'

Later they ate a kind of rice gruel, thick and salty.

Willie thought, 'They've been living like this for centuries. I have been practising my yoga, so to speak, for a few days, and have become obsessed by it. They have been practising a profounder kind of yoga, every day, every meal. That yoga is their life. And of course there would be days when there would be nothing at all to eat, not even this gruel. Please, let me be granted the strength to bear what I am seeing.'

And for the first time in his life Willie that evening fell asleep in his dirt. He and his guide rested all the next day in the hut while the owner went out to do his work. The next afternoon they began to walk again. They halted at night in another village, and spent the night again in a hut with a calf and hens. They ate rice flakes. There was no tea, no coffee, no hot drink. The water they drank was dirty, from a muddy brook.

Two days later they had left fields and villages behind and were in a teak forest. They came by moonlight that evening to a clearing in the forest. There were low olive-coloured plastic tents around a cleared area. There were no lights, no fires. In the moonlight shadows were black and sharp.

Willie's guide said, 'No talking. No questions.'

They ate quite well that evening, groundnut, rice flakes, and wild meat. In the morning Willie considered his companions. They were not young. They were city people, people who would have had each man his own reason for dropping out of the workaday world and joining the guerrillas.

During the day Willie thought, 'Kandapalli preached the Mass Line. Kandapalli wished the villagers and the poor to fight their own battles. I am not among the poor and the villagers in this camp. There has been some mistake. I have fallen among the wrong people. I have come to the wrong revolution. I don't like these faces. And yet I have to be with them. I have to get a message out to Sarojini or to Joseph. But I don't know how. I am completely in the hands of these people.'

Two evenings later a rough man in military uniform came to him and said, 'Tonight, man from Africa, you will do sentry duty.'

That night Willie cried, tears of rage, tears of fear, and in the dawn the cry of the peacock, after it had drunk from its forest pool, filled him with grief for the whole world.

THREE

The Street of the Tanners

THERE WERE ABOUT forty or fifty people in the camp. Word went around, spread from newcomer to newcomer, that there were ten, even twenty, camps like this one in the liberated areas, the areas under the control of the guerrillas; and this gave a general confidence, even brought about a kind of swagger in the recruits, especially after olive uniforms were handed out. This happened on the fourth day. Somewhere, Willie thought, thinking back to what he had heard of the guerrillas in his part of Africa, some cloth-seller had been made to pay his dues to the movement in this cheap, lightweight olive cloth; and some village tailor had been asked to do some rough sewing. A peaked cloth cap came with the uniform; just above the visor was a star in red satin. The uniform and the cap spoke of drama, coming suddenly to forty or fifty lives; it also spoke reassuringly of organisation; and it gave everyone a new, easy, sheltering identity.

It was a training camp. The sentry, not speaking, making no sound, woke them up one by one while it was still dark. The rule of the camp was that there was to be no sound and no light at night. Afterwards there came the calls of the noisy peacocks and other forest birds, fully a mile off, one bird in particular giving strident, desperate-sounding calls of alarm when it thought that some predator was getting too close to its eggs. At about six there was the roll call, and then for three hours they jogged and did physical exercises and sometimes practised crawling on the ground with a gun in their hands. For breakfast they had peanuts and rice flakes. And then they were lectured on guerrilla tactics. They were to make no sound when they were in the forest; they were to communicate by making bird calls, and they spent much time practising these bird calls. They were all very serious; no one laughed when the bird whistles went wrong. After lunch – which could mean deer or frogs or goat: this was not a vegetarian movement – they rested until mid-afternoon; and then they drilled and exercised for an hour and a half. The worst time then followed: the long evening, eleven hours long, without lights or proper speech, everyone talking only in whispers.

Willie thought, 'I have never known such boredom. Ever since I have come to India I have known these terrible nights of boredom. I suppose it is a kind of training, a kind of asceticism, but for what I am not sure. I must look upon it as another chamber of experience. I must give no sign to these people that I am not absolutely with them.'

When he was staying at the Neo Anand Bhavan he had bought some pre-stamped air-letter sheets. He began one hot afternoon in his oppressive plastic tent to write a letter to Sarojini. It was the only time he could write. *Dear Sarojini, I think something terrible has happened. I am not with the people we talked about. I don't know how it's happened, but I believe I am with Kandapalli's enemies.* He thought that was too open. He crossed out

Kandapalli's name, and then decided that it was too dangerous for him to write to Sarojini. He put the letter aside, in the kind of canvas back pack he had been given and looked out through the flap at the white, melancholy light of the forest clearing and the exercise ground.

He thought, 'This light denies everything. It denies beauty. It denies human possibility. Africa was gentler, as Joseph suggested. Perhaps I have been too long away. But I mustn't think too much along those lines. The cause we talked about in Berlin is still good and true. That I know.'

The rule in the camp, enunciated by the leader – a man of about forty, who looked like a businessman or civil servant, and had possibly been a member of the cadets at his school – the rule was that the recruits should not ask too many questions of their fellows. They should simply accept them as wearers of the red star. And Willie lost himself in conjecture about the people around him. They were all people in their late thirties or early forties, Willie's age, and he wondered what weakness or failure had caused them in mid-life to leave the outer world and to enter this strange chamber. He had been away from India too long. He couldn't assess the backgrounds of the people around him. He could only try to read the faces and the physiques: the too-full, sensual mouth in some speaking of some kind of sexual perversion, the hard mean eyes in others, the bruised-seeming eyes of yet others that spoke of hard or abused childhoods and tormented adult lives. That was as far as he could read. Among these people seeking in various ways to revenge themselves on the world, he was among strangers.

On the tenth or eleventh night there was a great disturbance in the camp. The sentry panicked and began to shout, and all the camp was filled with alarm.

Somebody shouted, 'The Greyhounds!'

That was the name of the special anti-guerrilla force within the police. They used guerrilla tactics: they were said to specialise in speed, secrecy, and surprise, the three S's, and they attacked first. This was their well-publicised reputation, and a number of terrified recruits ran out from their plastic tents and made for the forest.

It was a false alarm. Some animal had stumbled into the camp and frightened the sentry.

Gradually then people were called back, shame-faced, many of them only in their underclothes, and angry, full of a new rage.

Willie thought, 'Until tonight they thought they were the only ones with guns and training and discipline, the only ones with a programme. It made them brave. Now they have an idea of an enemy, and they are not so brave. They are only meaner. They will be very nasty tomorrow. I will have to be careful with them.'

Nothing was said by the leader that night. He was concerned in his businessman's or bureaucrat's way only to restore order. At dawn the routine of the camp was as before. It was only after breakfast (peanuts, rice flakes, the usual), and when the 'military theory' class was to begin, that the leader spoke to the camp; and then he spoke not as a man wishing to enforce discipline, but as a man fearful of a mass desertion, fearful of violence and the break-up of his camp. He knew his audience. At the beginning of his talk they were restive, like people who had been found out and in childlike pique had returned to their old bruised identities, ready to forgo the shelter and comfort of their olive uniforms and the red satin star on their caps, which only a few days before had appeared to make a new life so easy for them. They were waiting for rebuke, foreheads furrowed, eyes narrow and mean, lips pursed, cheeks puffed out: middle-aged men full of childhood pique but capable of adult rage. They were not going to put up with rebuke. When it became clear that the leader had no intention of mocking them they gradually calmed down.

Willie thought, 'Kandapalli was right. If I was concerned with making a revolution for the defeated and the insulted, if like Kandapalli I could cry easily at the thought of people's unrevenged sorrows over the centuries, these are not the men I would want with me. I would go to the poor themselves.'

The leader said, 'The sentry made a mistake last night and gave us all a big fright. I don't think the sentry should be blamed. He is not used to the forest and wild animals, and too much was placed anyway on the shoulders of one man. From tonight we will have two sentries. But what happened last night shows how important it is for us at all times to be on our guard. We must always imagine that the enemy is observing us, and we must expect him at every turn of every road. Something is always to be learned from a misadventure, and as a result of last night we will develop our exercises. We will attempt over the next few days to get everyone familiar with certain defensive procedures. These procedures should become second nature to us all, at any time of day or night, and that will help in the next emergency.'

And for the next week or so military theory was not the boy-scout business of crawling on the ground with a gun and making bird whistles to the man in front. They practised protecting the camp. In one exercise they established a perimeter around the camp; in the other they fanned out far on two sides to prepared positions and waited to ambush any assault party.

Willie thought, 'But what will happen when battle is joined, when the other side attacks? We are not being trained for that at all. This is just the beginning of military theory. This is nothing. All these people will be good for will be to fire a gun at someone who can't fire back. And that is really what they want.'

But there was calm in the camp. Everyone was now waiting for orders.

The leader came to Willie one day and said, 'Headquarters is taking an interest in you. They are detailing you for a special job. You will be leaving in two days. Get your things ready. You will go to the town of Dhulipur. Bhoj Narayan will go with you. He was the sentry who gave the false alarm. But that's not why we are sending him. We are sending him because he is one of the best. We have rented a room for the two of you. We will give you a hundred and fifty rupees. At the end of two weeks we will send you more. You are to stay in your room for further instructions.'

As the leader spoke Willie found it easy to imagine him in a double-breasted suit. He was a man of the comfortable middle class, in his forties, fluent, experienced, easy in manner, confident, rather like a university teacher or a box-wallah executive for a big company. Willie could imagine him as the boy sergeant of the cadets at his school, playing the non-commissioned officer to the junior army officer who came twice a week to train and inspect the cadets. What had caused him to drop out of that easy life? Was it too great a security, was it a conviction that it would be easy for him to return to that world? Willie studied his face, looking for a clue in the smooth skin, the bland features, the too-quiet eyes, and then the idea, transmitted from the man himself, came to him. 'His wife despises him, and has been cuckolding him for years. This is how he intends to revenge himself. What mischief is this elegant man going to cause?'

* * *

IT WAS A DIFFICULT journey to Dhulipur. It took more than a day. Willie put on his civilian clothes (themselves theatrical, a semi-peasant disguise), took some rations from the camp, hung the long fine peasant towel over his shoulder, and put on his leather slippers. They were still new. The slippers were to protect him from scorpions and other dangerous creatures, but it was hard for Willie, too used to socks, to walk in slippers. For much of the time his bare heels slipped off the shiny leather and trod the ground. Bhoj Narayan knew the way. First they walked out of the teak forest. That took more than three hours. Then they came to villages and little fields.

There was a peasant or a farmer Bhoj Narayan knew in one village, and to his thatched house they went in the afternoon when it was hot. The man was out, but his wife was welcoming. Willie and Bhoj Narayan sheltered in the open secondary hut, with cool thatched eaves that hung welcomingly low, shutting out much of the glare. Willie asked the woman of the house for *sattoo*, for which he had developed a taste; and he and Bhoj Narayan moistened it with a little water and ate and were content. The *sattoo* was made from millet. Before the sun went down the master of the house came, dark and sweated from his labours. He asked them to stay for the night in the open hut where they were. The calves were brought in, with their fodder. Rice gruel was offered to Willie and Bhoj Narayan. Willie was for accepting, but Bhoj Narayan said no, the millet *sattoo* was quite enough. Willie allowed himself to be guided by that. And then it was night, the long night that began when it was dark, with the fields outside where village people did everything they had to before settling down to sleep.

Early in the morning they left, to walk the five miles to the bus station. There they waited for a bus; when it came it took them to a railway station; and there they waited for a passenger train to take them to the town of Dhulipur. They arrived in the afternoon.

Bhoj Narayan was now very much in command. He was a big dark man with broad shoulders and a slender waist. He had not talked much to Willie so far, following the rule of the camp, but now in the town he became more communicative as he began looking for the district in which the room had been hired for them. They looked and looked. When they asked, people looked at them in a strange way. At length, disbelievingly, they came to the tanners' area. The smell of decomposing flesh and dog excrement was awful.

Willie said, 'At least no one will come looking for us here.'

Bhoj Narayan said, 'They are testing us. They wish to see whether we will break. Do you think you can stand it?'

Willie said, 'It is possible to stand anything. We are tougher than we think. The people who live here have to stand it.'

The house in which the room had been rented for them was a small low house with a red-tile roof in a street of small low houses. There was an open gutter outside, and the walls of the rented room (shown them by one of the cricket people Joseph had talked about) had the same mottled multi-coloured quality as the walls of the Neo Anand Bhavan, as though all kinds of liquid impurities had worked their way up like a special kind of toxic damp.

Willie thought, 'I must do something to fight this smell. I must try to overcome it mentally.'

But he couldn't. And then, as he had done at various points in his recent journey (and just as sometimes in the past, feeling lost in Africa, unable to pick his way back to safety or to what he would be easy with, and with no one to confess his anxiety to, he had taken to counting the different beds he had slept in since he was born, to keep track of things), so now in the street of the tanners he began re-living the stages of his descent in the past year. From the desolation and real scarcities of a broken-down estate house in an abandoned Portuguese colony in Africa; to the flat in Charlottenburg in Berlin which at first had seemed to him a place looted and bare and unkempt and cold, speaking of post-war neglect, and full of earlier ghosts he could scarcely imagine; to the airport town in India, to the Riviera Hotel, to the Neo Anand Bhavan, to the guerrilla camp in the teak forest, and now this shock of the tanneries in a small town he didn't know and wouldn't be able to find on a map: separate chambers of experience and sensibility, each one a violation with which he in the end would live as though it was a complete world.

It was in this great stench of the street of the tanners that that evening he and Bhoj Narayan became close. As though it had needed that particular calamity (as it appeared) to bring them together. They went out walking, away from the smoky flambeaux of the tanneries, to the dim fluorescent lights of what to Willie now seemed the purer town, the bazaar (its flies now asleep) and the area around the railway station.

Willie said, 'They've given us one hundred and fifty rupees for fourteen days. That's ten rupees a day. In Berlin you wouldn't be able to buy a cup of coffee with that. Do you think they expect us to spend our own money?'

Bhoj Narayan said, with a touch of sternness, 'We should do what they say. They have their reasons.'

And Willie understood that Bhoj Narayan was a true man of the movement, the man in charge of this mission, and had to be heeded.

They went to the bazaar and spent five rupees on dal, cauliflower, and pickles; and another two rupees on coffee. They walked then in the half darkness of the town, talking of their past, each man identifying himself in a way that hadn't been permitted in the camp. Willie spoke of England and his eighteen years in Africa.

Bhoj Narayan said, 'I heard something about that. We must seem like nothing to you.'

Willie said, 'It seems more exciting than it was. Words can give wrong ideas. The names of places can give wrong ideas. They have too many grand associations. When you are in the place itself, London, Africa, everything can seem ordinary. At school we learned a little comic poem by William Blake. I don't think I remember it all. *There was a naughty boy, And a naughty boy was he. He ran away to Scotland, The people there to see. There he found that the ground was as hard, And the cherry was as red, As in England. So he stood in his shoes and he wondered.* That was me. That was why I came looking for you. I was unhappy where I was. I had a strong idea that my place was in this world here.'

In the darkness as they walked Willie saw the post office. He thought, 'I must try to pick my way back here tomorrow.'

Bhoj Narayan said his ancestors had been peasants. They had been driven out of their land and village by a great famine at the end of the nineteenth century. They were a backward caste. They had gone to a new British-built railway town, and there his grandfather had found work of some sort. His father had finished school and found a job in the state transport system. He had then become an accountant. His mother's family had had the same kind of history. They had a cultured background. They were musicians. But they were of the same backward caste.

Willie said, 'You are telling me a success story. Why are you in this movement? Why are you throwing everything away? You are a middle-class man now. Things can only get better for you and your family.'

Bhoj Narayan said, 'Why are you in it?'

'A good question.'

Bhoj Narayan said with a little irritation, 'But why?'

Willie, backing away from his earlier evasiveness, and the social distance it implied, said, 'A long story. I suppose it's the story of my life. I suppose it's the way the world is made.'

'Same here. With people of feeling things can never be cut and dried. When you buy a machine you get a book of instructions. Men are not like that. I am proud of my family, proud of what they have done in the last hundred years. But at the same time I'll tell you. When in the old days I heard about a landlord being killed, my heart sang. I wanted all the feudals to be killed. I wanted them all to be hanged and stay hanging until the flesh fell off their skeletons.'

Willie recognised Joseph's language.

Bhoj Narayan said, 'And I didn't want others to do the killing. I wanted to be there myself. I wanted to show myself to them before they were killed. I wanted to see the surprise and fright in their eyes.'

Willie thought, 'Is this true? Or is he trying to impress me?' He considered the features of the dark man, tried to imagine his family, tried to imagine the powerless past. He said, 'I believe the famine that drove your people out of their village was the famine that drove my great-grandfather, my father's grandfather, out of their ancient temple. Isn't it strange? We are linked more closely than we thought. And I discovered some years ago that Rudyard Kipling wrote a story about that famine. A love story, an English love story.'

Bhoj Narayan was not interested. They walked back towards the street of the tanners, to undress and wait for the night to pass; and Willie was locked then in that new chamber of consciousness, of smell and awfulness, but with the conviction that he would soon be living in it as in a complete world, and would survive.

In the morning he picked his way to the post office. On the old single-page air-letter that he had not finished – where he had scratched out Kandapalli's name and then had been worried about going on – he wrote: *I believe I am among the enemies of the man we talked about. I am not master of my movements. I will be staying here for two weeks. Please write me at the poste restante of this town. This letter will take one week to get to you. Your letter will take a week to get to me. I am depending on you.*

He and Bhoj Narayan went to the bazaar at midday. The food was fresher at midday than in the evening. They ate with relish and then, as they walked about the town, Bhoj Narayan told more of his story. There was no need for Willie to probe.

Bhoj Narayan said, 'I thought in my second year at the

university I should give up my studies and join the guerrillas. I used to go with some friends to the tank on the edge of the town. I suppose it's my old background, but I've always liked green. Grass and trees. It's the way the world should be. We used to talk about what we might do. About joining the guerrillas. But we didn't know how to go about doing anything. I could only think of approaching one of our teachers. He said he didn't know how to put me in touch with the guerrillas. But he did. A man from the engineering department of the town came to see me at the students' hostel one day. He gave me a date when he would be coming to take me to see the people I wanted to see. I promised to come with my friends. But the friends didn't turn up when the time came. They were too frightened. They were too worldly. They loved life too much. So I went on my own. That was how it began. That was three years ago.'

'So it's worked out for you?'

'It's worked out. I've lost a couple of friends. It took me six months to get used to it. I also miss the jokes. In the movement you can't make jokes. And you can't make jokes with the peasants. They absolutely don't like it. Sometimes I feel they will kill you if they think you are teasing them. You have always to say literally what you mean. If you are used to the other way of talking, it's not always easy.'

* * *

So the days passed, ten rupees a day; and with the companionship of Bhoj it was not disagreeable. But as their money dwindled, and no replacement money came, and no instructions, Willie began to be anxious.

Bhoj Narayan said, 'We must ration our money now. We have thirty rupees left. We must spend five rupees a day on food. When we start doing that ten rupees a day will seem like luxury. It will be good discipline.'

'Do you think they have forgotten us?'

'They have not forgotten us.'

On the fifteenth day, when they had been living on five rupees a day for three days, Willie went to the post office. A letter from Sarojini was waiting for him in the poste restante. The sight of the German stamp lifted his heart.

Dear Willie, I don't know how to tell you. I suppose when one is trying to arrange things long distance mistakes in communication can occur. I don't know whether Joseph is responsible or whether somebody else is responsible. The movement, as you know, has split, and what has happened is that you are among psychopaths. In every underground movement, and I mean every underground movement, there is an element of criminality. I have seen plenty of them and I know. I should have told you when you were here, but I thought you were an intelligent man and would find out on your own and know how to deal with it when the time came. I don't have to tell you to be careful. Some of the people around you are what is known in the movement as action men. That means they have killed, and are ready to kill again. They can be boastful and wild. The comfort is that you are all serving the same cause in the end, and the time may come one day when you may be able to cross over and join Kandapalli's people.

He crumpled up the letter and threw it, with its precious German stamp, on a pile of wet and rotting garbage outside the bazaar. Inside the bazaar Bhoj Narayan said, 'This is our last day with money.'

Willie said, 'I feel they have forgotten us.'

'We have to show our resourcefulness. We must start looking for work after we have eaten. There would be part-time work in a place like this.'

'What work can we do?'

'That's the trouble. We have no skill. But we will find something.'

They ate small portions of rice and dal in leaf plates. When they came out Bhoj said, 'Look. Black smoke in the sky a few miles away from here. Chimneys. Sugar factories. It's the grinding season. Let us have a walk.'

They walked to the edge of the town and then they walked through the semi-countryside to the factory, the chimneys getting taller all the time. Trucks loaded with canes passed them all the time, and ahead of them were bullock carts also loaded with canes. It was chaos in the factory yard, but they found a man of authority. Bhoj Narayan said, 'Leave the talking to me.' And five minutes later he came back and said, 'We have a job for a week. From ten at night to three in the morning. We will be picking up wet bagasse after the canes have been crushed. We will be taking the bagasse to a drying area. When the stuff is dry they use it as fuel. But that's not our problem. Twelve rupees a day, a good deal less than the official minimum wage. You wouldn't be able to buy a cup of coffee in Berlin. But we are not in Berlin, and in some situations you don't argue. I told the foreman we were refugees from another country. It was my way of telling him that we weren't going to make trouble. Now we should walk back to the street of the tanners and rest for the night. It will be a long walk there again and a long walk back in the morning.'

And so for Willie the room in the street of the tanners changed again, and became a place of rest before labour. And became, early next morning, just before six, a place where, having walked back in the darkness and bathed off the sticky, sugary bagasse wet from their bodies at the communal tap (fortunately running at that hour), Willie and Bhoj Narayan fell into deep and exhausted sleep, in a kind of brutish contentment.

Willie woke from time to time to the physical aches of his over-exercised body, and then in his half-slumber he saw again the ghostly half-lit scene in the factory yard with the ragged cricket people, his fellow workers, for whom this nightly labour was not a joke or a little out-of-hours drama, a break in routine, but a matter of life and death, walking to and fro in a kind of slow hellish silhouetted dance to the flat wide concrete drying place with small baskets of wet bagasse on their heads, and then with empty baskets in their hands, with others in the distance taking the night's dried bagasse to feed the factory furnace, the flames from the bagasse leaping an extraordinary beautiful turquoise and casting an extra pale green glow on the small dark bodies, shining and wasted: about sixty men in all doing what ten men with wheelbarrows could have done in the same time, and what two simple machines would have done with little fuss.

He woke just before one, reflecting, as he looked at it, that his Rolex watch was like a memory, and a need, of another world. Bhoj Narayan was still sleeping. Willie didn't wish to disturb him. As soon as he could he went out and made for the town away from the street of the tanners. He had an air-letter form and a Pentel pen. He looked for what was known in small towns like this as a hotel, but was only the roughest kind of café or tea shop. Bhoj Narayan had discouraged this kind of adventure. Willie found his hotel. He asked for coffee and steamed rice-cakes. It came with two kinds of chutney and two kinds of dal, and it seemed like the height of luxury, though a month before this hotel, where flies, nimbler than the people, swarmed everywhere and fed on everything, would have worried him. The lean waiter, physically just above the cricket class, with thick oily hair, wore a tunic suit in white drill. It was black and dirty wherever it could be dirty, especially around the bulging side pockets, as though that kind of dirt was a mark of service and hard work. Clearly only one clean suit a week was allowed to the waiter, and this day was near the end of the allotted week.

The waiter wiped the marble table dry for Willie, the flies swarming up in irritation, making for Willie's and the waiter's hair; and Willie took out his air-letter and wrote.

Dear Sarojini, I don't have to tell you that I came into this thing with the purest of hearts and the wish to do what with your teaching and the promptings of my own mind had begun to seem to me to be right. But now I must tell you I feel I am lost. I don't know what cause I am serving, and why I am doing what I do. Right now I am working in a sugar factory, carting wet bagasse from ten at night to three in the morning for twelve rupees a day. What this has to do with the cause of revolution I cannot see. I see only that I have put myself in other people's hands. I did that once before, you will remember, when I went to Africa. I intended never to do it again, but I find now that I have. I am with a senior man of the movement here. I am not easy with him, and I don't think he is easy with me. I have run away from the room we share to write this letter. I believe he is one of the action men you wrote me about. He told me that the peasants don't like jokes, and can kill people who they feel are teasing them. I feel the same is true of him. He asked me why I had joined the movement. I couldn't of course tell him the whole story in two sentences and I said, 'Good question.' As though I was in London or Africa or Berlin. He didn't like that, and I couldn't laugh it off. I have made a few more stumbles like that with him, and the result is I am afraid to talk freely to him, and he resents this. He is the leader. He has been in the movement for three years. I have to do what I am told, and I feel that in a few weeks I have lost my freedom for no good reason that I can see. I am thinking of running away. I have two hundred marks from the Berlin money. I suppose I can change this at a bank, if they don't get too suspicious, and then I can go to a railway station, and pick my way back to our family house. But that would be a kind of death for me, too. I don't want to return to that horrible family unhappiness. I am sorry to be writing like this. I don't know how long I will be in this town and whether it will be worth your while to write me at the poste restante. I will give you a new address as soon as I can.

Bhoj Narayan was still in his canvas cot when Willie got back to the street of the tanners. Willie thought, 'I am sure he knows where I've been and what I've been doing.'

To avoid questions, he said, 'I went to the town and had a coffee and an idli. I needed it.'

Bhoj Narayan said, 'It's only twelve rupees a night at the sugar factory. Go easy. There might be hard days ahead.'

Willie, sleepy again after his breakfast, undressed and got into his little cot. The thought of the long day weighed on him, and the thought of the labour of the night.

He thought, 'Is there a point to all of this? There is a point for Bhoj Narayan. He knows what is being planned and how what we are doing here fits in. He has complete faith in it. I don't have that faith. All I need now is the strength to go on, the strength just for tonight. Let me pray that that strength comes to me from some quarter, some very deep part of my spirit. That is how I must start living now, one day at a time, or one half-day at a time. I have sunk to the depths. I thought this street of the tanners was the limit. But the ghostly bagasse workers have taken me down several notches, and they will be there tonight again, surviving in all their wretchedness. Perhaps I needed to know about these true survivors. Perhaps this exposure to human nullity will do me good, will make me see more clearly.'

He surrendered to pictures of the turquoise flames on the small bodies of the night workers. The pictures became distorted, lost their sequence, and he fell asleep. The light had almost gone when he awakened. Bhoj Narayan was not in the room, and he was thankful for that. He dressed and went to the bazaar and had a little leaf-cup of curried chickpeas. It was like excess, after the morning's feast. It filled him up, and he was able when he came back to the room to wait patiently until eight, when Bhoj Narayan came back and it was time for them to start walking to the sugar factory.

And somehow, as if in answer to his need, the strength came to him for the labour of the night. What had been new and debilitating the previous night, in labour and images, was routine on this second night; that helped. After an hour (the Rolex marking off the time, as in his other life or lives) the comforting idea came to him that it was like doing a long and difficult drive in Africa. The thought of it was worrying beforehand, but once you started it became quite all right, quite mechanical: the road itself seemed to take you where you were going. All you had to do was to be calm and allow yourself to go.

Afterwards they stood in line with the others, sweated,

coated with the sticky grey bagasse, wet, to get their twelve rupees.

Bhoj Narayan said, 'Honest labour.'

Willie didn't know how to deal with that. He didn't know whether Bhoj Narayan was speaking ironically, mocking the way an employer or factory foreman might have spoken, or whether he was being serious and encouraging, and meant that this hard labour of theirs in the bagasse yard was serving the cause and for that reason was to be cherished.

When Willie woke up the next day Bhoj Narayan was not in the room, and it occurred to Willie that he had probably gone out to make some roundabout contact with the movement. Bhoj Narayan's attitude was still that everything was all right, that in due course fresh money and new instructions would come; and Willie no longer raised the matter with him.

It was one o'clock, an hour later than Willie had awakened the day before. His body was getting used to the hours; with a mind racing ahead to alarm, he thought that perhaps in two or three days he would be spending most of the hours of daylight in stupefied sleep, his most alert hours the hours of his bagasse labour.

He went to the hotel he had used the previous day and ordered coffee and steamed rice-cakes. The routine was comforting. The undersized waiter with his thick oily hair was still in his very dirty white drill uniform. It was perhaps a little dirtier now, or much dirtier; at this stage of grey and black degrees of dirt were hard to assess.

Willie thought, 'We will be doing the bagasse job for six more days. Perhaps then we'll be somewhere else. Perhaps I will never see this waiter in a clean uniform. I am sure that is how he sees his uniform: always white and clean and ironed. Perhaps if he sees his uniform as it is he will lose all his style. His life will change.'

He went afterwards to the post office, and tapped at the poste restante counter, to see whether by some miracle there was another letter from Sarojini. Pigeon holes against the dark wall were full of letters of various sizes. The clerk when he came didn't bother to look. He said, 'Nothing today. Perhaps in three days. That's when we get the air mail from Europe.'

He walked in the dingy business area of the little town. Monsoon and sun had mottled the walls and done away with their original colour. Only the signboards, shrill and competing, were new and bright with paint. He passed a branch of the Bank of Baroda. It was very dark inside. The ceiling fans turned slowly, not disturbing the jagged paper piles on desks, and the clerks at the counter were behind a metal grille.

Willie said, 'Would it be possible to change some German marks here?'

'If you have a passport. Twenty-four rupees to a mark. We have a minimum charge of a hundred rupees. You have your passport?'

'Later. I will come back later.'

The idea of running away had come to him only the day before when he was writing to Sarojini. And he thought now, 'If I change a hundred marks I will get twenty-three hundred rupees after the charges. That will be enough to get me where I am thinking of going. I must guard those marks with my life. Bhoj Narayan must never know.'

Bhoj Narayan said nothing about what he had done in the morning. But he had begun to worry. And three days later, when only three days of their work in the sugar factory were left to them, he said to Willie, 'I feel there has been a calamity of some sort. We have to learn to live with the idea of calamity. I've never been let down before. And my feeling is that we should start thinking of making our way back to the camp in the teak forest.'

Willie thought, 'That's what you will be doing. You will be doing it on your own. I have my own plans. I will get away and make a fresh start. This is a mistake.'

The waiter was in a clean uniform that day. It altered him. He smiled and was full of welcome. There were the merest smudges on his pockets where for two or three hours he had been dipping his hands to fish out change.

Willie thought, 'I never thought I would see this. It must be a sign.' And when he went to the post office the man said, 'Something for you. I told you it was going to come in three days.'

Dear Willie, Our father is ill. Neither you nor I have been in touch with him for many years, and I suppose if you asked me I would have said that I was waiting for him to die, so that no one would be able to see what I had come from. I don't know how you feel, but my shame was very great, and my happiest day was when Wolf came and took me away from that dishonest mess of a family and an ashram. But this news of the illness of the old man makes me think of things from his point of view. I suppose with age one can begin to do things like that. I see how damaged he was, through no fault of his own, and I see how he did the best with what was available to him. We are of another generation and another world. We have another idea of human possibility and we must not judge him too harshly. My heart is telling me that I should go and see him, although I know in my bones that when I get there I will find the same old mess and will be ashamed of them all and pining to leave all over again.

Willie thought, 'The waiter's clean white uniform was a sign. That idea of changing a hundred marks into rupees and making my way back to the ashram was a bad idea. It is cowardly. It is against all my knowledge of the world. I must never think of it again.'

When he went back to the street of the tanners he said to Bhoj Narayan, 'You are right. We should start thinking of making our way back to the camp. If there has been a calamity they will need us all the more.'

They were very close then, and that afternoon in the town, and walking to the factory, and during the hours of work and during the walk back just before dawn. And Willie for the first time felt something like companionship and affection for the dark man.

He thought, 'I have never had this feeling for any man. It is wonderful and enriching, this feeling of friendship. I have waited forty years for it. This business is working out.'

They were awakened about noon by a commotion outside their house: many harsh voices speaking at once. The harsh voices were the voices of the tanners, as though they had developed this special grinding quality of voice to compensate for the high smell in which they lived. The light around and above the door was dazzling. Willie was for looking out. Bhoj Narayan pulled him to one side. He said, 'Somebody is looking for us. It is better for me to deal with it. I will know how to talk.' He dressed and went out into the commotion, which immediately became more of a commotion, but then was stilled by the authority of his new voice. The voices moved away from the house, and a few minutes later Bhoj Narayan came back with a man in what Willie could now recognise as the peasant disguise people in the movement used.

Bhoj Narayan said, 'I never thought we were going to be let down. But we almost gave you up. We've been living on air for a week.'

The mock-peasant said, wiping his face with the long thin towel hanging over his shoulder, like an actor growing into his part, 'We've been under great pressure. The Greyhounds. We've lost some people. But you were not forgotten. I've brought you your money, and your instructions.'

Bhoj Narayan said, 'How much?'

'Five hundred rupees.'

'Let's go into the town. There are now three of us outsiders in one little room in the settlement, and we've drawn a lot of attention to ourselves. That could be unhealthy.'

The mock-peasant said, 'I had to ask. Perhaps I didn't use the right words. And they became suspicious.'

Bhoj Narayan said, 'You probably tried to be funny.'

He and the newcomer walked ahead. They all came together again at the hotel where Willie had his coffee and rice-cakes. The waiter's uniform was degrading fast.

Bhoj Narayan said to Willie, 'The leadership are taking quite an interest in you. You've hardly been in the movement, but already they want you to be a courier.'

Willie said, 'What does a courier do?'

'He takes messages from one area to another, passes on instructions. He's not a fighter, he never knows the whole situation, but he's important. He might do other things as well, depending on the situation. He might ferry arms from point A to point B. The point about a good courier is that he has to look OK everywhere. He must never stand out. And you do that very well, Willie. Have you ever watched a street? I have, watching for policemen in disguise, and it doesn't take long to spot the people in a street who don't belong. Even trained people. They can't help it. They give themselves away in twenty ways. But for some reason Willie looks at home everywhere. Even in the bagasse yard he looked at home.'

Willie said, 'It's the one thing I have worked at all my life, not being at home anywhere, but looking at home.'

FOUR

Safe Houses

THE MOVEMENT HAD suffered badly from police action in a certain sector, had lost a whole squad, and to take pressure off other squads in that sector the leadership – far off, mysterious – had decided to open a new front in another area which had so far, in the language of guerrilla war, been untroubled.

Until then for Willie the guerrilla territory had been a series of unconnected landscapes – forest, village, fields, small town. Now as a courier, with Bhoj Narayan as his guide and superior, the landscapes began to join up. He was always on the move, on foot in the villages, in three-wheeler scooters or buses on the highroads, or in trains. He was on no police list as yet; he could travel openly; this was part of his value as a courier. This being on the move pleased him, gave him a feeling of purpose and drama, though he could only intuit the general guerrilla situation. Part of his business as a man who travelled was to give encouragement, to exaggerate the extent of the liberated areas, to suggest that in many areas the war was almost on the point of being won, and required only one last push.

He spent more time in towns and it became possible for him

to receive letters from Sarojini. In the towns he also began to eat better food. Strangely, the food in the countryside – where the food was grown – was bad; in the town every day could be a feast day. In the villages, when times were good, the peasant heaped his plate or leaf with grain, and was content to add only flavourings of various sorts; in the towns even poor people ate smaller quantities of grain, and more vegetables and lentils. Because he was eating better Willie became less liable to small illnesses, and the depressions they could bring on.

And for the first time since his two weeks in the camp in the teak forest, he began as a courier to get some better idea of the people who were his comrades in the movement. His impressions in the camp had not been good, but now with his deep relationship with Bhoj Narayan, a relationship which in the beginning had not gone well, he controlled his wish to see the flaws in people.

Once every two weeks or so there would be a meeting of senior people from various sectors. Willie helped to arrange these meetings. He was present at many of them. They were usually in a town and they could be risky, since any unusual gathering would have been spotted by the local people and reported to the police. So each man or each couple of men had their own contact in the town, and aimed to arrive at the contact's house in the early evening, after a journey which could be quite long, could last a day or more, could involve day-long walks on the embankments between fields, away from the dangerous public roads. They came in clothes that would not draw attention. Disguise mattered. The instructions were that on the road they should dress as they might have dressed in the villages. Goatherds or weavers, or people who were pretending to be those things, wore blanket shawls which hid almost everything about a man.

It was from the contact that people found out when they arrived where in the town the meeting was to be. Sometimes they went then to the roof of the contact's house and changed into less sweated clothes; or they changed from workaday country clothes, the local loincloth and the long shirt with big pockets at the sides and the brightly-coloured thin towel on the shoulder, to town clothes, trousers and shirt or long tunic. Sometimes, for all their revolutionary talk, they wished to wear trousers to be seen as trousers-people, to give themselves a little more authority with their fellows during the discussions. They took off their rough village slippers once they were inside the meeting house; but their feet remained scratched and marked with deep dirt even after washing and, with the scattering of grubby blanket shawls, gave the gathering a village feel.

People came to the town to talk, to receive instructions, to do their self-criticism sessions. But they also came to eat, to savour the simplest town food, even to taste proper granular salt. And this suppressed simple greed led to an inverted kind of boasting, with people talking competitively of the austerity of their lives in the villages.

At one of his first meetings – in a railway settlement, in a railway house, where the furniture in the main room had been pushed back to the walls, and people were sitting on mattresses and sheets on the floor – Willie heard a pale-complexioned man say, 'I have been eating cold rice for the last three days.' Willie didn't treat this as a friendly conversation starter. He took it literally. He didn't believe it, disliked the boasting, and he fixed his eyes on the man's face a little longer than he should. The man noticed, and didn't like it. He returned Willie's gaze, hardness for hardness, while continuing to speak to the room. 'But that's no hardship for me. It's the way I lived as a child.' Willie thought, 'Oh, oh. I've made an enemy.' He tried afterwards to avoid the man's gaze, but he was aware all evening of the man's malevolence growing. The occasion was poisoned for him. He remembered his early distrust of Bhoj Narayan, the way he had judged a man who had never left India by the standards of another country. He didn't know how to retrieve the situation with the eater of cold rice, and he learned later that evening that the man was the head of a squad, and perhaps a good deal more within the movement, a senior and important man. Willie was only a courier, doing what was thought of as semi-intellectual propaganda work, and on probation; it would be some time before he was admitted to membership of a squad.

Willie thought, 'I once unthinkingly said "Good question" to Bhoj Narayan, and for a time earned his hatred. Out of old habit, when this man was talking about eating cold rice, I looked at him more mockingly than I knew. And now he is my enemy. He will want to put me down. Like Bhoj Narayan with some other people, he will want to see the mockery in my eyes replaced by fear.'

His enemy was known as Einstein, and over the next few months Willie picked up various pieces of his story, which was legendary in the movement. He came of a peasant family. A primary school teacher spotted his mathematical talent and pushed him up as far as he could in a country setting. No one in that family had ever had higher education, and immense sacrifices were made, when the time came, to send the young man to a neighbouring small town where he could go to a university. A room, more properly a space, six feet by four feet, was rented in the verandah of a washerman's house for fifteen rupees a month. The smallness of his living space, and the tininess of the sums he dealt in was part of the romance of his story.

Einstein's routine as a student in the washerman's house was famous. He rose at five, rolled up his bedding, and cleaned out his living space (Willie, old ways clinging to him, didn't think that could take long). Then he washed his pots and pans (he kept them separate from the washerman's) and boiled his rice over firewood in the kitchen part of the verandah. Willie noticed in the story that there was no room in Einstein's student timetable for the gathering of firewood; perhaps on firewood days Einstein was up at four. He ate his rice when it was ready and went to his classes. When he came back in the afternoon he washed his clothes; he had only one suit of clothes. Then he cooked some more food, perhaps rice again, and ate and went to sleep. In between chores he did his studying.

The examinations for the Bachelor of Science degree came. Einstein found that he was at sea with the very first problem of the first paper. His mind went blank. He thought he should write a letter of apology to his father for his failure. He began to write, but then as he wrote an entirely novel way of solving the first problem presented itself to him. The rest of the examination came easily to him, and his novel solution of the first problem created a stir in the university. Everybody got to know about the letter of apology out of which, as in a dream, the solution had come; and it began to be said that he was in the great line of Indian twentieth-century mathematical geniuses. This talk, which he encouraged, began at last to affect him. He published a mathematical paper in an Indian journal. It was well received, and he thought that it had fallen to him to correct Einstein. This soon became a mania. He lost his university job and could get no other. He published no other paper. He returned to his village, dropped all the trappings of education (trousers, shirt tucked in, shoes and socks), and dreamed of destroying the world. When the movement appeared, he joined it.

Willie thought, 'This man cannot start a revolution. He hates us all. I must make my way to Kandapalli and the other side.'

Then there came to him, at the poste restante of one of the towns he regularly visited, a letter from Sarojini.

Dear Willie, Our father is seriously ill and all his ashram work is suspended. I know you will feel that this is no great loss to the world, but I have begun to have other ideas. The ashram was a creation, say what you will about it. I suppose that is the effect the prospect of death has on us. The other news, which is just as bad, and perhaps even worse from your point of view, is that Kandapalli is not well. He is losing his grip, and nothing is weaker than a revolutionary who is losing his grip. People who admired the strong man and wished to share in his strength run from the weak man. His weakness becomes a kind of moral failing, mocking all his ideas, and that I fear is what is happening to Kandapalli and his followers. I feel I have landed you in a mess. I don't know whether it is possible for you to get back to Joseph, or whether Joseph himself is part of the problem.

Willie thought, 'It is too late now to worry about Joseph and his vicious son-in-law, filling that flat with tension. No one more vain and vicious than the low wishing to set the record straight. I was worried about that son-in-law as soon as I saw him, with his twisted self-satisfied smile.'

* * *

BHOJ NARAYAN SAID one day, 'We have an interesting new recruit. He owns a three-wheeler scooter-taxi. He comes of a simple weaver-caste background, but for some reason – perhaps a teacher, perhaps the example of a friend or distant relation, perhaps some insult – he was granted ambition. That's the kind of person who's attracted to us. They've begun to move, and they find they want to move faster. In the movement we've done research on those people. We've studied caste patterns in the villages.'

Willie thought, 'You are my friend, Bhoj Narayan. But that's your story too. That's why you understand him.' And then a little later, not wishing to betray his friend even in thought, this extra idea came to Willie: 'Perhaps it's my story as well. Perhaps that's where we all are. Perhaps that's why we are so hard to manage.'

Bhoj Narayan said, 'He sought our people out. He invited them to his house and gave them food. When the police repression was bad he offered his house as a hiding place. I think he might be useful in our courier work. We should go and check him out. His story is like Einstein's, but without the brilliance. He went to a little town to study, but he didn't get a degree. The family had to call him back to the village. They couldn't afford the ten or twelve rupees rent for a space in the town, or the twenty or thirty rupees for the boy's food. It's pathetic. It makes you want to cry. He suffered when he went back to the village. He had got too used to town life. Do you know what town life was for him? It was going to a little tea shop or hotel and having a coffee and a cigarette in the morning. It was going to a half-rupee seat in a rough little cinema. It was wearing shoes and socks. It was wearing trousers and tucking in his shirt and walking like a man, not flopping about with country slippers and inside a long shirt. When he went back to the family's weaver-caste house in the village he lost all of that at one blow. He had nothing to do. He wasn't going to be a weaver. And he was bored out of his mind. You know what he said? "In the village it's pure nature, not even a transistor." Just the long, empty days and the longer nights. In the end he got a bank loan and bought a scooter-taxi. At least it got him out of the village. But really it was his boredom that brought him to us. Once you learn about boredom in the village you are ready to be a revolutionary.'

One afternoon a week or so later Willie and Bhoj Narayan went to the scooter-man's village. This wasn't a village of uneven thatched roofs and dirt roads, the village of popular imagination. The roads were paved and the roofs were of local red curved tiles. Weavers were a backward caste, and the dalit or backward-caste area of the village began at a bend in the main village lane, but if you didn't know it was a dalit area you would have missed it. The houses were like those that had gone before. The weavers sat in the late-afternoon shade in the yards in front of their houses and spun yarn into thread. The looms were in the houses; through open front doors people could be seen working them. It was an unhurried scene of some beauty; it was hard to imagine that this spinning and weaving, which looked so much like some precious protected folk craft, was done only for the village, for the very poor, and was a desperate business for the people concerned, run on very narrow margins. The spinning wheels were home-assembled, with old bicycle rims for the main wheels; every other part seemed to be made from twigs and twine and looked frail, ready to snap.

The scooter-man's scooter was in his front yard, next to a spinning wheel. He lived with his brother and his brother's family and the house was larger than the average. The two bedrooms were on the left, the rooms with the looms were on the right. The rooms were no more than ten or twelve feet deep, so that you were hardly in the house when you were out of it. At the back of the house on one side was the open kitchen and a large basket with corn-cobs, bought for fuel. On the other side was the outhouse. Some richer person's field came right up to the plot, right up to where the scooter-man's brother had planted a fine-leaved tree, as yet quite small and slender, which in a couple of seasons would be cut down and used as fuel.

Space: how it always pressed, how in all the openness it always became minute. Willie was unwilling to work out the living arrangements of the house. He imagined there would be some kind of loft in each of the bedrooms. And he understood how, to a young man who had known the comparative freedom of a small town, to be reduced to the small space of this weaver's house, and to have nothing to do, would be a kind of death.

They brought out low benches for Willie and Bhoj Narayan, and with ancient courtesies, as though they were very rich, they offered tea. Old deprivation showed on the face of the wife of the brother. Her cheeks were sunken and she looked about forty, though she could have been no more than twenty-five or twenty-eight. But Willie at the same time was moved to notice the care with which the brother's wife had dressed for the occasion, in a new sari of muted colours, grey and black in a small oblong pattern, with a fringe of gold.

The scooter-man was beside himself with pleasure to have Willie and Bhoj Narayan in his house. He spoke a little too freely of his admiration for the movement, and from time to time Willie noticed a kind of disturbance in the brother's eyes.

Willie thought, 'There's a little trouble here. Perhaps it's the difference in ages, perhaps it's the difference in education. One brother has been a trousers-man and has learned boredom. The older brother hasn't. He or his wife may feel that they are sinking too deep in something they don't understand.'

Afterwards, when Bhoj Narayan asked Willie, 'What do you think?' Willie said, 'Raja is all right.' Raja was the name of the scooter-man. 'But I am not so sure of the brother or the brother's wife. They are frightened. They don't want trouble. They just want to do their weaving work and earn their four hundred rupees a month. How much do you think Raja borrowed from the bank for his scooter?'

'A scooter costs about seventy or seventy-five thousand rupees. That's new. Raja's scooter would have cost a good deal less. He's probably borrowed thirty or forty thousand. The bank wouldn't have given him more.'

'The elder brother probably thinks about that every night. He probably believes that Raja is over-educated and has got above himself and is heading for a fall.'

Bhoj Narayan said, 'They adore Raja. They are very proud of him. They will do what he wants them to do.'

* * *

TWO OR THREE times a month they called out Raja to do some work for the movement. He took Willie or Bhoj Narayan or some others to where they had to go in a hurry. And, having this facility now, Willie went often to the post office in small towns, to check his poste restante letters from Germany. They got to know Willie in these post offices; they didn't always ask him to show his passport. That had seemed to him charming, the Indian friendliness people spoke about; it occurred to him only later to be worried.

And then, after some months, Raja began to ferry supplies, with Willie or Bhoj Narayan, or on his own. There was a space below the passenger seat of the scooter, and it was also easy to fit a false floor. The pick-up and drop-off points always changed; it was understood they were only stages in a kind of relay. Bhoj Narayan acted as a coordinator; he knew a little more than Willie, but even he didn't know everything. Supplies, mainly weapons, were being assembled for a new front somewhere. After all its recent losses the movement was cautious. It was using many couriers, each courier being used only once or twice a month; and supplies were being sent in small quantities, so that discovery or accident would result only in a small local loss, nothing to alter the larger plan.

Raja said to Willie one day, 'Have you ever seen the police headquarters? Shall we go, just to have a look?'

'Why not?'

It had never occurred to Willie to go looking for the adversary. He had lived for too long now with his disconnected landscapes, his disconnected duties, with no true idea of the results of his actions. It hadn't occurred to him that this other, well-mapped view of the area was also open to him, would be as easy as opening a book. And when they were on the main road, heading for the district headquarters, it was for a while like returning to an earlier, whole life.

The landscape acquired a friendlier feel. The neem and flamboyant shade trees beside the road, though for stretches the line of trees was broken, spoke of some old idea of benevolence that was still living on. The road acquired another feel, the feel of the working world, with the pleasures of that world – the truck stops with big painted signs, the cola advertisements, the smoky black kitchens at the back with earthen fireplaces on high platforms, and the brightly painted plastic tables and chairs (everything painted the colour of the cola advertisements) in the dusty yards at the front – so different in mood and promise from the self-sacrificing pleasures Willie had been living with for more than a year. Where there was water there were friendly small fields of paddy, maize, tobacco, cotton, sometimes potatoes, sometimes peppers. The fields of the liberated areas Willie knew had fallen into ruin: the old landlords and feudals had run away years before from the guerrilla chaos, and no secure new order had been established.

It was easy for Willie to return to old ways of feeling, and it was a shock when they came to the district headquarters, to the police area at one end of the little town, in a terrible noise of twenty or thirty taxi-scooters like Raja's, and in a brown-blue billow of exhaust smoke, to see the stained old sandbags (speaking of sun and rain and sun again) and machine guns and the crumpled, much used uniforms of the Central Reserve Police Force outside police headquarters, uniforms that spoke of a deadly seriousness: to see this effect of the disconnected things he had been doing, to understand in a new way that lives were at stake. The police parade ground, perhaps also the playing ground, was sandy; the kerbstones of the roads within, the camp roads, were newly whitewashed; the shade trees were big and old: like the rest of that police area, they would have had a history: they probably came from the British time. Raja, shouting above the screech and scrape of scooters, excitedly told Willie where in the main two-storeyed building the police commissioner's rooms were, where the police guest rooms were, and where elsewhere in the compound, at one side of the parade or playing ground, the police welfare buildings were.

Willie was not excited. He was thinking, with a sinking heart, 'When they were telling me about what the guerrillas were doing, I should have asked about the police. I never should have allowed myself to believe that there was only one side in this battle. I don't know how we make mistakes like that. But we do.'

Not long after this Raja was admitted to a training camp. He stayed for a month, then went back to his scooter work.

It was then that things began to go wrong for him.

Bhoj Narayan said to Willie one day, 'It's terrible to say, but I think we are having trouble with Raja. Both his last deliveries of supplies were captured by the police just where he deposited them.'

Willie said, 'It might be an accident. And possibly the people who received them were to blame.'

Bhoj Narayan said, 'I have another reading. I feel the police have been bribing his elder brother. Perhaps bribing both brothers. Thirty thousand rupees is a big debt.'

'Let us leave it for the time being. Let us not use him.'

'We'll do that.'

Two weeks later Bhoj Narayan said, 'It's as I feared. Raja wants to leave the movement. We can't allow that. He'd have us all picked up. I think we'll have to go and see him. I have told him we are coming to talk it over. We should aim to get there just when the sun sets. We'll take another scooter.'

The sky was red and gold. The few big trees about the weavers' area were black. In a house about a hundred yards away there was a cooking fire. It was the house of a family who made bidi leaf-cigarettes. If they rolled a thousand cigarettes a day they made forty rupees. This meant they made twice as much as a weaver for a day's work.

Bhoj Narayan said to Raja and his brother, 'I think we should go inside the house.'

When they went in the elder brother said, 'I asked him to leave. I didn't want him to get killed. If he gets killed we will have to sell the scooter. We will make a loss on that and we will still have to pay off the debt to the bank. I wouldn't be able to do it. My children will become paupers.'

The elder brother's wife, who on the previous occasion had worn her best sari, with the gold fringe, but was now wearing only a peasant woman's skirt, said, 'Maim him, sir. Take away an arm or a leg. He will still be able to sit at a loom and do something. Please don't kill him. We will become beggars if you do.' She sat on the floor and held Bhoj Narayan's legs.

Willie thought, 'The more she begs and pleads, the angrier he will get. He wants to see the fear in the man's eyes.'

And when the shot was fired, and Raja's head became a mess, the elder brother's eyes popped as he stared at the ground. That was how they left him, the elder brother, staring and pop-eyed next to the home-made looms.

All the way back to their base they were grateful for the stutter of the scooter.

A week later, when they met face to face again, Bhoj Narayan said, 'Give it six months. In my experience that's what it takes.'

* * *

FOR SOME WEEKS afterwards Willie marvelled at himself. He thought, 'When I first met Bhoj Narayan I didn't like him. I was uneasy with him. And then somehow when we were together in the street of the tanners, and I was very low, I found a companionship with him. That companionship was necessary to me. It helped me through a bad patch, when I was sinking into old ways of feeling, old ways of wishing to run away, and that feeling of companionship is now what is uppermost when I think of him. I know that the other Bhoj Narayan, the man I distrusted, is still there, but now I have to look very hard for him. The later man is the man I know and understand. I know how he thinks and why he does what he does. I carry the scene in the house with the looms in my head. I see the scooter in the yard next to the spinning wheel with the old bicycle rim. I see that poor elder brother with the popping eyes, and understand his pain. And yet I do not think I will willingly betray Bhoj Narayan to anyone. I do not think there is any point. I haven't worked out why I feel there is no point. I could say various things about justice and people on the other side. But it wouldn't be true. The fact is I have arrived at a new way of feeling. And it is amazing that it should have happened just after fourteen or fifteen months of this strange life. The first night, in the camp in the teak forest, I was disturbed by the faces of the new recruits. Later I was disturbed by the faces at the meetings in the safe houses. I feel I understand them all now.'

* * *

THEY WENT ON with the slow, careful labour of taking supplies to where a new front was to be opened, working like ants digging out a nest in the ground or taking leaf fragments to that nest, each worker content and important with his minute task, carrying a speck of earth or a bitten-off scrap of a leaf.

Bhoj Narayan and Willie went to a small railway town to check that the deliveries there were secure. This town was one of the places where Willie picked up his poste restante letters. He had last visited it with Raja, and had had the feeling then – from the too familiar, too friendly clerk – that he had been overdoing the trips to the post office in Raja's scooter and had been making himself too noticeable there as the man who got letters from Germany. Until then he had thought of the poste restante as quite safe; very few people even knew of the facility. But now he had a feeling of foreboding. He examined all the dangers that might be connected with the poste restante; he dismissed them all. But the foreboding remained. He thought, 'This is because of Raja. This is how a bad death lays a curse on us.'

The railway workers' colony was an old settlement, from the 1940s perhaps, of flat-roofed two-roomed and three-roomed concrete houses set down tightly together in dirt roads without sanitation. It might have been presented at the time as a work of social conscience, a way of doing low-cost housing, and it might just about have looked passable in the idealising fine line (and fine lettering) of the architect's elevation. Thirty-five years on, the thing created was awful. Concrete had grown dingy, black for two or three feet above ground; window frames and doors had been partially eaten away. There were no trees, no gardens, only in some houses little hanging pots of basil, a herb associated with religion and used in some religious rites. There were no sitting areas or playing areas or washing areas or clothes-drying areas; and what had once been clean and straight and bare in the architect's drawing was now full of confused lines, electric wires thick and thin dipping from one leaning pole to the next, and the confusion was fully peopled: people compelled here by their houses to live out of doors in all seasons: as though you could do anything with people here, give them anything to live in, fit them in anywhere.

The safe house was in one of the back streets. It seemed perfect cover.

Bhoj Narayan said, 'Stay about a hundred feet behind me.'

And Willie dawdled, his heels slipping off the smooth leather of his village sandals and trailing on the dirt of the street.

Some scrawny boys were playing a rough kind of cricket with a very dirty tennis ball, a bat improvised from the central rib of a coconut branch, and a box for a wicket. Willie saw four or five balls bowled: there was no style or true knowledge of the game.

Willie caught up with Bhoj Narayan at the house.

Bhoj Narayan said, 'There's no one there.'

They went around to the back. Bhoj Narayan banged on the flimsy door, which was rotten at the bottom where rain had splashed on it for many seasons. It would have been easy to kick it in. But sharp, acrid voices from three houses at the back called out to them: women and men sitting in the narrow shadow of their houses.

Bhoj Narayan said, 'I am looking for my brother-in-law. His father is in hospital.'

A wretchedly thin woman in a green sari that showed up all her bones said, 'There's no one there. Some people came for him one morning and he went away with them.'

Bhoj Narayan asked, 'When was that?'

The woman said, 'Two weeks ago. Three weeks.'

Bhoj Narayan said under his breath to Willie, 'I think we should get out of here.' To the woman he said, 'We have to take the message to other relatives.'

They walked back through the parody of the cricket game.

Bhoj Narayan said, 'We are still paying for Raja. Everybody he got to know with us is compromised. I let my guard down, I liked him so much. We have to give up this town. We are being watched even as we walk here.'

Willie said, 'I don't think it was Raja. It might have been Raja's brother, and he didn't really know what he was doing.'

'Raja or Raja's brother, we've taken a bad knock. We've lost a year's work. Lakhs of rupees in weapons. We were building up a squad here. Heaven knows what has happened in other sectors.'

They walked away from the railway colony to the older town.

Willie said, 'I would like to go to the post office. There might be a letter from my sister. And since we are not coming back here this might be my last chance for a while to hear from her.'

The post office was a small, much decorated British-built stone building. It had ochre or magnolia walls edged with raised masonry painted red; it had deep, low stone eaves in the Indian style; and a semi-circular stone or masonry panel at the top of the façade gave the date 1928. Obliquely opposite across the thoroughfare was a tea shop.

Willie said, 'Let's have a tea or a coffee.'

When the coffee came Willie said, 'I have to tell you this. I have become nervous of the post office. I came here too often with Raja. You know how he was. Itchy feet. He always wanted to be on the road. I would come here even when I knew that there wouldn't be a letter from my sister. You could say that sometimes I came with Raja only for the company and the ride. The clerk became friendly. It was nice in the beginning, being known. Then it worried me.'

Bhoj Narayan said, 'I will go for you.'

He took a sip of coffee, put the cup down, and made his way across the bright road to the post office doorway, dark below the low stone eaves. He was swallowed up in the gloom and at the same time Willie saw four or five men in varying costumes detaching themselves from the fixed postures in which they had been sitting around the dark mouth of the post office. A second later these men, all together now, were hurrying Bhoj Narayan to what had looked like a taxi but now showed itself to be an unmarked police car.

After the car drove away Willie paid for the coffee and crossed the bright road to the poste restante counter. The clerk was new.

He said to the clerk, 'What was all that about?'

The clerk said, with his too formal English, 'Some malefactor. The police were waiting for him for a week.'

Willie said, 'Can I buy stamps at this counter?'

'You do that at the front.'

Willie thought, 'I must leave. I must leave fast. I must go to the railway station. I have to go back to base as fast as I can.'

And then, with every new thought that came during his fast walk in the afternoon sun, he understood his predicament more and more clearly. Sarojini's letter would now be in the hands of the police. Perhaps earlier letters as well. Everything was now known about him. He was now on the police list. He no longer had the protection of anonymity. And it was only many minutes later, after he had digested these new facts about himself, that he began to live again those very simple two or three minutes of Bhoj Narayan's walk and capture. It was Bhoj Narayan's boast that he knew how to study a street, to see who didn't belong. The gift had failed him at the end. Or he hadn't thought to use it. Perhaps he hadn't understood the danger. Perhaps he had been too disturbed by what had happened before in the railway colony.

At the railway station he saw from the dust-blown, faded black-and-white boards that the next train going in the direction he wished to go was an express and not a passenger train. Passenger trains were slow, stopping at all the stations on the way. The express train would take him many miles beyond where he would normally get off. It would commit him to walking at night through villages and across fields, exciting dogs in villages and birds in open areas, being always at the centre of a great commotion; or he would have to ask at some peasant's or outcast's hut at the edge of a village to be put up for the night, and take his chance in an open shed, with the chickens and the calves.

The express train was due in just over an hour. The idle thought came to him that the Rolex on his wrist would give him away to anyone on the lookout for a fugitive with German connections. Then that simulated anxiety became real, and he began to wonder whether he had been followed from the town, whether some expert police street-watcher hadn't spotted him as an intruder, not a local, in the tea shop opposite the post office.

There was a way at ground level over the tracks to the platform at the other side. This way was busy. There was also an old timber bridge, with a walkway between high half-walls (high, perhaps, to prevent people throwing themselves in front of trains). There were only half a dozen people there. They were young people; they were on the bridge for the adventure and the view. Willie went and stood with them and, knowing that only his head and shoulders showed, tried to become a watcher of crowds. In no time he was fascinated, seeing how unselfconscious people were in their movements, how unique each man's movements were, and how much of the person they revealed.

He saw nothing to worry him, and when the express came in, and the crowd appeared to roar, and the hucksters put an extra edge into their cries that lifted them above the general roar, he ran down and forced himself into a third-class compartment that was already quite packed. The open windows had horizontal metal bars; there was fine blown dust everywhere; everything was warm, and everyone smelled of old clothes and tobacco. When the express moved off again into the sunlight he thought, 'Luck has been with me. And for the first time here I have been on my own.'

Not far from the passenger-train halt where he would have preferred to get off the track had a sharp bend. Even express trains slowed down there, and Willie, feeling that luck was now with him, was planning to jump off the express at that point, to save himself a long night's march in unfamiliar territory. That point was about two hours away.

He thought, 'I am on my own. Bhoj Narayan is no longer with me. I suppose I will have a rough time with some people now.'

He considered the people in his compartment. They would have been like the poor Bhoj Narayan and his family had risen out of in two or three generations. All that work and ambition had now been wasted; all that further possibility had been thrown away. He had told Bhoj Narayan, when they had talked of these things a long time before, and before they had become friends, that Bhoj Narayan's family story was a success story. But Bhoj Narayan had not replied, had not appeared to hear. The same was true, though in a much smaller way, of Raja's upward movement from the weaver caste. That, too, was full of further possibility, and that, too, had come to nothing. What was the point of those lives? What was the point of what could be seen as those two suicides?

Many minutes later, a little nearer the jumping-off point when the track curved, Willie thought, 'I am wrong. I am looking at it from my own point of view. Everything was the point for Bhoj Narayan. He felt himself to be a man. That was what the movement and even his suicide – if we think of it like that – gave him.'

And then a little later, almost before he jumped, Willie thought, 'But that is romantic and wrong. It takes much more to be a man. Bhoj Narayan was choosing a short cut.'

The express slowed down, to about ten miles an hour. Willie jumped on to the steep embankment and allowed himself to roll down.

The daylight was going. But Willie knew where he was. He had a walk of three miles or so to a village and a hut, more a farmhouse, whose owner he knew very well. The monsoon was over, but now, as if out of spite, it began to rain. Those three miles took a long time. Still, it could have been worse. If courage had not come to him, and he hadn't jumped off the train at that dangerous steep bend, he would have been taken many extra miles to where the express stopped: a day's journey on foot, at least.

It was just before eight when he came to the village. There were no lights. People went to sleep early here; nights were long. The village street ran along the mud-and-wattle front wall of Shivdas's high farmhouse. Willie shook the low door and called. Presently Shivdas called back, and soon, wearing almost nothing, a very dark and tall and gaunt man, he opened the low door and let Willie into the kitchen, which was at the front of the house, behind the mud-and-wattle street wall. The thatch was black and grainy from years of cooking smoke.

Shivdas said, 'I wasn't expecting you.'

Willie said, 'There's been an emergency. Bhoj Narayan has been arrested.'

Shivdas took the news calmly. He said, 'Come, dry yourself. Some tea? Some rice?'

He called to someone in the next room, and there was movement there. Willie knew what that movement meant: Shivdas was asking his wife to give up their bed to the visitor. It was what Shivdas did on such occasions. The courtesy came instinctively to him. He and his wife then left the thatched main house and moved to the low, open, tile-covered rooms at the side of the courtyard at the back, where their children slept.

Less than an hour later, lying in Shivdas's bed below the high, black, cool thatch, in a warm smell of old clothes and tobacco which was like the smell of the third-class railway compartment of just a couple of hours before, Willie thought, 'We think, or they think, that Shivdas does what he does because he is a peasant revolutionary, someone created by the movement, someone new and very precious. But Shivdas does what he does because he is instinctively following old ideas, old ways, old courtesies. One day he will not give up his bed to me. He will not think he needs to. That will be the end of the old world and the end of the revolution.'

FIVE

Deeper in the Forest

He got to his base – it had been his and Bhoj Narayan's, his commander – late the next afternoon. It was a half-tribal or quarter-tribal village deep in the forest and so far not touched by police action; it was a place where he might truly rest, if such rest was possible for him now.

He arrived at what some people still called the hour of cow-dust, the hour when in the old days a cattle boy (hired for a few cents a day by the village) drove the village cattle home in a cloud of dust, and the golden light of early evening turned that sacred dust to soft, billowing gold. There were no cattle boys now; there were no landowners to hire them. The revolutionaries had put an end to that kind of feudal village life, though there were still people who needed to have their cattle looked after, and there were still little boys who pined to be hired for the long, idle day. But the golden light at this time of day was still considered special. It lit up the open forest all around, and for a few minutes made the white mud walls and the thatch of the village huts and the small scattered fields of mustard and peppers look well cared for and beautiful: like a village of an old fairytale, restful and attractive to come upon, but then full of menace, with dwarves and giants and tall wild forest growth and men with axes and children being fattened in cages.

This village was for the time being under the control of the movement. It was one of a number of headquarters villages and was subject to something like a military occupation by the guerrillas. They were noticeable in their thin olive uniforms and peaked caps with a red star: trousers-people, as the tribals respectfully called them, and with guns.

Willie had a room in a commandeered long hut. He had a traditional four-poster string bed, and he had learned like a villager to store small objects between the rafters (of trimmed tree branches) and the low thatch. The floor, of beaten earth, was bound and made smooth with a mixture of mud and cowdung. He had got used to it. The hut for some months had become a kind of home. It was where he returned after his expeditions; and it was an important addition to the list he carried in his head of places he had slept in, and was able to count (as was his habit) when he felt he needed to get hold of the thread of his life. But now the hut had also become a place where, without Bhoj Narayan, he was horribly alone. He was glad to have got there, but then, almost immediately, he had become restless.

The rule of privacy, of not saying too much about oneself, and not inquiring into people's circumstances in the world outside, which had been laid down during his first night in the camp in the teak forest, that rule still held.

He knew only about the man in the room next to his. This man was dark and fierce and with big eyes. When he was a child or in his teens he had been badly beaten up by the thugs of some big landlord, and ever since then he had been in revolutionary movements in the villages. The first of those movements, historically the most important, had faded away; the second had been crushed; and now, after some years of hiding, he was on his third. He was in his mid or late forties, and no other style of life was possible for him. He liked tramping through villages in his uniform, browbeating villagers, and talking of revolution; he liked living off the land, and this to some extent meant living off village people; he liked being important. He was completely uneducated, and he was a killer. He sang dreadful revolutionary songs whenever he could; they contained the sum of his political and historical wisdom.

He told Willie one day, 'Some people have been in the movement for thirty years. Sometimes on a march you may meet one, though they are hard to find. They are skilled at hiding. But sometimes they like to come out and talk to people like us and boast.'

Willie thought, 'Like you.'

And repeatedly during the evening of his return, hearing the man next door singing his revolutionary songs again and again (the way some boys at Willie's mission school used to sing hymns), Willie thought, 'Perhaps some feeling of purpose will come back to me.'

Once or twice during the night he got up and went outside. There were no outhouses; people just used the forest. There were no lights in the village. There was no moon. He was aware of the sentries with guns. He gave the password, and then a little while later he had to give it again, so that as he walked he felt the strange word 'comrade' echoing about him, as question and reassurance. The forest was black, and full of sound: sudden wing-beating, amid cries of alarm and pain from birds and other creatures, calling for help that wouldn't come.

Willie thought, 'The most comforting thing about life is the certainty of death. There is no way now for me to pick my way back to the upper air. Where was the upper air? Berlin? Africa? Perhaps there is no upper air. Perhaps that idea has always been a mirage.'

In the morning someone knocked on the door of Willie's room and came in before Willie answered. The man who came in carried an AK-47. He was as pale as Einstein, but much smaller, about five feet. He was very thin, with a skeletal but handsome face and bony, nervous hands. Another six or seven inches would have given him an immense presence.

He said, 'My name is Ramachandra. I am a unit commander. Your unit commander now. You are no longer a courier. We have received instructions that you are to be admitted into my unit. You have proved yourself. Today or tomorrow we will be having a section meeting to discuss the new situation. The meeting will be here or somewhere else. I don't know as yet. You must hold yourself ready to start marching this evening.'

He had small, hard, mad eyes. He fingered his gun with his bony fingers all the time he spoke. And then, attempting another kind of style, he turned abruptly and walked out of the room.

Like Einstein, Ramachandra was a man of an upper caste, perhaps the highest. Such people were having a hard time in the world outside; populist governments had set up all kinds of barriers against them since independence; many of them, fearing slow impoverishment at home, were now migrating to the United States, Australia, Canada, England. Ramachandra and Einstein were doing something else. Within the movement, they were embracing their persecutors. Willie, with his mixed background – his upper-caste father, placid, inactive, with a strain of asceticism, always expecting things to work out, his more fiery mother, many stages down, wishing to seize the world – Willie understood these men very well.

He thought, 'I thought I had left all of this behind. But now it's all here, just as it was, leaping out at me. I have been around the world, but still it's here.'

* * *

THERE WAS NO night march through the forest for Willie, to his great relief. The section meeting was held in the village where he was. They assembled all the next day, arriving not in various disguises, as they did in the town, but in uniform; and in a great show of fellowship they ate the simple village food, peppery lentils and flat bread made of millet.

Einstein came. Willie had been fearing to meet him again, but now, after Ramachandra, Willie was ready to forgive the malevolence in his eyes and even ready to think that Einstein had softened.

There also came the leader of the camp in the teak forest, who all that time before had sent Willie with Bhoj Narayan to the street of the tanners. He was smooth and civil, even seductive, with wonderful manners, speaking softly and yet careful in his intonations, like an actor. Willie had mentally put him in a grey double-breasted suit and made him a university teacher or a civil servant in the world outside. Wondering what had driven a man apparently so complete to the guerrillas and their hard life in the bush, Willie following some kind of instinct had seen him as a man tormented by the infidelities of his wife. Willie had later thought: 'I wasn't making it up. I saw that because for some reason he wanted me to see it. It was the message he was transmitting to me.' Now, meeting the man again after two years, still seeing the far-off pain in his eyes, Willie thought, adhering half in a joke to his first assessment, 'Poor fellow. With that awful wife.' And treated him like that right through.

The meeting was in Ramachandra's hut. It began at about ten; that was the usual time for these section meetings. There was a pressure lamp. In the beginning it roared and was dazzling; then it settled down to a hum, and became duller and duller. Brown jute sacking had been spread on the earth floor, and over the sacking there were cotton sheets and blankets, with pillows and bolsters.

The civil man, the leader at the camp in the teak forest, gave the news. It was very bad. Much more had been lost than the men in the railway colony. They were only part of one squad, and three full squads had been wiped out by the police. All the weapons that had been assembled piece by piece over a year had been lost. That was a loss of many hundreds of thousands of rupees, and there had been nothing to show for it.

The leader said, 'In a war losses have to be digested. But these losses are exceptional, and we have to rethink our strategy. We have to give up our plan to take the war to the small towns at the fringe of our liberated areas. It was perhaps too ambitious at this stage. Though it should be said that in war ambition sometimes pays off. We will, of course, start up again in those places, or places like them. But that's in the future.'

Einstein said, 'The poison of Kandapalli's teaching is responsible for what has happened. The idea of organising the people through the people sounds pretty, and people abroad will applaud it. But we who know the reality know that the peasants have to be disciplined before they can become foot-soldiers of the revolution. You have to rough them up a little bit.'

A dark man said, 'How can you talk like this when you yourself are of a peasant family?'

Einstein said, 'That's why I talk as I do. I never hide what I come from. There is no beauty in the peasant. That is Kandapalli's teaching. He is a man of a high caste, though he suppresses his caste suffix. He is wrong because this movement is not a movement of love. No revolution can be a movement of love. If you ask me, I will tell you that the peasants ought to be kept in pens.'

Somebody else said, 'How can you talk in this cruel way when people like Shivdas serve the movement so loyally?'

Einstein said, 'Shivdas is loyal because he needs us. He wants people in the village to see how close we are to him. He uses our friendship to terrorise the villagers. Shivdas is very black and very thin and he gives us his bedroom and he talks revolution and land redistribution. But he is a crook and a thug. The big landowners and the old feudal officials have run away. There is no policeman or surveyor in his village, and every year Shivdas reaps many acres of other people's crops and ploughs many acres of other people's land. If people didn't think we were with him they would have killed him long ago. The day Shivdas thinks it will serve him better he will betray us to the police. The revolutionary has at all times to be clearsighted, and to understand the poor human material he might have the misfortune to work with. If Commander Bhoj Narayan hadn't been led astray by our African friend we wouldn't have had the calamity we have come here to discuss.'

People looked at Willie. Ramachandra's eyes were hard.

The man acting as chairman, the leader of the camp in the teak forest, and clearly now the section leader, said to Willie, 'I think you should have the opportunity to say something.'

Willie said, 'The commander is right. I feel responsible. I feel especially responsible for what happened to Bhoj Narayan. He was my friend. I wish to say that too.'

Einstein looked appeased. And there was a general relaxation in the meeting. Self-criticism was part of these meetings. When it came quickly it had a good effect: it bonded people together.

The leader said, 'Chandran has spoken generously. I think he should be commended for that.'

Gradually, then, through many interruptions, through inquiries about the loss of the squads and the arms, and the arrest of Bhoj Narayan, and through long discussions about the nature of the peasantry as compared with the nature of the urban proletariat (a favourite topic), the leader came to the new strategy that the movement had decided on.

The section leader said, 'We will give up taking the war to the small towns, as I said. Instead, we will push deeper into the forest. Each section will take over a hundred and fifty villages. We will administer these villages, and we will announce that we have expanded the liberated areas. This will help with the loss of morale. It will not be easy. It will be hard, but it is the way ahead.'

The meeting ended after three hours. Long before then they had said what they wanted to say. They began to repeat things.

They began to say 'Personally I feel' or 'I very much feel', to add passion to what they had said before; it was a sign they were flagging. The pressure lamp itself gradually dimmed; and then could not be pumped higher.

Afterwards – the pressure lamp fading fast to its limp brown mantle, the meeting breaking up, some people hanging around for a few last words, but standing now (in bare feet or olive socks) on the sheets and sacking and amid the pillows and bolsters where they had been sitting, others recovering their boots from the many boots at the doorway, and then picking their way with flashlights to their huts, the flashlights making the forest bigger and the surrounding night blacker – afterwards Einstein came to Willie just before he left the hut and said in a neutral voice, 'The weaver-caste man went to the police, didn't he?'

Willie said, 'It looks like it.'

'He paid the price. So I suppose the police will get Bhoj Narayan under Section 302. Did people see?'

Willie said, 'The brother.'

Einstein's eyes became far away. A second or two later he blinked, gave a little nod as if acknowledging something, and pressed his lips: a man filing away information.

Willie thought, 'I hope I haven't made another mistake.'

* * *

WITHIN A MONTH there began the push deeper into the forest to extend the liberated area. Every squad was given its own route, the list of villages it had to occupy and re-educate. Sometimes two squads might for a stretch follow the same route, and sometimes, exceptionally, two or three squads might camp together for a short time in one of the larger villages. Only people at the top knew how the squads were deployed and what the strategy was; only they knew the extent of the new liberated area. Everybody else took the hard campaign on trust: the long marches in the forest, the poor food and bad water, the days spent among nervous, passive villagers and tribal people, who (prepared by a tough 'warm-up' group that had been sent on ahead) from time to time were assembled and made to speak of their 'problems', or simply clapped their hands and sang village songs. The squad leader, if he could, might offer a solution of the problems that he had heard about. If he couldn't, he spoke (always in the same simple words and slogans) of the idea and promise of the liberated area; he laid down a few of the new rules, and the people's new loyalties. And then the squad marched on, with a promise to return in some months, to see how people were getting on with their new gift of freedom.

It was a strange time for Willie, a step down into yet another kind of life: patternless labour, without reward or goal, without solitude or companionship, without news of the outside world, with no prospect of letters from Sarojini, with nothing to anchor himself to. In the beginning he had tried to hold on to his idea of time, his idea of the thread of his life, in his old way, counting the beds he had slept in since he was born (like Robinson Crusoe marking each day with a notch on a piece of wood, as he had thought, going back to one of the books of his mission school). But that counting of beds had become harder and harder with the undifferentiated days of marching, the villages almost all the same. Many months had passed since the life of marching and camping began; perhaps a year, perhaps more. What had been painful in the beginning, stretching out the days, had become habit. He felt his memory slipping, like time now, and with that slipping of memory the point of the mental exercise disappeared. It became too strenuous, too frustrating; it caused his head to hurt. He gave it up; it was like shedding a piece of himself.

In the squad the nearest thing to companionship was with Ramachandra, the commander. What separated Willie from the rest of the squad was what attracted Ramachandra.

One day they were resting in the forest. A villager and his wife passed by, the woman with a bundle on her head. The villager greeted Willie and Ramachandra. Willie called back, 'Are you going far?' The man said they were going on a visit to some relations many miles away. Then with a smile he said, 'If I had a camera I would give you a good memory of this moment. "Lost in the woods".' And he laughed.

Ramachandra was at once on his guard. He asked Willie, 'Are they mocking us?'

Willie said, 'No, no. He was only being friendly. Though I must say I've never heard a villager making such an elaborate joke. He didn't just say we looked lost, which was all that he meant. He brought in the camera, for the joke. He probably got it from a film.'

After the villager and his wife had passed Ramachandra said, 'They say that your father is a temple priest. An upper-caste man. If that is true, why are you here? Why aren't you in England or the United States? That's where many of my relations are.'

Willie outlined his life in England, Africa and Berlin. In the forest the very names were full of dazzle, even when Willie (not wishing to arouse jealousy and careful not to overdo the personal drama) talked of failure and humiliation and hiding. Ramachandra showed no jealousy. His eyes softened. He wanted to hear more. It was as though Willie, in those far-off places, was experiencing for him as well. And from time to time thereafter, but never too often, and never wishing to appear too friendly, he sought Willie out to talk of far-off things.

About two weeks later he said, 'I was not like you. You are middle class. I was a country boy. I was poor. But you must understand. When I was poor and in the country I wasn't thinking all the time that I was poor. That's what a lot of people in the movement don't understand. When I was in the country I used to think that our life was just a regular kind of life. I used to graze cattle with a low-caste boy, a harijan, as people said in those days. Imagine: grazing cattle and not thinking anything of it. The harijan boy used to come home with me sometimes. My father didn't mind. He thought the boy was ambitious and he thought that was what mattered in people. My mother didn't mind either, but she refused point blank to wash any cup or glass the boy used. So I washed any glass or cup the boy used. I wonder if the boy knew. You know what happened to him? He was ambitious – my father was right. He is a senior teacher now, that boy, as oily as a paratha and as fat as a barrel. And I am here.'

Willie, thinking hard, as though there were still any number of traps he had to avoid with Ramachandra, said, 'He is where he wants to be. You are where you want to be.'

Ramachandra said, 'It was only when I went to the town, to go to a college, that I understood how poor we were. You are used to seeing me in uniform. But when I first went to the town I used to wear a long shirt and pyjama. Our politicians make a point of wearing country clothes, to show how much they care for the common man, but for true country people those clothes can be a cause for shame. When I first went to the town I was ashamed of my clothes all the time. My college friends noticed. They were richer than me. Or let's say they had a little more money than me. They took me to a tailor and had a suit stitched for me. Two or three days later we went to the shop and they helped me put the suit on. I could hardly believe it when I looked down at myself. All that fine cloth. I wondered whether I would ever have the courage to go out into the street wearing all that cloth. It's not so easy now to remember those first few moments of wearing a suit – I've got so used to it. Then the tailor asked me to look at myself in the long mirror. That was another shock. The country boy had vanished. A city man was looking at me. But then something unexpected happened. I became full of sexual rage. I was a city man. I had a city man's needs. I wanted a girl. But no girl would look at me.'

Willie considered the pale, pared-down, handsome face set on the thin, small body, still not much more than the body of the small boy grazing cattle in the village. The body seemed to mock the beauty of the face, to render it null; the eyes that could appear so hard were really also full of pain.

Willie said, 'All of us from the subcontinent have trouble with sex. We are too used to our parents and families arranging it for us. We can't do it for ourselves. If I didn't have that trouble I wouldn't have married the girl I did. I wouldn't have gone to Africa and wasted eighteen years of her life and mine. If I had been easier about sex, if I had known how to go out and get it, I would have been another kind of man. My possibilities would have been endless. I can't even begin to work them out. But without that talent I was doomed. I could get only what I got.'

Ramachandra said, 'It was better than what I got.'

Willie, picking up just a hint of jealousy in Ramachandra's eyes, thought it better to let the subject drop.

And it was Ramachandra who, in a roundabout way, returned to the topic many days later, when they were on the march.

He said, 'What books did you read when you were young?'

Willie said, 'I had a lot of trouble with the books we were told to read. I tried reading *The Vicar of Wakefield*. I didn't understand it. I didn't know who those people were, or why I was reading about them. I couldn't relate it to anything I knew. Hemingway, Dickens, Marie Corelli, *The Sorrows of Satan* – I had the same trouble with them and all the others. In the end I had the courage to stop reading them. The only things I understood and liked were fairy stories. Grimm, Hans Andersen. But I didn't have the courage to tell my teachers or my friends.'

Ramachandra said, 'My college teacher asked me one day – I was already a trousers-man, I should tell you – "Haven't you read *The Three Musketeers*?" When I said no he said, "You've missed half your life." I looked hard for that book. It wasn't an easy book to find in our small town. What a letdown it was! I didn't know where I was or who those people in costume were. And you know what I thought? I thought my teacher – he was an Anglo-Indian – had said that thing about missing half my life because his teacher had said the same thing to him. I felt that thing about *The Musketeers* had come down the generations, from schoolteacher to schoolteacher, and nobody had told them to stop. Do you know what was easy for me, what I could understand right away and relate to my needs? Lenin, Marx, Trotsky, Mao. I had no trouble with them at all. I didn't find them abstract. I gobbled them up. The only thing I could read apart from that were the Mills and Boon books.'

Willie said, 'Love stories for girls.'

'That's why I read them. I read them for the language, the conversation. I thought they would teach me how to approach girls at the college. I felt that because of my background I didn't have the correct language. I couldn't talk about films and music. A certain kind of language leads to a certain kind of talk and then sexual experience – that was what I thought. So after classes I would go home and read my Mills and Boon and learn passages by heart. I would practise this language on the girls in the cafeteria at the college. They would laugh. One girl didn't laugh. But after a while she got up and went off with the boy she was waiting for. She had been using me as a convenience. I hated that girl especially. I became full of sexual rage, as I told you. I wished I had stayed in my country clothes and never left my village. I wished I had never allowed my friends to put me in a suit. That rage grew and grew. I began to feel I was sitting on a spring. It was that rage that led me to the movement. Somebody from the movement at the college preached hatred of girls. He preached it as a kind of new moralism. He used to say, "The first sacrifice is your sexuality, comrade." Others said the same thing. I heard them say that the revolutionary was really an ascetic and a saint. The ascetic is very much in our tradition, and I was attracted to it. It is something I preach myself to our squad. I have killed two people who went against the teaching. I killed a man who raped a tribal girl, and I killed a man whom I saw fondling a village boy. I didn't ask him for any explanations. I stripped that second fellow of all identification and left his body for the villagers to dispose of as they wished.'

Willie noticed how unwilling Ramachandra was in any account of his sexual unhappiness to acknowledge his small size. He talked of everything else: his background, his clothes, his language, the village culture; but he left out what was obvious and most important. It was like the self-criticism sessions they had at formal meetings, where truth was often what was evaded, as Willie himself had evaded the truth when talking about the arrest of Bhoj Narayan and the loss of his squad. Willie admired Ramachandra for not complaining of his size, for the pretence that as a man he was like others, able to talk of more general issues. But no amount of concealment, no amount of sympathy, could do away with Ramachandra's grief and incompleteness. And often, when he saw the fine-featured man asleep, Willie was full of affection for him.

Willie thought, 'When I first saw Bhoj Narayan I saw him as a thug. But then I became friendly with him and lost that vision. When I first saw Ramachandra, handling his gun with his small bony hands, I saw him as a killer and a fanatic. Now already I am losing that vision of him. In this effort of understanding I am losing touch with myself.'

On another day Ramachandra asked Willie, 'Why did you leave your wife?'

Willie said, 'I was in Africa. A Portuguese colony on its last legs. I had been there for eighteen years. My wife was from that colony. I was living in her big house and on her land, twenty times more land than anyone here has. I had no job. I was just her husband. For many years I thought of myself as lucky.

Living where I did – very far from home: India was the last place I wanted to be – and in that high colonial style. Because you must understand I was poor, literally without money, and when I met my wife in London, at the end of my useless college course, I had no idea at all what I might do or where I might go. After fifteen or sixteen years in Africa I began to change. I began to feel that I had thrown away my life, that what I had thought of as my luck was no such thing. I began to feel that all I was doing was living my wife's life. Her house, her land, her friends, nothing that was my own. I began to feel that because of my insecurity – the insecurity I had been born into, like you – I had yielded too often to accidents, and that these accidents had taken me further and further away from myself. When I told my wife I was leaving her because I was tired of living her life she said something very strange. She said it wasn't really her life. I have been thinking of that in the past two years, and I believe now that what my wife was saying was that her life was as much a series of accidents as I thought mine was. Africa, the Portuguese colony, her grandfather, her father. At the time I saw it only as a rebuke, and I was in no mood to accept it. I thought she was saying that my life with her had given me strength and spirit and knowledge of the world: these were her gifts to me, and I was now using them to spoil her life. If I had thought she meant what I now believe she did, I would have been very moved, and I might never have left her. That would have been wrong. I had to leave her, to face myself.'

Ramachandra said, 'I feel that everything about my birth and life was an accident.'

Willie thought, 'That is how it is with all of us. Perhaps men can live more planned lives where they are more masters of their destiny. Perhaps it is like that in the simplified world outside.'

* * *

THEY CAME TO a village which was unlike the villages or forest settlements they had been marching through for the past year. This village would have been the seat of a small feudal lord in the old days. A tax-farmer, Ramachandra said: the collector of the forty or fifty kinds of tax these wretched villagers had had to pay in the old days: the virtual owner of twenty or thirty or more villages. The big house, too grand for the setting, was still there on the outskirts of the village. It was empty now, but (of old respect, perhaps, or fear of malign spirits) no squatters had moved in, and all over the whole spreading complex – the front vestibule, the brick-paved courtyards, the suites of now doorless rooms – there was the damp, dead, tainted smell of the rotting masonry of a long-abandoned mansion. This smell came from bats and their accumulated, cushiony droppings and from colonising pigeons and wilder birds who had left a crust of white, gritty splashes on the walls, splash upon splash upon splash. It would have been a distasteful labour to clear the house of what bats and birds had left behind, but even then it would have taken a long time, if the house were repeopled, to give it the smell of human life again.

For a long way outside the village the lord's lands could still be seen: overgrown fields, unirrigated and dried up, untended orchards of lemons and sweet limes with long, straggly branches, acacia and neem growing everywhere.

Ramachandra said, 'These villagers can make you want to

cry. Most of them don't have land, and for three years at least we've been trying to get them to take over these six hundred acres. We've held any number of meetings with them. We've told them about the wickedness of the rule of the old days. They agree with all of that, but when we tell them that it is up to them now to take over and plough these acres, they say, "It's not our land." We will talk for two hours and they will appear to agree with you, but then at the end they will say again, "It's not our land." You can get them to clean out water-tanks. You can get them to build roads. But you can't get them to take over land. I begin to see why revolutions have to turn bloody. These people will begin to understand the revolution only when we start killing people. They will have no trouble understanding that. We have started at least three revolutionary committees in this village and in many of the others. They have all faded away. The young men who join us want blood. They have been to high school. Some even have degrees. They want blood, action. They want the world to change. All we give them is talk. That is Kandapalli's legacy. They see nothing happening and they drop out. If we were ruling the liberated areas with an iron hand, as we should, we would have all those six hundred acres cleared and ploughed in a month. And people would have had some idea of what the revolution means. We have to do something this time. We've heard that the family of the old tax-collector is trying to sell this land. They ran away at the time of the first rebellion and they have been living in some city or other ever since. Living in the old parasitic way, doing nothing. Now they are poor. They want to sell this land in some shady deal to a rich local farmer, a kind of Shivdas figure. He lives about twenty miles away. We are determined to prevent this deal. We want the land to be occupied by the villagers, and it looks as though this time we will have to kill some people. I think we will have to leave some people behind here to enforce our will. This is where Kandapalli has been undermining us. Crying for the poor, hardly able to finish a sentence, impressing everybody, and doing nothing.'

They came to the lord's house. It was two storeys high and the outer wall was blank. The vestibule went through the lower floor of the house. On either side of the vestibule was a high platform two or three feet wide set into an alcove in the thick wall. Here in the old days the doormen would have watched or slept or smoked water pipes and simpler visitors would have waited. This style of house – courtyards alternating with suites of rooms with a central passageway, so that it was possible from the front to see down a tunnel of light and shade right through to the back – this style of house would have been an ancient way of building here. Many farmers had simpler versions of the big house. It spoke of a culture that, in this respect at least, was still itself; and Willie in the foul smell of the half-rotten big house found himself moved by this unexpected little vision that had been granted him of his country. The past was terrible; it had to be done away with. But the past also had a kind of wholeness that people like Ramachandra couldn't begin to care about and couldn't replace.

It was as Ramachandra had prophesied at the village meeting the next evening. They came respectfully in their short turbans and in their loincloths long or short and in their long shirts, and they listened and looked wise. The uniformed men of the movement let their guns be seen, as Ramachandra had ordered. Ramachandra himself looked impatient and hard and tapped his bony fingers on his AK-47.

'There are five hundred or six hundred acres here. A hundred of you could take over five acres each and start ploughing, start bringing it back to fertility.'

They made a kind of collective sigh, as though that was something they longed for. And yet, when Ramachandra questioned people individually, the reply was only, 'The land is not ours.'

He said to Willie afterwards, 'You see how fine old manners and fine old ways equip people for slavery. It's the ancient culture our politicians talk about. But there is something else. I understand these people because I am one of them. I just have to pull a little switch in my head and I know exactly what they are feeling. They accept that some people are rich. They don't mind that at all. Because these rich people are not like them. The people like them are poor, and they are determined that the poor shall remain poor. When I tell them to take ten acres each, do you know what they are thinking? They are thinking, "I don't want Srinivas to get ten acres of land. It will make him intolerable. Better if I don't get ten acres if it prevents Srinivas and Raghava from getting ten more acres. Only the gun can bring revolution. I am thinking that this time we will have to leave half a squad here to bring them to their senses.'

That evening he said to Willie, 'I feel we are always taking one step forward and then two steps back, and the government is always there waiting for us to fail. There are some people in the movement who have been in all the rebellions and have spent thirty years doing what we do. They are people who really don't want anything to happen now. For them revolution and hiding and knocking on villagers' doors and asking for food and shelter for the night has become a way of life. We have always had our hermits wandering about the forest. It's in our blood. People applaud us for it, but it's got us nowhere.'

He was becoming wild, passion overcoming the regard he had for Willie, and Willie was glad when they separated for the night.

Willie thought, 'They all want the old ways to go. But the old ways are part of people's being. If the old ways go people will not know who they are, and these villages, which have their own beauty, will become a jungle.'

They left behind three men of the squad, to talk about the need to plough the lord's land.

Ramachandra, more philosophical this morning, like a cat that has abruptly forgotten its rage, said, 'They won't do anything.'

A mile out of the village young men began to come out of the forest. They walked in step with the squad. There was no mockery in them.

'Our recruits,' Ramachandra said. 'You see. High school boys. As I told you. For them we are a vision of the life they once had. But they didn't have the money to stay on in the small town they went to for their education. We are for them what the London-returned and America-returned boys were for you. We will let them down, and I feel it is better to let them go at this stage.'

At noon they rested.

Ramachandra said, 'I haven't told you why I joined the movement. The reason is actually very simple. You know about the college boys who befriended me in the town and bought a suit for me. There was a teacher at that college who for some reason was very nice to me. When I got my diploma I thought I should do something in return for him. You know what I thought? Please don't laugh. I thought I should ask him to dinner. It was something that was always happening in the Mills and Boon books. I asked him whether he would like to have dinner with me. He said yes, and we fixed a date. I didn't know what to do about that dinner. It tormented me. I had never given anyone dinner. A crazy idea came to me. There was a rich family in the town. They were small industrialists, making pumps and things like that. Dazzling to me. I didn't know these people, but I took my courage in both hands and went to their big house. I put on my suit, the one that had given me so much joy and pain. You can imagine the cars in the drive, the lights, the big verandah. People were coming and going, and no one noticed me at the beginning. Halfway down the drawing room there was the kind of bar that people in these modern houses have. No one was paying me too much attention, with all the crush, and I felt that I could even sit at the bar and ask the bowtied servant for a drink. He was the only one I felt I could talk to. I didn't ask him for a drink. I asked him who the owner of the house was. He pointed him out to me, sitting on an open side verandah with other people. Sitting out in the cool night air. A sturdy rather than plump middle-aged man with thin hair smoothed back. With my heart in my boots, as the saying is, I went to the verandah and said to the great man, in the presence of all the people there, "Good evening, sir. I am a student at the college. Professor Coomaraswamy is my teacher, and he has sent me to you with a request. He very much would like to have dinner with you on – I gave the date – if you are free." The great man stood up and said, “Professor Coomaraswamy is greatly admired in this town, and it would be an honour to have dinner with him.” I said, “Professor Coomaraswamy particularly wants you to host the dinner, sir.” The Mills and Boon books had given me this language. Without Mills and Boon I couldn’t have done any of it. The great industrialist looked surprised but then said, “That would be an even greater honour.” I said, “Thank you, sir,” and almost ran out of the big house. On the day I put on my suit of pain and joy and took a taxi to my professor’s house. He said, “Ramachandra, this really gives me great pleasure. But why have you come in a taxi? Are we going far?” I didn’t say anything, and we drove to the industrialist’s. My professor said, “This is a very grand house, Ramachandra.” I said, “For you, sir, I want nothing but the best.” I led him to the open verandah, where the industrialist and his wife and some other people were sitting, and then again I almost ran out of the house. The next day in the college my professor said, “Why did you kidnap me last night and take me to those people, Ramachandra? I didn’t know who they were, and they didn’t know anything about me.” I said, “I am a poor man, sir. I can’t give someone like you dinner, and I wanted only the best for you.” He said, ‘But, Ramachandra, my background is like yours. My family were just as poor as you.’ I said, ‘I made a mistake, sir.’ But I was full of shame. That was where that suit and Mills and Boon had taken me. I hated myself. I wanted to wipe out everyone who had witnessed my shame. I imagined the laughter of all those people in the verandah. I felt I couldn’t live in the world unless those people were dead. Unless my professor was dead. I have almost forgotten what they looked like, but that shame and anger is still with me.’

I said, 'Little things drive people more than we sometimes imagine. I have so many causes of shame. In India, London, and Africa. They are fresh after twenty years. I don't think they will ever die. They will die only with me.'

Ramachandra said, 'That is what I feel too.'

* * *

LATER THAT AFTERNOON a group of young men came out of the forest as the squad marched by. They had been waiting for the squad perhaps all day; time here was almost without value. And it was possible to tell from their bright faces and eager manner that these young men were potential recruits, young men imprisoned in their village and dreaming of breaking out: dreaming of the town and modern dress and modern amusements, dreaming of a world where time would have more meaning, dreaming perhaps also, the more spirited among them, of upheaval and power. Such groups had been attaching themselves to the squad at various stages of the march; their names and parentage and villages had been noted down. But this group of young men was different from others. These young men had news; their news made them frantic.

They sought out the man with the important gun, recognising him as the commander. Ramachandra and they talked. After a while Ramachandra signalled to the column to halt.

Ramachandra said, 'They say there's an ambush prepared for us higher up.'

Willie said, 'Who?'

'It could be anybody. If it's true. It could be the police. It could be Kandapalli's supporters. It could be men hired by that big farmer who wants to buy the land from the old feudal. They would regard us as enemies. It could even be villagers who have become tired of having us in their villages and want now to get rid of us. They know we don't mean business. It is part of the mess we are in here. Everybody feels the old world is changing and nobody can see a clear way ahead. We have thrown away our chance and now there are hundreds of causes. If we had proper military training we would know how to deal with an ambush. But we didn't want to use guns. We just did the boy-scout and cadet stuff. Shouldering arms and presenting arms and standing at ease. That is all right if you are the only one with a gun. But now there is someone else with a gun, and I don't know what to do. All I feel is that I should go forward and try to kill him. I can't ask you to follow me since I don't know what to do. If there is an ambush and something happens to me you should go back on your tracks. Now make yourselves scarce.'

Willie said, 'Ramachandra.'

'I have a good gun.'

They waited in that part of the forest until it was dark. Then one of the young men who had brought the news of the ambush called to them from the forest path.

'They killed him.'

'Who was it?'

'The police. He crept right up to them and sprayed them with his gun. He killed three. That gave him away, and they killed him. This will get into the papers, I tell you.'

Willie said, 'He killed three?'

'Yes, sir.'

It was like good news, after all. Willie thought, 'He honoured his name in the end. In the Indian epic, Ramachandra is the highest kind of man. He is much more than a religious man. You can depend on him in all circumstances to behave well, to do the right thing.'

The young man who had brought the news said, 'Terrible for you, to lose a gun.'

Some time later – when (according to Ramachandra's last order) they were going back on their tracks, staying off the main forest path, moving slowly in the darkness, determined to march all night if they had to, to get away from the police party, if the police were following – when they had been some time on this silent, half-blind march, Willie thought, 'I didn't think of the dead policemen. I've forgotten myself. Now I'm truly lost. In every way. I don't know what lies ahead or behind. My only cause now is to survive, to get out of this.'

SIX

The End of Kandapalli

AFTER TWO ANXIOUS days they came again to the village with the lord's abandoned mansion, the lord's abandoned straw-coloured fields (with the vivid green of fast-growing parasitic vines), and the orchards where branches had outgrown their strength, where starved-looking leaves, not the right colour, were few on spindly crusted twigs, and fruit was scattered and deceptive, with wasps making nests within the rotted, grey-white skins of sweet limes and lemons.

It was a different village for them. They had been stars for the two weeks they had been there. They had had guns and uniforms and peaked caps with the star the colour of blood, and their words had mattered (even if no one had really believed in them). Now that had changed; all the village knew about the police ambush and the death of the menacing squad commander. With no particular aggression, merely going about the small details of day-to-day village life with the self-righteous intensity of men who knew what was what, the villagers seemed to see through the returning men in uniform.

They looked for the three men they had left behind to organise the take-over of the lord's land. It seemed staggering now, that they should have thought of attempting such a thing. It must have been awful for the three men. No one in the village knew where they were. No one even seemed to remember them. And it soon became clear to the remnant of Willie's squad and Keso, the fat, dark stand-in commander, a failed medical student, that these men had deserted. Keso knew about desertions.

They had been given the use of huts when they had occupied and liberated the village. Now Keso thought it would have been wrong to ask and perhaps even dangerous to spend the night in the village. He ordered that they should continue on their march, doing what Ramachandra had said, going back the way they had come, stage by stage to base.

Keso said, 'You can't help feeling that Ramachandra was right. We would have achieved a lot more if we had killed a few of these people whenever we liberated a village. We would also have been safer now.'

They didn't know the forest well enough to stay away from the paths and avoid the villages. They began to think of the villagers as enemies, though they depended on them for water and food. Every night they camped half a mile or so outside a village; every night (with a remnant of their very rough military training) they posted an armed member of the squad as a sentry. That fact became known about them; it saved them from being looted by certain village people.

On the way out, Willie now realised, and during all his time with the movement, he had lived with the pastoral vision of the countryside and forest that was the basis of the movement's thinking. He had persuaded himself that that was the countryside he saw; he had never questioned it. He had persuaded himself that outside the noise and rush and awfulness of cities was this quite different world where things followed an antique course, which it was the business of the revolution to destroy. This pastoral vision contained the idea that the peasant laboured and was oppressed. What this pastoral vision didn't contain was the idea that the village – like those they had liberated on the march (and then let go of) and might one day with luck liberate again – was full of criminals, as limited and vicious and brutal as the setting, whose existence had nothing to do with the idea of labour and oppression.

Willie wondered how on the way out he had failed to see these village criminals. Perhaps Ramachandra with his bony nervous fingers on his AK-47 had caused them to lie low. Now in every village the depleted squad was beset and provoked by criminals. In one village there was a pale-complexioned man on a horse and with a gun – how could they have ever missed him? – who came to their evening camp and shouted, 'You are CIA, CIA. You should be shot.' Keso decided that they shouldn't respond. It was the best thing to do, but it wasn't easy. The man on horseback was a village thug, acting up for the village, making a show of the fearlessness which a while before he had preferred to hide.

In some villages there were people who had got it into their heads that the squad were travelling gunmen who could be hired to kill an enemy. The people who wanted someone killed usually didn't have money, but they thought they could nag or cajole the men into doing what they wanted. Perhaps this was how they lived, begging for favours in everything. This way of life showed in their wild eyes and wasted bodies.

Willie remembered one of the things Ramachandra used to

say: 'We must give up the idea of remaking everybody. Too many people are too far gone for that. We have to wait for this generation to die out. This generation and the next. We must plan for the generation after that.'

So stage by stage they went back, for Willie the vision of pastoral undoing itself, as if by a kind of magic. Roads that had been made by the squad with the help of villagers had disappeared; water-tanks that had been cleared of mud had become clogged again. Family disputes, infinitely petty, about land or bore-wells or inheritances, that had been brought to Ramachandra as squad leader for his adjudication, and appeared to have been set right by him, raged again; at least one murder had occurred.

One day, outside a village, a dark middle-aged man came up to the marching squad. He said to Keso, 'How long have you been in the movement?' And it was as if he had spoken merely to let them hear his beautiful educated voice and understand that, in spite of his peasant clothes and the thin towel-scarf over his shoulders, he was a townsman.

Keso said, 'Eight years.'

The stranger said, 'When I meet people like you – and I do meet people like you from time to time – I can't help thinking that you are only captains and majors. Beginners, on the first rung of ascension. Don't mind it. I have been in the movement, in all the movements if you prefer, for thirty years, and I see no reason why I can't go on for another thirty. If you are on your toes all the time you can't be caught. That's why I think of myself as a general. Or, if you think that is too boastful, a brigadier.'

Willie said, 'How do you spend your time?'

'Avoiding capture, of course. Apart from that I am intensely bored. But in the middle of this boredom the soul never fails to sit in judgement on the world and never fails to find it worthless. It is not an easy thing to explain to outsiders. But it keeps me going.'

Willie said, 'How did you start?'

'In the classical way. I was at the university. I wished to see how the poor lived. There was a certain amount of excited talk about them among the students. A scout for the movement – there were dozens of them around – arranged for me to see the poor. We met at a railway station and travelled through the night in a third-class coach on a very slow train. I was like a tourist, and my guide was like a travel courier. We came at last to our poor village. It was very poor. It never occurred to me to ask why my guide had chosen this particular village or how the movement had found it. There was no sanitation, of course. That seemed a big thing then. And there was very little food. My guide put questions to people and translated their replies for me. One woman said, "There has been no fire in my house for three days." She meant she hadn't cooked for three days and she and her family hadn't eaten for three days. I was immensely excited. At the end of that first evening the villagers sat around a fire in the open and sang songs. Whether they were doing that for us or for themselves, whether they did it every evening, I never thought to ask. All I knew was that I passionately wished to join the movement. The movement of the time, the movement of thirty years ago. That was arranged for me by my guide. It took time. I left the university and went to a small town. I was met by contacts. They said they were posting me to a particular village. It was a long walk from the small town. The main road became a dirt road, and then night came. It was March, so it was quite pleasant, not hot. I was not frightened. And then I came to the village. It was not too late. As soon as I saw the village I saw the house of the big landlord. It was a big house with a neat thatched roof. The poor people didn't have neat thatched roofs. Their eaves were untrimmed. That big landlord was the man I had to kill. It was quite remarkable, on my very first day seeing the house of the man I had to kill. Seeing it just like that. If I was another kind of person I would have thought it was the hand of God. Setting me on my path. Those were my instructions, to get the big landlord killed. I wasn't to kill him myself. I was to get some peasant to do it. That was the ideology of the time, to turn the peasants into rebels, and through them to start the revolution. And, would you believe, just after seeing the house, in the darkness, I saw a peasant coming back from his work, late for some reason. Again, the hand of God. I introduced myself to the peasant. I said straight out, "Good evening, brother. I am a revolutionary. I need shelter for the night." He called me sir and invited me to his hut. When we got there he offered me his cowshed. It is the classic story of the revolution. It was a terrible cowshed, though now I have seen many much worse. We had some dreadful rice. The water came from a little stream. Not some story-book purling English stream, clear as crystal. This is India, my masters, and this was a dreadful muddy runnel. You had to boil whatever you could wring out of the smelly mess. I talked to my host about his poverty and his debt and the hardness of his life. He seemed surprised. I then invited him to kill his landlord. I was pushing it, don't you think? My first night and everything. My peasant simply said no. I actually was quite relieved. I wasn't hardened enough. I would have wanted to run away if the man had said, "What a good idea, sir. It's been on my mind for some time. Come and watch me knife the bastard." What my peasant said was that he depended on his landlord for food and money for three months. To kill the landlord, he said, giving me some of his own wisdom in exchange for my theories, would be like killing the goose that laid the golden egg. His speech was full of sayings like that. I ran away as soon as I could the next morning. It's a classic revolutionary story. Most people would have gone back to the town and taken a bus or train home, and gone back to their studies and to screwing the servant girls. But I persevered. And here you see me, thirty years later. Still going among the peasants with that philosophy of murder.'

Willie said, 'How do you spend the day?'

Keso said, 'It was what I was going to ask him.'

'I am in somebody's hut. I have spent the night there. No worries about rent and insurance and utilities. I get up early and go to the fields to do my stuff. I have got used to it now. I doubt whether I could go back to sitting in a little room with four walls. I go back to the hut, have a little of the peasant's food. I read for a while. The classics: Marx, Trotsky, Mao, Lenin. Afterwards I visit various people in the village, arranging a meeting for some future date. I return. My host comes from the fields. We chat. Actually, we don't. It's hard to talk. We don't have anything to say to one another. You can't make yourself part of the life of the village. After another day or two I am off. I don't want my host to get tired of me and tip off the police. In this way every day flows past, and every day is like every other day. I feel the life I am describing is similar to that of a high-powered executive.'

Willie said, 'I don't understand that.'

Keso said, 'I don't understand it either.'

The stranger said, 'I mean the boredom. Everything is laid on for them. Once you get into those outfits you are all right for life. British American Tobacco, Imperial Tobacco, Unilever, Metal Box. They tell me that at Imperial the big boys just have lunch and go around checking the dates on cigarette packs in the shops.'

He had become agitated at the hint of distrust, and he spoke defensively. A little of his rhetorical style had gone. He didn't wish now to stay with the squad, and as soon as he could – at the sight of a cluster of huts where he might go and rest – he excused himself.

Keso said, 'Do you think he ever worked in one of those big companies?'

Willie said, 'I feel he might have applied and failed. Probably if they had taken him at Metal Box or one of the others he would never have come out to the countryside and started asking peasants to kill people. That thing he said about captains and majors and being himself a general, that probably tells us that he tried for the army and the army didn't want him. I'm a little angry with him.'

'That's extreme.'

'I am angry with him because at first I thought that in spite of his clowning manner there was some wisdom in him, something I could use. I was listening very carefully, thinking that later on I would work out everything he was saying.'

Keso said, 'He's mad. I think he's never been arrested because the police don't think it is worth their while. The peasants probably think he is a joke.'

Willie thought, 'But probably we are all like that to the villagers. Probably without knowing it we've all become a little mad or unbalanced. Keso would have liked to be a doctor. Now he lives this life and tries to tell himself it is real. It's always easy to see the other man's strangeness. We can see the madness of those villagers who wanted us to kill people for them. Those men with the badly made, twisted faces, as though they had literally had a terrible time being born. We can't see our own strangeness. Though I have begun to feel my own.'

* * *

THEY CAME AT last to the base, where Willie had a room of his own. The wish of the high command to extend the liberated areas had failed; everyone knew that. But in spite of the general gloom Willie was happy to be in a place where he had already been. He felt he had ceased to be flung into space; he felt he might once again come to possess himself. He liked the low clean thatched roof – so protecting, especially when he was on his string bed – where he could store small things between the thatch and the rafters; he liked the plastered beaten-earth floor, hollow-sounding below his feet.

Willie was hoping to see the section leader again, the man with the soft, educated manner. But he was not around. The news was that he had deserted, had surrendered to the police after elaborate negotiations. He had claimed the bounty that had been offered for his arrest; guerrillas who surrendered could claim this bounty. Then he had made his way back to the big city from which he had come. There for some days he had stalked his estranged wife before shooting her dead. No one knew where he was now. Perhaps he had killed himself; more likely, with the freedom of movement his bounty would have given him, he was at large in the immense country, using all his guerrilla's skill for disguise and concealment, and was perhaps even now shedding his old personality and the pain he had carried for years.

The news would have made a greater stir if at about the same time the police hadn't arrested Kandapalli. That was by far the bigger event, though Kandapalli had now lost most of his following and was so little a security risk that the police took no special precautions when they arrested him or when they took him to court. What was most notable about him was the clippings book he carried with him all the time. In this book he had pasted newspaper photographs of children. There was some profound cause for emotion there, in the photographs of children, but Kandapalli couldn't say; his mind had gone; all that was left him was this great emotion. Willie was profoundly moved, more moved than he had been in Berlin when he had first heard of Kandapalli from Sarojini: his passion for humanity, his closeness to tears. There was no means of being in touch with her now, and for some days, in a helpless kind of grief, which held grief for himself and the world, and every person and every animal who had been wounded, Willie tried to enter the mind of the deranged man. He tried to imagine the small old schoolteacher choosing pictures from the newspapers and pasting them in his book. What pictures would have attracted him, and why? But the man eluded him, remained a prisoner of his mind, forever in solitary confinement. The thought of the derangement of the mind, where no one could now reach him, the unimaginable twists and turns from present to past, was more affecting than news of the death of the man would have been.

Even enemies of the man were moved. Einstein thought that the movement should make some gesture, to show solidarity with the old revolutionary. He brought the matter up at the formal meeting of the section.

He said, 'His disgrace disgraces us all. We have quarrelled with him, but we owe it to him to do something. We owe it to him for reviving the movement at a bad time, when it had been crushed and was all but dead. I propose that we kidnap a minister of the central government or, if that is beyond us, a minister of the local state. We will make it clear that we are doing it as a gesture in support of Kandapalli. I volunteer myself for the action. I have done some research. I have a certain man in mind, and I know when it can be done. All I need are three men and three pistols and a car. I will need another man to stand at the traffic lights near the minister's house and to stop the cross-traffic for three or four seconds while we are making our getaway. This man will make believe he is doing it for the minister. The action itself should take no more than two minutes. I have actually done a dry run, and that took one minute and fifty seconds.'

An important squad leader said, 'We shouldn't do anything more at the present time to encourage the police to come down harder on us. But please outline your plan.'

'The minister's house is at Aziznagar. We need to be there a week in advance, or four days at least, to get used to the layout of the streets. We will need a car. We will hire it from somewhere else. Three of us will sit in the car in the morning just outside the gates. The minister's house is hidden from the street by a high wall. Perfect for us. A guard will come and ask us what we are doing. We will mark this guard down as the man to deal with when the time comes. We will say we are students from college – I will find out which one to say – and we want to ask the minister to come and talk to us or something like that. I will judge when the crowd is thinning and the time is ripe. I will get out of the car and walk past the guard to the minister's front door. As I walk one of the men with me will shoot the guard in the hand or the foot. I will now be in the minister's house. I will shoot anyone who is in my way. I will burst into the minister's office or greeting room with a great deal of noise and shouting. I will shoot at his hand, rapid fire, shouting all the time. He will be very frightened. As soon as he is wounded I will hustle him out of the front door to the car blocking the gate. I have studied his physique. I can do it. I can hustle him out. All this has to be done with coolness and precision and determination. There will be no hesitation at any stage. We drive past the traffic lights, which will be fixed for us. Two minutes. Two bold, cool minutes. The action will be good for us. It will tell people we are still around.'

The squad leader said, 'It's nice and simple. Perhaps too simple.'

Einstein said, 'The most effective things are simple and direct.'

Keso said, 'I am worried about the traffic lights. Wouldn't it be better to put them out of action?'

Einstein said, 'Too early, and they'll fix them. Too late, and there'll be a jam at the intersection. Better someone walking to the intersection, if the lights are against us when we appear, and this person, very cool, pulling on official-looking white gloves and stopping the cross-traffic. If the lights are with us we have to do nothing at all.'

The squad leader said, 'Is there a policeman or a police box at the intersection?'

Einstein said, 'I wouldn't have wanted to do it if there was a police box. When we have passed, this person will walk calmly to the other side of the road, taking off his gloves, and will get into a car or a taxi, which will then leave the scene. So perhaps we will need a second car. If anyone at all notices they will think it's another Indian street joker. Four men, two cars, three pistols.'

Keso said, 'I feel you are determined to do this, whatever we say.'

Einstein said, 'I think it will be a challenging thing to do. And it will be unexpected, since we have nothing against this particular minister. I like the unexpectedness. I think it will set an example to our people. Too many of us, when we plan a military action, can think only in the most banal way. So the other side are always waiting for us, and we fill the jails.'

Afterwards Einstein and Willie talked.

Einstein said, 'I hear you had a rough time during that push into the interior. Extending the liberation area. The strategy was poor, and some people paid the price. We spread ourselves too thinly to do anything.'

'I know, I know.'

'The leaders are letting us down. Too much high living. Too many conferences in exotic places. Too much jostling to go abroad to do publicity and raise funds. By the way. You remember that weaver-caste fellow who betrayed us to the police a couple of years ago?'

Willie said, 'The Bhoj Narayan business?'

'He wouldn't be giving any evidence against anybody. I

don't think they would be booking Bhoj Narayan under Section 302.'

Willie said, 'What a relief.'

'I wanted you to know. I know how close you two were.'

'Are you going to do that action?'

'I mustn't talk any more about it. You can talk these things away, you know. It's like mathematics when you're young. It comes to you without your knowledge, when you are most silent.'

Willie thought of the little weaver colony as he had last seen it: the red sky, the clean front yards where yarn was spun into thread, the three-wheeler taxi-scooter in front of the house where Raja lived with his elder brother. He remembered the cooking fire, festive-looking in the fading light of day, in the half-open kitchen of the leaf-cigarette makers a hundred yards away: people twice as well off, or half as poor, as the weavers: that early fire seeming to mark the difference between them. He remembered the elder brother's wife in her cotton peasant skirt falling to the floor of the little house before Bhoj Narayan, holding his knees, and pleading for her brother-in-law's life beside the home-made loom.

He thought, 'Who here would know that I cared for those men? Perhaps both brothers are better off dead. Perhaps it's as Ramachandra said. For people like Raja and his brother the damage is already too great. This generation is lost, and perhaps the next as well. Perhaps both brothers have been spared an untold amount of useless striving and needless pain.'

* * *

EVERY TWO WEEKS now there were district meetings. Squad leaders or their representatives came from liberated areas in different parts of the forest in a kind of mimicry of old-fashioned social life. The news they brought, unofficially, was of police arrests and the liquidation of squads, but the fiction of successful revolution and the ever expanding liberated areas was still maintained, at least in the formal discussions, so that these discussions became more and more abstract. They might debate, for instance, with great seriousness, whether landlordism or imperialism was the greater contradiction. One man might become vehement about imperialism – which in the setting really felt very far away – and afterwards someone might say to Willie, 'He would say that, of course. His father is a landlord, and when he is talking about imperialism what he is really saying is, "Whatever you people do, stay away from my father and family." Or they might debate – they did it every two weeks, and everyone knew what would be said on either side – whether the peasantry or the industrial proletariat was going to bring about the revolution. In spite of all the killings, the movement was becoming more and more a matter of these abstract words.

In the middle of this came news of Einstein's action. He had done it all as he had said, and it had failed. Einstein had said that the high wall of the minister's official house was good for the action because it would hide Einstein and his friends in the kidnap car. But his research was not as thorough as he had boasted at the sector meeting. What the wall also did was to hide the full security arrangements of the house from Einstein. He had thought that there was only one armed guard and he was at the gate. What he discovered, on the day of the action, and seconds away from the intended kidnap, was that there were two further armed guards inside. He decided to call the whole thing off, and almost as soon as he had entered the yard he pushed his way back past the guard at the gate and got into the car. The lights were against them, but the man they had deputed to stop the cross-traffic did his job beautifully, walking slowly to the middle of the road, pulling on big white gloves and stopping the traffic. Some people had thought that this was the weakest part of the plan. As it turned out, this was the only part that worked. And, as Einstein had said, it was hardly noticed.

When he reappeared among them he said, 'Perhaps it's for the best. Perhaps the police would have come down really hard on us.'

Willie said, 'You were pretty cool, to cancel at the last moment. I probably would have pressed on. The more I saw myself getting into a mess, the more I would have pressed on.'

Einstein said, 'All plans should have that little room for flexibility.'

A senior man of the council of the movement came to the next section meeting. He was in his sixties, far older than Willie had expected. So perhaps the boastful madman who had talked about being in all the movements for thirty years was right in some things. He was also something of a dandy, the senior man of the council, tall and slender and with beautifully barbered, glossy grey hair. This again was something Willie didn't expect.

Einstein, to turn the talk away from his own abandoned plan, said to the man of the council, 'We really should stop talking about the liberated areas. We tell people in the universities that the forest is a liberated area, and we tell people in the forest that the universities are a liberated area. Unlikely things happen:

these people sometimes meet. We are fooling nobody, and we are putting off the people we want to recruit.'

The man of the council fell into a great rage. His face became twisted and he said, 'Who are these people who will want to question me? Have they read the books I have read? Can they read those books? Can they begin to understand Marx and Lenin? I am not Kandapalli. These people will do as I say. They will stand when I tell them to stand, and sit when I tell them to sit. Have I made this long journey here to listen to this kind of rubbish? I might have been arrested at any time. I have come here to talk about new tactics, and I get this tosh.'

His rage – the rage of a man who had for too long been used to having his own way – clouded the rest of the meeting, and no one raised any further serious points.

Later Einstein said to Willie, 'That man makes me feel like a fool. He makes us all fools. I cannot imagine that we have been doing what we have been doing for his sake.'

Willie said (a little of his ancient London college wit unexpectedly coming back to him, overriding his caution), 'Perhaps the big books he has been reading have been about the great rulers of the century.'

* * *

THE NEW TACTICS that should have been discussed at that meeting came directly from the council as commands. Liberated areas were henceforth to be isolated and severely policed; people in these areas were to know only what the movement wanted them to know. Roads and bridges on the perimeter were to be blown up. There were to be no telephones, no newspapers from outside, no films, no electricity. There was to be a renewed emphasis on the old idea of liquidating the class enemy. Since the feudal people had long ago run away, and there was strictly speaking no class enemy left in these villages, the people to be liquidated were the better off. The revolutionary madman Willie and Keso had met had spoken of the philosophy of murder as his revolutionary gift to the poor, the cause for which week after week he walked from village to village. Something like this philosophy was brought into play again, and presented as doctrine. Murders of class enemies – which now meant only peasants with a little too much land – were required now, to balance the successes of the police. Discipline in the squads was to be tightened up; squad members were to report on one another.

Willie was reassigned to a new squad, and found himself suddenly among suspicious strangers. He lost his room in the low-eaved hut, which he had grown to think of as his. His squad was a road-destroying and bridge-destroying squad, and he lived in a tented camp, again constantly on the move. He became disorientated. He remembered the time when it consoled him, gave him a hold on things, to count the beds he had slept in. Such a hold was no longer possible for him. He wished now passionately only to save himself, to get in touch with himself again, to get away to the upper air. But he didn't know where he was. His only consolation – and he wasn't sure how much of a consolation it was – was that, amid all the strangers whose characters he didn't want to read, whom (out of his great fatigue and disorientation now) he wished to keep as mysteries – his only consolation was that at the two-weekly meetings of the section he continued to see Einstein.

Now there came the order for the squad to get villagers to kill better-off farmers. This was no longer optional, a goal that might be reached one day when conditions were suitable. This was an order, like a retail chain ordering its managers to improve sales. The council wanted figures.

Willie and another man from the squad went with a gun to a village at dusk. Willie remembered the madman's story of going to a village after nightfall and asking the first labourer he saw to kill the landlord. That had happened thirty years ago. And now Willie was living through it again. Only, now there was no landlord.

They stopped a labourer. He was dark, with a short turban, and had rough, hard hands. He looked well fed.

The man with Willie said, 'Good evening, brother. Who is the richest man in your village?'

The villager seemed to know what they were leading up to. He said to Willie, 'Please take your gun and go away.'

The man with Willie said, 'Why should we go away?'

The villager said, 'It will be all right for you two. You will go away to your nice houses. At the end of this business, if I follow you, I will get my arse beaten by somebody or other. Of that I am absolutely sure.'

The man with Willie said, 'But if you kill the rich man, that will be one less man to oppress you.'

The villager said to Willie, 'You kill him for me. Besides, I don't know how to use a gun.'

Willie said, 'I'll show you how to use a gun.'

The villager said, 'It really will be much simpler for everybody if you killed him.'

Willie said, 'I'll show you. You hold it like this, and look down here.'

Down the sight of the gun a farmer came into view. He was coming down a slight hill. He was at the end of his day's labour. Willie and the man with him and the villager were hidden by a thicket beside the village path.

Looking down the gunsight at the man, the gun moving minute distances as if in response to the uncertainty or certainty in his mind, the scale of things altered for Willie, and he played with that change of scale. Something like this had happened in Portuguese Africa when, after a mass killing of settlers, the government had opened the police rifle range to people who wished to learn to shoot. Willie knew nothing of guns, but that change of scale in the world around him when he looked down the gunsight entranced him. It was like focusing on a flame in a dark room: a mystical moment that made him think of his father and the ashram where he dispensed this kind of enlightenment.

Somebody said, 'You have the rich man in your sights.'

Without looking at the speaker Willie recognised the voice of the commander of his new squad.

The commander, not a young man, said, 'We've been worried about you for some time. You cannot ask a man to do something you can't do yourself. Shoot. Now.'

And the figure who had been trembling in and out of the gunsight half spun to one side, as though he had been dealt a heavy blow, and then fell on the path on the slope.

The squad commander said to the shocked villager, 'You see. That's all there is to it.'

When his blood cooled Willie thought, 'I am among absolute maniacs.'

A little later he thought, 'That was my first idea, in the camp in the teak forest. I allowed that idea to be buried. I had to do that, so that I could live with the people I found myself among. Now that idea has resurfaced, to punish me. I have become a maniac myself. I must get away while I still have time to return to myself. I know I have that time.'

Later the squad commander said, and he was almost friendly, 'Give it six months. In six months you will be all right.' He smiled. He was in his forties, the grandson of a peasant, the son of a gentle clerk in government service; a life of bitterness and frustration showed in his face.

* * *

HE WOULD WALK to where the road had not been blown up. Just under ten miles. It was a simple village road, two strips of concrete on a red dirt surface. No buses plied on that road, no taxis or taxi-scooters. It was a guerrilla area, a troubled area, and taxis and scooters were nervous of getting too near. So he would have to make himself as inconspicuous as he could (the thin towel-shawl, the long shirt with the big side pockets, and trousers: trousers would work) and walk from there to the nearest bus station or train station.

But at that point this dream of escape broke down. He was on a police list, and the police would be watchful at bus stations and train stations. It was possible for him, as a member of the movement, to hide when he reached the open, so to speak; the movement had a network. As a man running away from the movement, and hiding from the police, he had no protection. Not on his own. He had no local contacts.

He thought he would wait until the section meeting and open himself to Einstein. It was risky, but there was no one else he felt he could talk to.

All his doubts about Einstein fell away as soon as he talked to him.

Einstein said, 'There is a better way. A shorter way. It will take us out to another road. I will be coming with you. I am tired, too. There are two villages on the way. I know the weavers in both villages. They will put us up for the night, and they will arrange for a scooter to take us on our way. Past the state border. They have friends on the other side. Weavers have their networks too. You can see that I have been researching this trip. Be careful of these people here. Play along with them, if you have to. If they think you are deserting, they will kill you.'

Willie said, 'Weavers. And scooters.'

'You are thinking it's like Raja and his brother. Well, it is like that. But that's how things sometimes happen. A lot of weaver people working their way up go into scooters. The banks help them.'

Over the days of the meeting they talked of escape.

Einstein said, 'You can't just go and surrender to the police. They might shoot you. It's a complicated business. We have to hide. We might have to hide for a long time. We will do it first with some weaver people in the other state, and then we will move on. We have to get some politicians on our side. They would like to claim the credit for getting us to surrender. They would negotiate with the police for us. It might even be the man I planned to kidnap. That's the way the world is. People are now on this side, now on that. You didn't like me when you first saw me. I didn't like you when I first saw you. The world is like that.

Close your mind to nothing. There is something else. I don't want to know what you might have done while you were in the movement. From now on, just remember this: you have done nothing. Things happened around you. Other people did things. But you did nothing. That is what you must remember for the rest of your life.'

* * *

IT TOOK SIX months. And for periods this undoing of their life in the movement was like a continuation of that life.

On the first night, before they reached the weavers' hut where they were to sleep, they took off their uniforms and buried them, not willing to risk a fire, and not wanting to burn the uniforms in the presence of their weaver hosts. There followed long days of hot, bumpy journeys over different kinds of road in three-wheel taxi-scooters that were low to the ground, the two of them now in one scooter, now (Einstein's idea, for the security) in separate scooters. The taxi-scooter hood was deep but narrow, like a pram's, and the sun always angled in. On busier roads fumes and brown exhaust smoke blew over them from all sides, and their skin, stinging from the sun, smarted and became gritty. They rested at night in weaver communities. The small, two-roomed houses seemed to have been built more to shelter the precious looms than the people. There was really no space for Willie and Einstein, but space was found. Each house they came to was like the one they had left, with some local variation: uneven thatch instead of tiles, clay bricks instead of plastered mud and wattle. At last they crossed the state border, and for two or three weeks the weaver network on the other side continued to protect them.

Willie now had a rough idea where they were. He had a strong wish to be in touch with Sarojini. He thought he might write and ask her to send a letter to the poste restante of a city where they were going.

Einstein said no. The police now understood that ruse. Poste restante letters were not common, and the police would be looking for poste restante letters from Germany. Because of the weavers they had had a comparatively easy journey so far, and Willie might think they were overdoing the caution; but Willie had to remember that they were on a shoot-on-sight police list.

They moved to one city, then to another. Einstein was the leader. He was trying now to get someone in public life to talk to the police.

Willie was impressed. He asked, 'How do you know all of this?'

Einstein said, 'I had it from the old section leader. The man who went out and then killed his wife.'

'So he was planning his break-out all the time I knew him?'

'Some of us were like that. And sometimes those are the very people who stay and stay, for ten, twelve years, and become quite soft in the head, unfit for anything else.'

For Willie this time of waiting, this moving to new cities, was like the time he had spent in the street of the tanners, when he didn't know what was going to follow.

Einstein said, 'We are waiting on the police now. They are going through our case. They want to know what charges have been laid against us before they can accept our surrender. They are having some trouble with you. Someone has informed on you. It's because of your international connections. Do you know a man called Joseph? I don't recall a man called Joseph.'

Willie was about to speak.

Einstein said, 'Don't tell me anything. I don't want to know. That is our arrangement.'

Willie said, 'There is actually nothing.'

'That is almost the hardest thing to deal with.'

'If they don't accept my surrender, what then?'

'You hide, or they kill you or arrest you. But we'll cross that bridge when we come to it.'

Some time later Einstein announced, 'It's all right, for both of us. Your international connections were not so menacing, after all.'

Einstein telephoned the police, and the day came when they went to the police headquarters of the town where they were. They went in a taxi and Willie saw a version of what Raja out of his own excitement had shown him in another town a long time ago: an army-style area created in the British time, the now old trees planted at that time, whitewashed four or five feet up from the ground, the white kerbstones of the lanes, the sandy parade ground, the stepped pavilion, the welfare buildings, the two-storey residential quarters.

The superintendent's office was somewhere there, on the lower floor. When they entered the office, the man himself, in civilian clothes, stood up, smiling, to welcome them. The gesture of civility wasn't at all what Willie was expecting.

He thought, 'Bhoj Narayan was my friend. My heart went out to Ramachandra. Without Einstein I wouldn't have known how to get here. But the man in front of me in this office is much more my kind of person. My heart and mind reach out at once to him. His face radiates intelligence. I have to make no allowances for him. I feel we are meeting as equals. After my years in the bush – years when in order to survive I made myself believe things I wasn't sure of – I feel this as a blessing.'

SEVEN

Not the Sinners

HE THOUGHT AT the end of that civil session with the superintendent, a man at once educated and physically well exercised, that he was in the clear, and he continued to think so even when he was separated from Einstein and taken to a jail in an outlying area. Perhaps because of the difficulties he and Einstein had had in arranging their surrender, and because Einstein, explaining the delays, had at a certain stage talked of the police having to 'go through' their cases, Willie had confused the idea of surrender with the idea of amnesty. He had thought that after he had gone to the police headquarters and surrendered, he would be released. And he continued in that hope even when he was taken to the jail, and checked in, as it might be into a rough country hotel, but by rough country staff in khaki. There was a certain repetitiveness about this checking in. The new arrival felt less and less welcome after each piece of the jail ritual.

'All this is unnerving to me, of course,' Willie thought, 'but it is an everyday business to these jail officers. It would be less disturbing to me if I put myself in their place.'

This was what he tried to do, but they didn't appear to notice.

At the end of his checking in he was lodged in a long room, like a barrack-room, with many other men. Most of them were villagers, physically small, subdued, but consuming him with their bright black eyes. These men were awaiting trial for various things; that was why they were still in their everyday clothes. Willie did not wish to enter into their griefs. He did not wish to return so soon to that other prison-house of the emotions. He did not want to consider himself one of the men in the long room. And out of his confidence that he was going soon to go away and be free of it all he thought he should write to Sarojini in Berlin – a jaunty, unsuffering letter: the tone was already with him – telling her of all that had happened to him in the years since he had last written.

But writing a letter wasn't something that could be done just like that, even if he had had pen or pencil and paper. He could think of writing that letter only the next day, and then the sheet of writing paper that the jailer brought him, as an immense favour, was like a much handled page of an account book, narrow, narrowly ruled, torn at the left edge along perforations, rubber-stamped in purple with the name of the jail at the top on the left, and with a big, black-stamped number on the right. That sheet of paper – thin, curling back on itself at the unperforated edge – cast him down, turned his mind away from writing.

Over the next two or three days he learned the jail routine. And, having put the idea of imminent release out of his mind, he settled into his new life, as he had settled into the many other lives that had claimed him at various times. The five thirty wake up, the stand-pipes in the yard, the formality of tasteless jail meals, the tedium of outdoor time, the long idle hours on the floor during lock-up time: he sought to adapt to it with an extension of the yoga (as he used to think of it) with which for a long time, since he had come back to India (and perhaps before, perhaps all his life) he had been facing everyday acts and needs that had suddenly become painful or awkward. A yoga consciously practised until the conditions of each new difficult mode of life became familiar, became life itself.

One morning, a few days after he had come in, he was taken to a room at the front of the jail. The superintendent he liked was there. He liked him still, but at the end of the interview, which was about everything and nothing, he began to feel that his case was not as easy as he had believed. Einstein had spoken of some trouble with Willie's 'international connections'. That could only mean Sarojini and Wolf, and that of course was where his adventure had started. But at the next interview, with the superintendent and a colleague of the superintendent's, nothing was said about that. There was the incident he had had to forget, the incident Einstein (who clearly knew more than he let on) said he didn't want to hear about. There had been witnesses, and they might have gone to the police. But nothing was said about that in the front room of the jail. And it was only during the fourth interview that Willie understood that the superintendent and his colleague were interested in the killing of the three policemen. Willie, when he thought of that, was more concerned with the pathos and heroism of Ramachandra; the policemen, unseen, unknown, had died far away.

In the earlier interviews, when he had been fighting phantoms, he had said more than he knew. He learned now that the superintendent knew the name of everyone in Ramachandra's squad and knew how close Willie was to Ramachandra. Since the superintendent also knew the police side of the story his idea of what had happened was more complete than Willie's.

Willie floundered. His heart gave way when he found that he was an accessory to the murder of three men and was going to be charged.

He thought, 'How unfair it is. Most of my time in the movement, in fact nearly all my time, was spent in idleness. I was horribly bored most of the time. I was going to tell Sarojini in that semi-comic letter that I didn't write how little I had done, how blameless my life as a revolutionary had been, and how idleness had driven me to surrender. But the superintendent has quite another idea of my life as a guerrilla. He takes me twenty times more seriously than I took myself. He wouldn't believe that things merely happened around me. He just counts the dead bodies.'

* * *

WILLIE HAD LONG ago given up counting the beds he had slept in. The India of his childhood and adolescence; the three worried years in London, a student, as his passport said, but really only a drifter, willing himself away from what he had been, not knowing where he might fetch up and what form his life would take; then the eighteen years in Africa, fast and purposeless years, living somebody else's life. He could count all the beds of those years, and the counting would give him a strange satisfaction, would show him that for all his passivity his life was amounting to something; something had grown around him.

But he had been undone by the India of his return. He could see no pattern, no thread. He had returned with an idea of action, of truly placing himself in the world. But he had become a floater, and the world had become more phantasmagoric than it had ever been. That unsettling feeling, of phantasmagoria, had come to him the day when poor Raja, with boyish excitement, had taken him for a ride in his three-wheel scooter, to show him 'the enemy': the local police headquarters with its old trees and sandy parade ground, watched over at the gate by heavily armed men of the reserve police force standing behind stained and dirty sandbags that had gone through a monsoon. Willie knew the road and its drab sights. But everything he saw on his excursion that day had a special quality. Everything was fresh and new. It was as though after being a long time below ground he had come up to the open. But he couldn't stay there, couldn't stay with that vision of freshness and newness. He had to go back with Raja and his scooter to the other world.

Phantasmagoria was confusing. He had at some time lost the ability to count the beds he had slept in; there was no longer any point; and he had given up. Now, in this new mode of experience that had befallen him – interviews, appearances in court, and being shifted about from jail to jail: he had had no idea of this other, whole world of prisons and a prison service and criminals – he started again, not going back to the very beginning, but starting with the day of his surrender.

The day came when he thought he should write to Sarojini. The jaunty mood had long ago left him; when at last he lay face down on the coarse, brightly coloured jail rug on the floor and began writing on the narrow ruled paper he was surprised by grief. He thought of his first night in the camp in the teak forest; all night the forest was full of the flappings and cries of birds and other creatures calling for help that wouldn't come. The writing posture was awkward, and the narrow lines, when he tried to write between them, seemed to cramp his hand. In the end he thought he shouldn't extend his obedience to the ruled lines. He let his writing spread over two lines. He needed more paper and he found that there was no trouble about that, once it was signed for. He had thought that a letter from jail could be on only one sheet; he hadn't asked; he assumed that in jail the world had shrunk in every way.

Assuming that they made no trouble in the jail about his letter, it should get to Sarojini in Berlin in a week, assuming her address hadn't changed. Assuming that she replied right away, and assuming that the people in the jail made no trouble about it, her reply would get to him in a week. Two weeks, then.

But two weeks passed, and three weeks, and four weeks. And there was no letter from Sarojini. The waiting was a strain, and a way of dealing with it was to give up altogether, to say that nothing was going to come. This was what Willie did. And, as it happened, his court life and jail life at this time had become dramatic.

He was sentenced to ten years imprisonment. He told himself it could have been worse. The jail to which he was finally taken had a big board above the front gate. On this board was painted in tall, narrow letters HATE SIN NOT THE SINNER. He saw it from the prison van as he went in, and he often thought about it. Was it Gandhian, this expression of a difficult kind of forgiveness, or was it Christian? It could have been both, since many of the mahatma's ideas were also Christian. He often imagined the letters on the other side of the front wall of the jail. What was painted on the inside of the wall was THANK YOU FOR YOUR VISIT. This was not meant for the prisoners, but for visitors.

One day he had a letter. The stamps were Indian, and on the Indian envelope (no mistaking that) the address of the sender was an address Willie knew well: it was the house where he had grown up, the address of his father's pathetic ashram. He would have been unwilling to unfold the pages (the jail people had cut the envelope open at the top) if he hadn't seen that the letter was not from his father, but from Sarojini, unexpectedly transported from Charlottenburg. She was instantly, in Willie's mind, stripped of the style Berlin had given her. She came back to him as she was twenty-eight years or so before, before Wolf, and travel, and her transformation. And it was as though something of that earlier personality had repossessed her as she wrote her letter.

Dear Willie, I left the Charlottenburg flat long ago, and your letter was passed on from one address to another and finally here. Berliners are very good about that sort of thing. I am sorry you have had so long to wait for a reply. It must have been awful for you. And all the time I was so close to you, less than a day away. But please don't think I will come to see you if you don't want it. In London when I went to see you that time at the college you didn't like it too much. I remember that. And all I wanted was to do good. It is my curse. The business went so wrong so quickly for you. What can I say? I will never forgive myself. That is no consolation for you, I know. You were sent to the wrong people, and as it turned out the other lot were not going to be much better. You were going to be snookered either way.

I came here because I needed a rest from Berlin, and I thought I should come and be with our father, who is near the end. I have told you this before, but I think now he was a finer man than any of us gave him credit for. Perhaps in the end one way of life is as good as any other, but that probably is what defeated people have to tell themselves. I am not too happy with what I have done, though everything was always done with the best of intentions. It is awful to say, but I believe I have sent many people to their doom in many countries. I know now that in the last few years the intelligence people of various countries followed us wherever we went. People trusted us because of what we had done, and we let nobody down. But then in these last few years the people we persuaded to let us make films about them were later picked up one by one. I can give you a list of the countries. It wasn't always like that, and Wolf had nothing to do with it. He is as much of a dupe as the rest of us.

I don't know how I can live with this idea. I was acting for the best, but when the chips were down people would say I was acting for the worst. Perhaps the best thing now would be for someone to bump me off in revenge.

I have nothing more to say just now. You wouldn't believe from what I have written that my heart is breaking. If I read this letter over I will scrap it and never start writing another. So I will send it as it is. Please let me know whether you want me to come and see you. A little money always comes in handy in jail. Please remember that.

It took him some time to digest all that was in the letter. He had felt at first that the letter, childish in parts, was emotionally false. But after some time, considering that when she wrote the letter she would have been surrounded by memories of childhood despair (which would have been like his own), he felt that everything was true. The news of betrayals did not surprise him; but that might have been because in these past few years he had got used to the fluidity, so to speak, of human personality as it adapted to new circumstances. What was upsetting was that for so long she (who had misled him) had been so near and in such a penitent mood. When the world had become phantasmagoric for him, during those desolate marches and bivouacs in the forest, fruitless and unending, he might at any moment have reached out a hand to her, so to speak, and been put in touch again with reality.

He waited for some days before writing. He wanted to clarify his thoughts and to find the right words. (There was no need for rush. Every everyday thing had to be stretched out now: a new form of yoga.) And this time her reply came in ten days.

Dear Willie, I was expecting some word of rebuke from you. There was none. You are a saint. Perhaps after all you are our father's son . . .

And all around him was the regimented, protected life of the jail: nine outdoor hours, fifteen hours of confinement.

THANK YOU FOR YOUR VISIT: that, for visitors, was on the inside of the front wall, at the end of the lane leading to the double main gate. For the prisoners there were smaller signs in sloping, racy lettering. *Truth always wins. Anger is a man's greatest enemy. To do good is the greatest religion. Work is worship. Non-violence is the greatest of all religions.* The time would come when he would cease to see the signs. But in the beginning, out of some kind of student's impishness, surviving in him though he was now not far off fifty, Willie thought he should write on a wall: *A stitch in time saves nine.* He never attempted it. Punishments were severe. But in his mind's eye he saw the sign sitting casually among the other pieties, and it amused him for weeks.

* * *

Willie shared a cell with seven or eight other prisoners. The number varied: some people came and went. The cell was quite big, thirty feet by ten or twelve feet, and for some prisoners it was bigger than anything they had known outside.

One or two prisoners had grown up in factory slums in a city, with brothers and sisters and parents all in one room. The standard room in those places was a cube, ten feet in all directions, with a loft about seven feet up that provided extra sleeping space (especially useful for night workers, who could sleep through the morning or afternoon while daytime family life went on below them). The man who told Willie this did so in a straightforward way at first, speaking of things that to him were quite straightforward, but when he saw that he was shocking Willie he began to swagger a little and exaggerate. In the end (Willie asked a lot of questions) the man had to admit, unwillingly, since it spoiled his story, that the one-room family life he was describing was possible only because so many things were done outside the room, in the wide corridor and in the yard. For the rest, the man said, it was like getting on a crowded bus. You didn't think you could get on, but somehow you did; once you were in, you didn't think you could last, but just a minute or two later, with the movement of the bus, everybody had shaken down and after a while everyone was quite comfortable. It was a little bit like jail, the man said. You didn't think you could do it, but then you found it wasn't so bad after all. A good roof, a ceiling fan in the really hot weather, a good solid concrete floor, regular food, a splash below the stand-pipe in the yard every morning, and even a little television, if you didn't mind standing up with the others to watch it.

This man's pleasure in the jail routine helped Willie. And even when, in the way of jails, the man had moved on, Willie remembered what he had said about 'shaking down' and added it to his yoga.

The people in the cell gradually changed until they were all like Willie, men of the movement who had surrendered. Their treatment then was much better, and the jail superintendent, as if explaining this, said one day, when he was doing his weekly round, with all his deferential officials, that they were now regarded as 'politicals'. The British, the superintendent said, had established this category of prisoner to deal with Gandhi and Nehru and the other nationalists who broke the law but couldn't be treated like other criminals.

Willie was excited by the prospect of favoured treatment. But his excitement didn't last long. The people in the political cells (there was another) were free, always within the jail routine, to organise their activities. And very quickly Willie saw that this favoured treatment had taken him back to what he had walked away from. The routine the politicals established was very much like the routine of the first camp in the teak forest, but without guns and military training. At five thirty they were awakened. At six they assembled outside, and then for two and a half hours they worked on the jail's vegetable plots and orchard. At nine they came back and had breakfast. After that they read the local regional newspapers (provided by the jail) and discussed the news. But the serious intellectual work of the morning was studying the texts of Mao and Lenin. This study, half pious, half mendacious, with people saying what they felt they had to say about the peasantry and the proletariat and the revolution, was sterile to Willie, always a waste of education and mind, and soon, in spite of the favoured treatment and even respect it secured in the jail, it became unbearable. He felt that what remained of his mind would rot away if for three or four hours a day he had to take part in these discussions. And even after the afternoon games and exercise, volleyball, jogging, which was meant to tire them out so that they could sleep, there were evening political discussions, shallow and lying and repetitive, with nothing new ever said, in the cell after lock-up time at six thirty.

Willie thought, 'I will not last. I will not shake down, as that man said people shook down in the crowded bus when the bus began to move. In the bus you can shake down because you are all body. You are not asked to use mind. Here you have to use mind or half-mind in a terrible, corrupting way. Even sleep is poisoned, because you know what you are going to wake up to. One terrible day follows another. It is extraordinary to think that people do this to themselves.'

One Monday, about two months later, when the superintendent was doing his round with his retinue of lesser jail officials, Willie broke out of the line of standing prisoners. He said to the superintendent, 'Sir, I would like to see you in your office, if that is possible.' The lower jail people, warder and head warder and chief head warder, were all for beating Willie back with their long staffs, but Willie's civility and educated voice and his calling the superintendent sir acted like protection.

The superintendent said to the jailer, 'Bring him to my office after the round.'

The hierarchy of the jail! It was like the army, it was like a business organisation, it was a little bit like the hierarchy of the movement. The foot-soldiers were the warder and head warder and chief head warder (though 'warder' sounded such a good, polite word). The officers were the sub-jailer and the jailer (in spite of the brutal, key-jangling associations of the word, more suited, Willie always thought, to the lower men who padded about outside the cells). Above the sub-jailer and jailer was the deputy superintendent of jails and, at the very top, the superintendent of jails. When a prisoner came to the jail, he might know nothing about the hierarchy that now ruled his life, might not be able to read the uniforms, but soon his reaction to uniforms and titles was instinctive.

The superintendent's office was panelled in some dark brown wood that had possibly been varnished. At the top of the wall a metal grille with a flat diamond pattern provided an air vent. On one panelled wall was a very large plan of the jail: the compounds, the cells, the assembly grounds, the vegetable garden, the orchard, the two perimeter walls, with every important exit marked with a thick red X.

On the superintendent's shoulders were the shining metal initials of the state prison service.

Willie said, 'I asked to see you, sir, because I wish to be moved from the cell where I am.'

The superintendent said, 'But it's the best cell in the jail. A nice, big space. A lot of open-air activity. And you have the most educated people there. Discussions and so on.'

Willie said, 'I can't stand it. I have had eight years of that sort of thing. I want to be with my own thoughts. Please put me among the ordinary criminals.'

'This is most unusual. It's very rough in the other cells. We are trying to treat you here as the British treated the mahatma and Nehru and the others.'

'I know. But please move me.'

'It will not be easy for you. You are an educated man.'

'Let me try.'

'All right. But let me do it in two weeks or so. Let people forget that you came to see me. I don't want them to believe that you asked to be moved. They might feel insulted, or they might think you were an informer, and they might make trouble for you in various ways. In a jail everybody is at war. You must remember that.'

Three weeks later Willie was moved to a cell in the other part of the jail. It was terrible. The cell was a long concrete room seemingly without furniture. All the way down the middle was a clear passageway about six feet wide. On either side of this passageway were the prisoners' floor spaces. Willie's strip of floor was about three feet wide, and he had a jail rug (in a bold blue pattern) on his strip of floor. That was all. No table, no cupboard: prisoners here kept such possessions as they had at the head of their floor space. Space was tight; one rug touched the other. The prisoners, sleeping or waking, kept their head against the wall and their feet pointing towards the passageway. Each rug had a different pattern and colour; this helped every man to know his space (and was also useful to the warders).

Willie thought, 'I can't go and ask the superintendent to move me back to the politicals. And when I think about it, I am not sure that I want to go back. They have that lovely vegetable garden and fruit orchard to work in. But all that discussion of the newspapers in the morning, which is no discussion at all, and all that study of Mao and Lenin in the evening is too big a price. Even in Africa among the settlers there was nothing quite so bad. Perhaps if I were a stronger man I could do it all and not be affected. But I am not strong in that way.'

That first evening as he was walking in the central open area between the jail rugs and the bed spaces, a very small man sprang up crying from one of the rugs and ran to his feet and held them. He was about four feet nine or ten inches, from Bangladesh, an illegal immigrant; whenever after each jail sentence he was taken to the border the Bangladeshis pushed him back, and he had some months of wandering until some new Indian jail claimed him. The sudden crying and leaping up and running to grasp the knees of some new official or visitor was one of his turns: something he did like a trained animal: his whole life was reduced to that.

A letter came from Sarojini. *Dear Willie, Our father is dead. He was cremated yesterday. I did not think to trouble you with this news, because I did not think you wanted to be troubled. Anyway, this is my news for you. I have decided to take over our father's ashram. My thoughts have been running in that direction for some time, as I think you know. I have no religious wisdom, and I will not be able to offer people anything of what our father offered them. I think what I will do is to turn the ashram into a place of quiet and meditation, something with a Buddhist slant, which I know a little about, from Wolf. How strange it is that I, who had so little use for this kind of place all my life, should now do this. But life does this to people sometimes. Let me come and see you. I will explain things more fully face to face . . .*

He got a sheet of ruled paper from the warder and, lying on his rug and twisting his body a little over his neighbour's space so that he could write on the low window sill of the cell, he wrote: *Dear Sarojini, You run from one extreme to the other. The idea of the ashram is an idea of death in life, and it goes against everything you have believed. What we discussed in Berlin remains true. I am grateful to you for making me face myself and what I come from. I consider that a gift of life. I am surrounded here by a kind of distress I don't know how to deal with, but the ashram is not the way. Nor was that foolish war which I went to fight. That war was not yours or mine and it had nothing to do with the village people we said we were fighting for. We talked about their oppression, but we were exploiting them all the time. Our ideas and words were more important than their lives and their ambitions for themselves. That was terrible to me, and it continues even here, where the talkers have favoured treatment and the poor are treated as the poor always are. They are mostly village people and they are undersized and thin. The most important thing about them is their small size. It is hard to associate them with the bigger crimes and the crimes of passion for which some of them are being punished. Abduction, kidnapping. I suppose if you were a villager you would see them as criminal and dangerous, but if you see them from a distance, as I still see them, although I am close to them night and day, you would be moved by the workings of the human soul, so complete within those frail bodies. Those wild and hungry eyes haunt me. They seem to me to carry a distillation of the country's unhappiness. I don't think there is any one single simple action which can help. You can't take a gun and kill that unhappiness. All you can do is to kill people.*

* * *

SAROJINI CAME TO see him. She wore a white sari – white the colour of grief – and of course she didn't have to wait with the others who had come to see prisoners in Willie's cell. Her manner, her speech, and her dress won her immediate regard, and she did not squat in the hot sun – in a low subdued queue, two persons wide – with the other visitors, under the gaze of the warders with their heavy staffs. She sat in a room in the front of the jail and Willie was called to see her. He liked her sari, and her general style, just as much as he had liked the jeans and chunky pullovers she had worn in Berlin.

She was enraged about the country people waiting in line in the sun to see their relations.

He said, 'They don't complain. They are happy to be in the queue. Some people make long journeys and wait all night and then in the morning they are turned away. Because they can't tip the warders, or because they didn't know they had to tip the warders. Money makes everything easy in the jail. The warders have to make a living, too, you know.'

'You are trying to shock me. But I expected that. It tells me you are in good spirits.'

'What we can really try to do is to get me in the hospital. There are about sixteen or twenty beds there. It's a big, airy room, quite bare, but one isn't looking for interior decoration in a jail. If we can slip the warders thirty or forty rupees a day, then my time in the jail becomes pure pleasure. I get an iron bed with a mattress, which is better than a rug on the floor, and all my meals are brought from the kitchen straight to me. Breakfast, lunch, and dinner in bed. Like a hotel.'

'What about the sick people?'

'They are where they belong, in the cells. What did you expect?'

She said, quite seriously, 'If I did it, would you go?'

'I might. I am getting tired of the cell. I also would like to get something to read. The other people can discuss Lenin and Mao until the cows come home. But the only thing they like you to read in the common cells is a religious book.'

'You'll be a mental wreck by the time you leave.'

'I think you are right. I am coming to the end of my mental resources. Once in Africa I had arranged to meet someone in the town on the coast. At a café or something. For various reasons I was terribly late. More than an hour. Yet when I went to the café the man was there, calmly waiting. He was a Portuguese. I apologised. He said, "There is no need. I have a well-stocked mind." I thought that was very grand. Probably he had heard it from somebody else, but I made it my ideal. After that, whenever I was in a doctor's waiting room, say, or a hospital out-patients department, I never ran to the dingy magazines to kill time. I examined my well-stocked mind. I've been doing a lot of that in my cell. But my mind is letting me down now. I am coming to the end of what it has. I've thought of our parents and my childhood. Actually, there's a lot there. I've thought of London. I've thought of Africa. I've thought of Berlin. Very important. I've thought of my years in the movement. If I were a religious man I would say that I was putting my spiritual life in order. Counting the beds I slept in.'

Two weeks after Sarojini's visit he was transferred to the hospital ward. He received books from her and began to read again. He was dazzled by everything he read. Everything seemed miraculous. Every writer seemed a prodigy. Something like this used to happen to him when very long ago, in another life, as it now seemed, he had tried to write stories and was sometimes stuck, his mind clogged. Those days usually occurred when he was deep in a story. He would wonder how anyone ever had the courage to write a sentence. He might even look at an aspirin bottle or a cough syrup bottle and marvel at the confidence of the man who had written the directions and warnings. In some such way now a deep regard came to him for everyone who could put words together, and he was transported by everything he read. The experience was glorious, and he would think that it was probably worth coming to jail just for this, this heightening of intellectual pleasure, this opening up of something in life he knew little of.

Something unusual happened five months or so after he had gone to the hospital ward.

The superintendent was doing his Monday morning round. Willie felt the superintendent's eyes on him and the first thought that came to him was that his time in the hospital ward was coming to an end. Sure enough, later that day a message came to Willie from the superintendent, relayed down the chain of command.

The next day Willie went to the superintendent's dark-panelled office with the diamond pattern in iron over the air vent.

The superintendent said, 'You are walking wounded, I see.'

Willie made a pleading gesture, asking for understanding.

'I will tell you why I called you. I've explained to you the privileged position you enjoy in the jail and which it is open to you at any moment to take advantage of. We operate under the same rules as in the British time. You gave an undertaking at the time of your surrender that you had done nothing that could be thought of as a heinous crime under Section 302. It was part of the package. All of you gave that undertaking. So we have the strange situation where hundreds, perhaps thousands, were killed by your movement, but we have not been able to find a single one of you who did anything. In all your statements it was always someone else who killed or pulled the trigger. Suppose now that there is someone in the jail who wishes to change that statement. Someone who is actually willing to say that X or Y or Z had actually done a particular killing.'

Willie said, 'Is there such a person?'

The superintendent said, 'There may be. In a jail everybody is at war. I told you that.'

* * *

HE WAS QUITE lucid in the superintendent's office. But later in his hospital bed his mind clouded and he was swamped by darkness. Cold fluids seemed to flow through his body. Something like real illness seemed to chill him. And yet all the time with the steadier part of his mind he was also thinking, as though he was filing away something for future use, 'This is beautifully done. If you have to betray and damage someone, this is the way to do it. When it is least expected, and with no calling card.'

A Gandhi-capped prisoner brought his dinner from the jail kitchen. It was what it always was. A plastic bowl of lentil soup, thickened perhaps with flour (you couldn't tell until you tasted it). And six pieces of flat bread, cooling and sweating fast.

When he woke up in the night, he thought, in the desolation of the hospital ward, 'Yesterday I was happy.'

He had trained himself to stay away from the vegetable patches and the orchard where the politicals worked. But the next morning when he went to have a look he saw the man whom he feared to see: Einstein. His mind had fastened on him as the betrayer, and this sighting of him for the first time in the jail grounds was like a confirmation. Einstein, intuitively disliked at first sight (and the memory of that first dislike was always with Willie), intuitively distrusted, then a companion in bad times, and now distrusted again. Willie knew that Einstein would have felt about him what he had felt about Einstein. He had grown to believe, especially in those last years in the forest, that there was a neat reciprocity in relationships. If you liked a man you would invariably get on with him; if you didn't feel easy with him he almost certainly felt the same way about you. In the jail Einstein and many of the others would have gone back to their hate, each man to his own, as to some secret treasure, something which in a time of uncertainty they could gaze on and be revivified. (Willie remembered the rhetorical and ignorant and boastful revolutionary they had met in the forest, a remnant of a long-defeated rebellion, who had been tramping through the villages for thirty years with his simple philosophy of murder, incapable now of any higher thought, and yet easily made timid.) It didn't take much to see how in the jail Einstein, daily cherishing the private treasure of his hate, and for no other reason, perhaps for no reward, would find immense satisfaction in this betrayal of Willie.

After that sighting of Einstein Willie went back to his hospital bed. He asked the warder for a sheet of writing paper and wrote to Sarojini.

Two weeks later she came to see him. When he told her what had happened she said, 'This is serious.'

And immediately he could see, in spite of her ashram life and white cotton sari, her fixer's mind at work. To agitate on behalf of political prisoners all over the world had been part of her political work. In the small room in the jail he could see her mind ranging fast over the possibilities.

She said, 'Who published your book in London? The book of stories.'

He told her. It seemed like another life now.

'A good left-wing firm. Was it in 1958?'

'The year of the Notting Hill race riots in London.'

'Clearly those riots had an effect on you?' She was like a lawyer.

'I don't know.'

'Whether you know or not, it may be a good line to take. Were you associated with anyone important? People coming to the college to talk, things like that.'

'There was a Jamaican. He went to South America to work with Che Guevara, but they threw him out. Then he went to Jamaica and ran a night club. I don't suppose that's much good to you. There was also a lawyer. He used to do little broadcasts for the BBC. That's how I met him. He helped a lot with the book.'

'Thirty years on he might be famous.'

He gave her the name, and she left him in an unreal mood, half living in the past and embarrassed by the dim memory of the false stories he had written in that time of darkness, half living in the hospital ward in the chill of his predicament.

* * *

ROGER, THE LAWYER, whose name Willie had given Sarojini, had written Willie a letter about the book a few weeks after it had been published. Willie had held on to the letter for years as to a magic charm. He had taken it to Africa and in the early years there he had often looked at it. *As the Latin poet says*, Roger had written in his old-fashioned educated way, *books have their destiny, and this book may live in ways that may surprise you.* Willie had seen in those words a kind of good prophecy. Nothing remarkable had befallen him, and in time he had put the prophecy aside. He had not thought to take the letter with him when he left Africa; and perhaps he would not have been able to find it: another thing lost in the mess of Africa at that time. But now in the jail Roger's words came back to him and, as before, he held on to them as to a piece of good prophecy.

It began to seem like that when some weeks later the superintendent sent for him again.

'Still walking wounded,' the superintendent said, making his old joke. Then he said, his voice changing, 'You never told us you were a writer.'

Willie said, 'It was a long time ago.'

'That's just it,' the superintendent said, lifting a sheet of paper from his desk. 'It says here that you were a pioneer of modern Indian writing.'

And Willie understood that just as his father, thirty years ago, had by his begging letters to great men in England set certain wheels in motion that had eventually taken him to London, so now Sarojini, out of her great political experience, had begun to act on his behalf.

Six months later, under terms of a special amnesty, Willie was once again bound for London.

EIGHT

The London Beanstalk

THE PLANE THAT took Willie to London taxied for a long time after it landed. It seemed to be going to the edge of the airport, and when at last people got off they had a very long walk back, matching the long taxiing out, to immigration and the centre of airport things. Luggage had to take a corresponding route back, and it was fifteen or twenty minutes before it began to arrive. Most of it was the pathetic luggage of the immigrant poor: cardboard boxes tied up with string; metal-edged wooden cases, new, but like old-fashioned steamer trunks, meant for bad weather at sea; enormous bulging suitcases (nearly all in some synthetic black material) that no man could easily shift or lift or carry by hand, and were meant more for the padded head of the Indian railway porter.

Willie felt old stirrings, the beginning of old grief. But then he thought, 'I have been there. I have given part of my life and I have nothing to show for it. I cannot go there again. I must let that part of me die. I must lose that vanity. I must understand that big countries grow or shrink according to the play of internal forces that are beyond the control of any one man. I must try now to be only myself. If such a thing is possible.'

Roger was at the barrier outside, camouflaged among the taxi-drivers with name cards and the large, buzzing family groups waiting for the travellers with heavy baggage. In spite of himself Willie was looking for a man thirty years younger, and Roger was not immediately recognisable. At first sight he was like a man in disguise.

Willie apologised for making him wait.

Roger said, 'I have learned to possess my soul in patience. The board told me that you had landed, and then it told me that you were most probably in the baggage hall.'

The voice and the tone were familiar. They recreated the vanished man, the man Willie remembered, who was now like someone hidden within the person before him. The effect was disturbing.

Later, when Willie's small suitcase was in the boot of Roger's car, and parking charges had been settled at the machine, Roger said, 'It's like being at the theatre. But in real life it's unnerving. The second act ends, and after the interval the man comes out with a powdered wig and a creased face. You see him as old. Old age can often look like a moral infirmity, and in real life to see someone suddenly old is like seeing a moral infirmity made suddenly clear. And then you understand that the other man is looking at you in the same way. Do you know anyone here? Have you kept in touch?'

'I used to know a girl at the Debenhams perfume counter. Hardly knew her, really. She was the friend of a friend, and all the time she was engaged to somebody else. The whole thing is too embarrassing to think about now. Do you think she would remember, after twenty-eight years?'

Roger said, 'She would remember. When she counts her lovers – and she would do that quite often – she would count you in.'

'How terrible. What do you think would have happened to her?'

'Fat. Faithless. Betrayed. Complaining about the wicked world. Vain. Talking too much. Commoner than ever. Women are more physical and more shallow than one imagines.'

Willie said, 'Will I have to be here now forever and ever?'

'It was part of the deal.'

'What will happen to me? How will I pass the time?'

'Don't think about it now. Just let it happen. Let it begin. Let it flow over you.'

'When I went to Africa I remember that on the first day I looked out of the bathroom window and saw everything outside through a rusty screen. I never wanted to stay. I thought that something was going to happen, that I would never unpack. Yet I stayed for eighteen years. And it was like that when I joined the guerrillas. The first night in the teak forest. It was too unreal. I wasn't going to stay. Something was going to happen and I was going to be liberated. But nothing happened, and I stayed seven years. We were always on the move in the forest. One day in a village I met a man, a revolutionary, who said he had been in the forest for thirty years. He was probably exaggerating, but he had been there a very long time. He was someone from the previous revolution. That revolution had died long before, but he had carried on. It had become a way of life for him, hiding, pretending to be a villager. Like an ascetic in his hermitage in the forest in an old story. Or like Robinson Crusoe, living off the land. The man was mad. His mind had stopped, like a dead clock, and he was still living with the ideas that were in his head when the clock stopped, showing the same time forever. Those ideas were very sharp, and when he talked of them he was like a sane man. There were people like that in the jail. I could always step back from myself, and consider my situation. But there were moments when I felt myself changing. The whole thing was so strange, such a string of unreal episodes, I feel in time I would have gone mad like the others. The brain is so delicate, and man can adapt to so many situations. That's how it's been for me. Has it been like that for you too? At least in some ways?'

Roger said, 'I would like to say that it's the same for all of us. But my life these last thirty years hasn't been like that. I have always felt myself in the real world. That may be because I have always felt that life had dealt me a good hand. It sounds smug, but there have been no surprises.'

Willie said, 'My life has been a series of surprises. Unlike you, I had no control over things. I thought I had. My father and all the people around him thought they had. But what looked like decisions were not decisions really. For me it was a form of drift, because I didn't see what else there was for me to do. I thought I wanted to go to Africa. I thought that something would happen and I would be shown the true way, the way meant for me alone. But as soon as I got on the ship I was frightened. And you – did you marry Perdita?'

'I couldn't tell you why. I suppose my sexual energy is low. There were six or seven people I might have married, and it would have always ended as it did with Perdita. It was a piece of good fortune for me that quite soon after our marriage she fell into a good and solid relationship with a friend of mine. This friend had a very big London house. It was something he had inherited, but that big London house excited Perdita. I was actually disappointed in her – her delight in the man's big house. But most people in this country have a streak of commonness. The aristocrats love their titles. The rich count their money all the time, and are always calculating whether the other man has less or more. The romantic middle-class idea in the old days was that the true aristocrats, and not the jumped-up middle class, never truly knew who they were. Not so. The aristocrats I have got to know always know who they are. They can be awfully common, those aristocrats. One man I know loves appearing among his dinner guests in a bathrobe, dishing out the drinks – and then going off to dress, after having humiliated all of us who were invited to his grand house. "What dressing up, my dear," he said to somebody afterwards, retailing the incident. "How grand we all were!" The "we", of course, was ironical. He meant "they", the guests he had made to come all dressed up. I was one of the guests, and I was the somebody he told the story to later. So I suppose Perdita's commonness is not so extraordinary. But I expected better of someone who had married me.'

Willie was recognising London names from the direction boards. But they were driving along a new highway.

Roger said, 'All this used to be part of your beat. Until they drove this road through it. I suppose that the common people are the only ones who are not common in the way I mean. Shallow and self-regarding and acting up to some idea of who they are. Anyway, there was Perdita having this relationship with this bounder with the big London house, everything satisfactory to all parties, the bounder having somebody's wife as his mistress,

Perdita intimate with a big London house and feeling quite adult. Then Perdita became pregnant. It was quite late for her, perhaps too late. The lover was alarmed. His love didn't extend that far – looking after a child forever and ever. So Perdita turned to me for support. I didn't like seeing her so wretched. I have a soft spot for her, you see. But I didn't understand the situation. I misread Perdita's passion, and said more or less that I was willing to surrender all rights, so to speak. Willing to let her go. I thought it was what she wanted to hear. But it made her hysterical, that two men should care so little for her. We had many a tearful session. For two or three weeks I dreaded going home. And then I said that the child was possibly mine and I was happy that a child was on the way. None of this was true, of course.

'I dreaded the arrival of the child. For some time I lived with the idea that I would leave Perdita, find some studio flat somewhere. In my imagination that studio flat became cosier and cosier and more and more removed from everything. It was immensely comforting. And then something happened. Perdita had a miscarriage. That was a mess. Just as I had been going into a shell, dreaming of my cosy little studio flat, so now she retreated into herself. She had a good long wallow. It was worse than before. There were days when I actually thought of not going home but of going to some hotel. She banned the lover, the bounder, my old legal friend. I began to think after some time that she was enjoying her situation, and I lived with her during this time as I would have lived with someone with a broken leg or arm, something dramatic to behold but not life-threatening.

'One day her scoundrelly lover sent her – would you believe

it? – a poem. I knew about it because it had been left out for me to see, on the sideboard in the dining room. It was a long poem. It wasn't a poem he had copied out, something he was quoting. It was a poem he said he had written for her. She knew that I looked down on the man with the big house as a kind of buffoon, and I suppose this was one in the eye for me. And, sure enough, the love-making of the two resumed, the afternoons in the big house or perhaps in my house, the excitement of the two. Though perhaps it wasn't excitement at this stage, perhaps just a resumed habit.

'I knew, of course, that the poem wasn't original. But just as sometimes we can be haunted by the ghost of earlier things in certain popular pieces of music, so I was haunted by this poem to Perdita. In a desultory way I began to look, and one day I found it. In a volume of W. E. Henley, a Victorian-Edwardian poet, a friend of Kipling. Never underestimate the power of bad art, Willie. I should have done nothing, should have let the lovers go on in their way, but I was irritated by the silliness or the self-satisfaction of Perdita – laying out the poem for me to see. I said to her one day, "Here is a nice book of poems for you, Perdita." And I gave her the Henley volume. It was wrong of me, but it gave me pleasure to think of the little scenes Perdita and her poet-lover were going to have. Of course they broke up for a while. But now I believe they've started up again.'

Now they had stopped outside Roger's house. It was a big house, semi-detached, but tall and big.

Roger said, 'And that's the private drama of this house. I suppose there is such a drama in every house here.'

Willie said, 'And yet you say your life has had no surprises.'

'I meant that. Whatever I had done, whoever I had married

or lived with, we would have arrived at a situation like the one I've been telling you about.'

In the quiet lamplit street, full of trees and shadows, the house was impressive.

Roger said, 'The little Marble Arch house was the seedcorn. I've been climbing up that property beanstalk all the time, and it's got me here. It is true of at least half the people on the street, though we might pretend otherwise.'

The house was big, but the room they went up to, two floors up, was small. Willie thought he could see Perdita's hand in it. He was moved. The stiff curtains were drawn. Opening them a little, he looked down at the trees and lamplight and the shadows and the parked cars. After a while he went down to the main room. Half of it was a sitting room, half a kitchen-dining room. He exclaimed at the wallpaper, the white paint, the cooker in the middle of the kitchen part of the room, the hood of the extractor. He said, 'Lovely, lovely.' The hobs on the cooker were ceramic hobs, flat with the surface. Willie exclaimed at that too. Roger said, 'You're overdoing it, Willie. There's no need. It's not so nice.' But then Roger, looking at Willie's face, understood that Willie was not exaggerating or mocking, that Willie was half-transported.

And, in fact, in Roger's house that first evening, Willie found himself full of every kind of sensual excitement. It was dark, but not yet absolute night. Through the uncurtained window at the back of the sitting room Willie could see the young black-trunked trees and the dark green gloom of the small garden at the back of the house. He thought he had never seen anything like it, nothing so benign. He couldn't take his eyes off it. He said to Roger, 'I've been in jail. We had an orchard to look after, but it was nothing like this. As guerrillas we walked through the forest, but that was hot forest, in stinging sun. Often on those walks I used to think I needed a narcotic. I liked the word. I would like to drink something now. In the forest we drank nothing. In Africa for eighteen years we drank Portuguese and South African wine.'

From far off, it seemed, Roger said, 'Would you like a glass of white wine?'

'I would like whisky, champagne.'

Roger poured him a large whisky. He drank it in a single draught. Roger said, 'It's not wine, Willie.' But he drank another glass in the same swift way. He said, 'It's wonderfully sweet, Roger. Sweet and deep. I have tasted nothing like it. No one told me that about whisky.'

Roger said, 'It's the effect of release. We got a man out from Argentina in 1977 or 1978. He had been horribly tortured. One of the first things he wanted to do when he came here was to go to the shops. One of the shops he went to was Lillywhites. It's bang on Piccadilly Circus. A sports shop. He stole a set of golf clubs there. He wasn't a golf player. It's just that he spotted the chance to steal. Some old guerrilla or criminal or outlaw instinct. He didn't know why he had done it. He dragged those clubs to the bus stop, and then he dragged them all the way from Maida Vale to the house, and displayed them. Like a cat bringing back a mouse.'

Willie said, 'In the movement we had to be austere. People boasted of their austerity, of how little they were making do with. In the jail the other prisoners had their drugs. But we politicals never did. We remained clean. It was part of our strength, oddly enough. But during the drive into London, while you were talking, I felt something strange happening to me. I began to understand that I was no longer in the jail, and some other person, not absolutely myself, began to crawl out as it were from hiding. I don't know whether I will be able to live with this new person. I am not sure I can get rid of him. I feel he will always be there, waiting for me.'

Then he found himself awakening from a heady heavy sleep. He thought after a while, 'I suppose I am in Roger's nice house, with the nice main room and the green garden with the small trees. I suppose Roger brought me up here.' Then a new thought, issuing from the new person who had possessed him, assailed him, 'I have never slept in a room of my own. Never at home in India, when I was a boy. Never here in London. Never in Africa. I lived in somebody else's house always, and slept in somebody else's bed. In the forest of course there were no rooms, and then the jail was the jail. Will I ever sleep in a room of my own?' And he marvelled that he had never had a thought like that before.

At some stage someone knocked on the door. Perdita. He wouldn't have spotted her in the street. But her voice was her own. He remembered her story and was stirred to see her. He said, 'Do you remember me?' She said, 'Of course I remember you. Roger's slender-waisted Indian boy. At least that was what was thought.' He didn't know what to make of that and left it unanswered. He put on the bathrobe in the bathroom of his room and went down to the main room with the centrally placed cooker below the hood. The night before its beauty had overwhelmed him. She gave him coffee from a complicated-looking contraption.

And then without warning she said, very simply, 'Who did

you marry?' Just like that, as though life was an old-fashioned story and marriage neatened everything, neatened and gave a point even to the fumblings of Willie nearly thirty years before. As though, in this matter of marriage, Willie had had a wealth of choice. Or perhaps none at all. As though in this view from the other side Willie, as a man, had a privilege she had never had.

Willie said, 'I met somebody from Africa and I went there and lived with her.'

'How wonderful. Was it nice? I often think it would have been nice in Africa in the old days.'

'When I was sitting in the jail in India we used sometimes to read items in the newspapers about the war in the place where I had been. We used to discuss it among ourselves. It was part of our political education, discussing these African liberation movements. Sometimes I would read an item about the actual region where I had been. Apparently the whole place had been destroyed. Every concrete building had been burnt. You can't burn concrete, but you can burn the windows and the roof rafters and everything inside. I often tried to imagine that. Every concrete building roofless and marked by smoke below the roofs and around the window openings. In the jail I used to make in imagination all the journeys I used to make, and I would imagine someone or some people making those journeys and setting all the concrete buildings alight. I used to try to imagine what it would have been like when nothing came from the outside world. No metal, no tools, no clothes, no thread. Nothing. The Africans had quite good skills in metal and cloth when they lived alone. But they hadn't lived alone for a long time, and they had forgotten those skills. It would have been interesting to see what would have happened when they were absolutely alone again.'

Perdita said, 'What happened to the person you went to Africa with?'

Willie said, 'I don't know. I suppose she went away. I don't imagine she would have stayed. But I don't know.'

'Oh, dear. Did you hate her so much?'

'I didn't hate her. I often thought of finding out. It was possible. I could have sent messages, from the forest or the jail. But I didn't want to get bad news. And then I didn't want to get news at all. I wanted to forget. I wanted to live my new life. But what about you, Perdita? How did things work out for you?'

'Do they work out for anybody?'

He considered her biggish belly – so ugly on a woman, so much uglier than on a man. Her skin was bad, coarse, caking. He thought, 'I never thought her pretty. But then I wished to make love to her, to see her undressed. So hard to imagine now. Was it age, my deprivation, my hormones, as they say? Or was it something else? Was it the idea of England that was still so strong at that time, and which cast a glow on its women?'

Perdita said, 'I don't imagine Roger had a chance last night to show you this.' She took a small paperback off the sideboard. Willie recognised his name and the name of the book he had written twenty-eight years before. She said, 'It was Roger's idea. It helped to get you released. It showed that you were a real writer, and not political.'

Willie didn't know the name of the paperback publisher. The printed pages were like those he remembered. The book would have been photographed from the original. The jacket copy was new: Willie read that his book was a pioneer of Indian post-colonial writing.

He took the book up to his little room in the big house. Nervously, fearful of encountering his old self, he began to read. And then very quickly he was drawn in; he shed his nerves. He ceased to be aware of the room and city in which he read; he ceased to be aware of reading. He felt himself transported, as if by some kind of time-travelling magic, into the time, twenty-eight years before, when he was writing. He felt he could re-enter even the sequence of the days, see again the streets and weather and newspapers, and become again like a man who didn't know how the future would unfold. He re-entered that time of innocence or ignorance, of not having a true grasp even of the map of the world. It was extraordinary then to come to himself from time to time and then going back to his book and re-entering that other life, living again the sequence of weeks and months, anxiety always below everything, before Ana and Africa.

He would have said, if he had been asked, that he had always been the same person. But it was another person who looked as from a great distance at his older self. And gradually, playing all that morning with the time capsule or time machine of the book, moving in and out of that earlier personality, as a child or someone new to air-conditioning might on a very hot day play with entering and then leaving cooler rooms, gradually there came to Willie an idea of the man he had become, an idea of what Africa and then the guerrilla life in the forest and then the prison and then simple age had made of him. He felt immensely strong; he had never felt like this before. It was as though he had managed to pull a switch in his head and seen everything in a dark room.

Perdita called him for lunch. She said, 'Normally I have a sandwich or something like that. But there is something special for you. Corn bread. I baked it yesterday. You don't have to eat it. I don't do these things very well, but I thought I should.'

It was oily and heavy. But the thought of Perdita baking this bad bread was oddly attractive to Willie.

He said, 'All the time I've been away I've had pictures of you in my head. I remember seeing you for the first time in the French restaurant in Wardour Street. I thought you were very stylish. I thought it was the stylishness of London. I hadn't met anybody like you. You wore striped gloves, whether of fabric or leather I couldn't say.'

She said, 'There was a fashion.'

He could see her thinking back, and he thought, 'The thirty years that have passed have been the true years of her life. She has no life now. No possibility. We have changed positions.' He said, 'And then I saw you at that party you and Roger gave at the Marble Arch house for the editor. The fat man. Somebody was talking. I looked across at you and found you looking at me. I held your gaze for a while and longed to make love to you. I tried some time later. I did it badly. But it took a lot of courage to try. I wonder if you knew that. Those two pictures of you have always been with me. In Africa in dark times, and everywhere else I've gone. I never thought it was going to be granted to me to be with you again.'

He got up and stood behind her chair and put his hands on her shoulders.

She said, 'Get back to your chair.'

She had said something like that twenty-eight years before, and he had been cowed. It had taken away all his sexual courage.

But now he pressed on her more firmly. Trusting to instinct – for he had never made such an attempt on a woman before – he kept his palms firmly on her and pushed down through some flimsy material to her small, slack breasts. He couldn't see her face (and he could see only a part of her body). This made him bolder. He left his palms on her breasts. For a while he stayed like that, not seeing her face, considering only her grainy greying hair. He said, 'Let's go up to my room.' He released his hold on her and she pushed her chair back and stood up. She then allowed herself to be led up to the little room. She disengaged herself from him and began to take her clothes off carefully. This is how she is with her afternoon lover, Willie thought, the man with the big house; she has only adopted me into the routine of her afternoon.

He, undressing as methodically as she, said, 'I will make love to you in the Balinese way.' It was half a joke, but only half, a way of re-presenting himself to her after the failure of all those years ago. The Balinese way was something he had picked up a long time before in Africa from a handbook of sex, serious perhaps, perhaps salacious – he no longer remembered. He said, 'The Balinese don't like pressing bodies together. In Bali the man sits on the woman. In this way a young man will not find it hard to make love to a very old woman.' His words had run away with him. But she appeared not to hear. And after all his abstemious years in the Indian woods and then in the Indian jail, the Balinese posture did come back to him; his knees and hips did not fail him. She was cooperative but withdrawn, as indifferent to his relief at managing the posture as she had been to his earlier words. She was very far from being a ruin. There were still areas of smoothness on her skin.

He considered the setting, the room she had decorated. The furniture – bed, table, chair – had been seemingly washed almost clean of its covering of paint or varnish or French polish, and the wood showed naked and old, with patches of white, perhaps a stubborn priming coat; or perhaps it was part of the bleaching style. The curtains were stiff and frilly, ivory or off-white with a small flower design in pale blue at wide intervals. The frilliness and stiffness suggested the curtains were about to billow inwards. This, together with the bleached furniture, suggested that the sea and healthy salt breezes were just outside. The previous day, in the flurry of arrival and later in his whisky stupor, Willie had seen all of this without truly noticing it. Now he saw how carefully it had been put together. The curtain material was repeated in the loose cover of the chair and in a kind of half frill around the top of the bleached table. The fluted wooden lampstand was bleached, with the usual flecks of white. The lampshade was royal blue. A tightly woven little basket of plaited straw held beautifully sharpened pencils of a cigar-box colour. Next to this was a dull globe of solid glass with pink-tipped matches in a little well in the middle. Willie had been puzzled by this the night before, and in the morning he had examined it. The glass globe was unexpectedly heavy. The dullness of the surface came from regular horizontal grooves that ringed it all the way down. Diagonal markings across the grooves led Willie to believe that to get a light you struck the pink-tipped match against the grooves. He did so; the match blazed; and then he had put the spent matchstick back in the well with the unused pink ones. It was still there. He thought that bit of style had come to Perdita from her own past, or was something she had wished as a girl to have one day in her own house.

And he became full of pity for Perdita, always withdrawn, always cooperative, her head on its side.

He thought, 'There's more of her soul in the decoration of this room than anywhere else, more even' – considering her from his sitting position – 'than in her used-up body.' And then, unexpectedly, with no great convulsion, she was satisfied, and her satisfaction led slowly to his own, which seemed to come from far away. He thought, 'I must never forget the Perditas. London would be full of them. I must never neglect the neglected. If I am to stay here it may be the way ahead.'

Carefully she picked up her clothes from the covered chair and went down to her own bathroom, leaving him to his. He thought, 'This is how it is with her when she is with her lover. This is the greater part of her life.' He wasn't expecting her to come back up, but she did. She was dressed again. He was back in the bed. She said, 'I don't know whether Roger has told you. He's involved with this awful banker and it's a mess.'

Willie said, 'I believe he told me about the banker. The man in a bathrobe.'

She went down again, and he returned to his own book, moving in and out of the past, in and out of his old self, immensely excited now by the room, the house, the great city outside. He stayed there, waiting – like a child, like a wife – for Roger to come back to the house. He fell asleep. When he woke up the light outside, beyond the ivory curtains, was going. He heard Roger come in. He heard him talking later on the telephone. There was no sound of Perdita. Willie wasn't sure whether he should dress and go down. He decided to stay where he was; and, like a child hiding, he was as quiet as he could be.

After a while Roger came up and knocked. When he saw Willie in bed Roger said, 'Lucky man.'

Willie hid his book and said, 'The first time I came to England I came by ship. One day, just before we got to the Suez Canal, the steward said the captain was coming to make his inspection. Just like the jail, really. The steward was agitated, the way the jailer and the others used to be agitated when the superintendent was making his round. I thought it didn't apply to me – the captain coming. So when he came in with his officers they found me half dressed on my bunk. The captain looked at me with hatred and contempt and never said a word. I've never forgotten that look.'

Roger said, 'Do you feel strong enough to come down for a drink?'

'Let me put on my clothes.'

'Put on your dressing gown.'

'I don't have one.'

'I am sure Perdita has put out a bathrobe for you.'

'I'll be like your banker.'

He went down in the bathrobe to the sitting room with the glorious green view, miraculous now in the fading light. There was no sight or sound of Perdita.

Roger said, 'I hope you'd want to stay here for a bit. Until you've found your feet.'

Willie didn't know what to say. He sipped the whisky. He said, 'Last night it was thick and sweet and deep. All the way through. Today only the first sip was sweet, and the very beginning of that sip. Now it's back to the whisky I remember. It seems to bind the taste buds on my tongue. I wasn't really a drinking man.'

Roger said, 'Today is one of the days I feel I didn't want to come home.'

Willie remembered something his wife Ana had said to him in Africa when things were beginning to go bad between them. She had said, 'When I met you I thought you were a man from another world.' The words, spoken simply, without anger, had struck at his heart: he had never known that was how he had appeared to her, a man in his own right, something he had longed to be. And the words had made him wish, hopelessly, with a quarter or less of himself, that he could have continued being that for her. He felt now that that was what he had become for Roger: a safe person, someone from another world.

The next afternoon, when he took Perdita up to the little room with the bleached furniture, he asked her, 'Where were you yesterday when Roger came home?' She said, 'I went out.' And Willie wondered, but didn't dare ask – feeling already a little of the humiliation that even a used-up woman could inflict on a man – Willie wondered whether she had gone to see her friend, the man who had copied out the poem by Henley and offered it as his own. He thought, as he sat on her, 'Should I send her away now?' It was tempting, but then he thought of all the complications that would ensue: he might even have to leave the house: Roger might reject him. So he stayed in the Balinese position. He thought, 'The fact that I can think as I am thinking shows that she cannot humiliate me.'

It might have been hard for Roger to come back to his house. But it wasn't like that for Willie. The house was in St John's Wood. It was a pleasure for him after his excursions in London to take the bus up the Edgware Road, get off at Maida Vale and walk away from the traffic and the noise to the trees and silence of St John's Wood. It was such a new world for him. Thirty years before, when he was packing up his few things to go to Africa, emptying his small college room, easily removing his presence, it had seemed to him that he was dismantling a life that couldn't be put together again. That life had been mean. He had always known that; he had tried all kinds of things to persuade himself that it was less so; he had devised time-tables to give himself the idea that his life was full and ordered. He was amazed now at the tricks he had used to fool himself.

He went to the places he had known. He thought in the beginning he would play the game he had played in India when he went back to join the guerrillas. He liked then seeing versions of his Indian world shrink, obliterating old memories, doing away with old pain. But his London world was not the world of his childhood; it was only the world of thirty years before. It didn't shrink. It stood out more sharply. He saw it all, all the separate buildings, as things made by men, made by many men at different times. It wasn't something simply there; and that change in his way of looking was like a little miracle. Now he understood that in the old days, in these places, there had always been, together with the darkness and incompleteness of his vision, a darkness in his head and a pain, a kind of yearning for something he didn't know, in his heart.

Now that darkness and weight were not with him. He stood unburdened before the buildings many different men had built. He went from place to place – the pretentious little college with its mock-Gothic arches, the fearful Notting Hill squares, the street with the little club north of Oxford Street, the small side street near Marble Arch where Roger had his house – everywhere seeing the little miracle happen, feeling the oppression lift, and feeling himself made anew. He had never had an idea – never, since childhood – what he might be. Now he felt he was being given some idea, elusive, impossible to grasp, yet real. What his essence was he still didn't know, though he had lived so long in the world. All that he knew at the moment was that he was a free man – in every way – and had a new strength. It was so unlikely, so unlike the person he had felt himself to be, at home, in London, and during the eighteen years of his marriage in Africa. How can I serve this person? he asked himself, as he walked about the London streets he had known. He could find no answer. He allowed the matter to go to the back of his mind.

The streets of the centre were very crowded, so crowded that sometimes it was not easy to walk. There were black people everywhere, and Japanese; and people who looked like Arabs. He thought, 'There has been a great churning in the world. This is not the London I lived in thirty years ago.' He felt a great relief. He thought, 'The world is now being shaken by forces much bigger than I could have imagined. Ten years ago in Berlin my sister Sarojini made me almost ill with stories of poverty and injustice at home. She sent me to join the guerrillas. Now I don't have to join anybody. Now I can only celebrate what I am, or what I have become.'

From these walks he returned to the big house in St John's Wood, to Roger, and, often in the afternoons, Perdita.

NINE

The Giant at the Top

AFTER TWO WEEKS his mood of exaltation abated and he began to be bored by the routine he had fallen into. Perdita herself became a burden, her body too familiar. Time lay heavily on his hands, and there was little he found he wanted to do. He had seen enough of London. His new way of looking no longer offered surprises. It no longer excited him to see the London of his past. To see it too often was to strip it of memories, and in this way to lose precious pieces of himself. The famous sights were like pictures now, taken in at a glance, hardly offering more than their postcard images – though sometimes he could still be startled by the river: the wide view, the light, the clouds, the unexpected colour. He didn't know enough of history and architecture to look for more; and the traffic and the fumes and the tourist crowds were exhausting; and in the big city he began to wonder, as he had wondered in the forest and in the jail, how he was going to make the time pass.

Roger went away one weekend. He didn't come back on the Sunday or the Monday. The house was dead without him. Perdita, strangely, seemed to feel it too.

She said, 'He's probably with his tart. Don't look so shocked. Hasn't he told you?'

Willie remembered what Roger had said at the airport about age showing in people as a kind of moral infirmity. He had said it almost as soon as they had met: it would have been uppermost in his mind just then, his way of preparing Willie for something like this moment.

The news came to him like a great sadness. He thought, 'I must leave this dead house. I cannot live in the middle of these two people.'

It was habit alone – not need, not excitement – that made him take Perdita up to his little room with its suggestions of sea and wind. Every occasion strengthened his determination to leave.

Roger came back during the course of the week. Willie went down one evening to have a drink with him.

He said, 'I have been waiting and waiting to taste whisky the way I tasted it that first evening here. Thick and sweet and deep. A child's drink, almost.'

Roger said, 'If you want to have that experience again you must spend many years in the bush and then go to jail for a while. If you break an ankle or a leg and you are in plaster for some weeks, you have a wonderful sensation the day they take the plaster off and you try to stand. It's an absence of sensation, and for the first few moments it's quite delicious. It quickly goes. The muscle starts building almost at once. If you want to have that sensation again you have to break your leg or ankle again.'

Willie said, 'I have been thinking. You and Perdita have been marvellous. But I think now that I should leave.'

'Do you know where you'll go?'

'No. But I was hoping you would help me find somewhere.'

'I will certainly do that when the time comes. But it isn't only a matter of finding somewhere. You will need money. You will need a job. Have you ever done a job?'

'I was thinking about that in the past few days. I've never done a job. My father never did a job. My sister has never done a proper job. We spent all our time thinking about the bad hand that had been dealt to us and not really preparing ourselves for anything. I suppose that's part of our situation. We can only think of revolt, and now when you ask me about what I think I can do I can only say nothing. If my father had a proper skill, or my mother's uncle, then I suppose I would have had a skill too. In all my time in Africa I never thought of acquiring a skill or profession.'

'You are not the only one, Willie. There are hundreds of thousands like that here. The society here gives them a kind of disguise. About twenty years ago I got to know an American black man. He was interested in Degas, quite seriously interested, and I thought he should follow this up professionally. But he said no, the civil rights movement was more important. When that battle had been won he could think about Degas. I told him that any good work he might do on Degas would in the end be serving his cause just as well as any political action. But he didn't see it.'

Willie said, 'It's changed now in India. If someone like my father was growing up now he would automatically be thinking of a profession, and I, coming after him, would automatically be thinking of a profession as well. It's the kind of change that's profounder than any guerrilla action.'

'But you mustn't be too romantic about work. Work is actually a terrible thing. What you must do tomorrow is to take a number sixteen bus to Victoria. Sit on the upper deck and look at the offices you pass, especially near Marble Arch and Grosvenor Gardens, and imagine yourself being there. The Greek philosophers never had to deal with the problem of work. They had slaves. Today we are all our own slaves.'

Idly, the next day Willie took a number sixteen bus and did as Roger suggested. He saw low, fluorescent-lit offices in Maida Vale and Park Lane and Grosvenor Lane and Grosvenor Gardens. It was another way of seeing the beautiful names of important streets in the great city, and his heart contracted.

He thought, 'There is work and work. Work as a vocation, one man's quest or self-fulfilment, can be noble. But what I am seeing is awful.'

When he saw Roger he said, 'If you will have me here for a while longer I will be grateful. I have to think out the whole thing. You were right. Thank you for saving me from myself.'

When Perdita came to his room the next morning she said, 'Has he told you about his tart?'

'We talked about other things.'

'I wonder whether he ever will. Roger's very sly.'

* * *

ROGER SAID TO Willie one day, 'I have an invitation for you from my banker. For the weekend.'

'The bathrobe man?'

'I've told him a little bit about you, and he's excited. He said, "From the Congress?" He's that kind of man. Knows everything, knows everybody. And, who knows, he might have some proposition for you. It's one of the reasons for his success. He's always on the lookout for new people. In that way you can say he's no snob. In another way, of course, he's snobbish beyond imagining.'

Two days before they left for the weekend Roger said, 'I think I should tell you. They unpack for you.'

Willie said, 'It sounds like jail. They're always unpacking for you there.'

'They take your suitcase, and when you go up to your room you find that one of those men in striped trousers has taken out all your clothes and other goods and spread them about in various suitable places. You are supposed to know where. So you have no secrets from the staff. It can be a great surprise. It's terribly shaming, the first time it happens. I've often thought I should insult them back by taking absolute rags in a filthy duffel bag, to show them how little I care for them. But I never do. At the last minute I get cowed. I can't help thinking of that scrutiny at the other end by servants, people technically below one, and I pack carefully, even in a slightly exhibitionist way. But you can do it. You can try to insult them. You're an outsider, and for them it doesn't matter what you do. Not many people know that that kind of big-house servant exists nowadays. They know that's what you are thinking, and they put on a special style. I am not easy with them. I find them a little sinister. I suppose they've always been sinister, those grand house servants. Nowadays they are embarrassing for everybody, I think, with the butler and the master acting it out, pretending that they are not out of the ordinary. My banker likes to pretend sometimes that everybody has a butler.'

When on the Friday they (and their suitcases) were in the taxi going to the railway station Roger said, 'It's actually because of Perdita that I became involved in this caper with the banker. I wished to impress her. I wished to show her that I knew a man with a house ten times bigger than her lover's big house, would you believe. I didn't want her to give up the lover. Far from it. I only wanted her to have an idea of his place in the scheme of things. I wanted her to feel a little squalid. What a calamity that's been for me.'

When they were in the railway station Roger said, 'I usually buy first-class tickets on these occasions. But I think this time I am going to buy second-class.' He lifted his chin as if to express his resolve.

Willie stood in the queue with him. When his turn came Roger asked for first-class tickets.

He said to Willie, 'I couldn't do it. Sometimes they meet you on the platform. I can say now that it's a foolish, old-fashioned thing about which I don't really care. But when the actual moment comes I don't think I would have the courage to be seen coming out of a second-class carriage by one of those awful servants. I hate myself for it.'

They were the only people in the first-class carriage. That was, strangely, a kind of letdown (since there was no one else to witness). Roger went silent. Willie searched for something that he might say to break the heavy mood, but everything he thought of seemed to refer in some way to their extravagant travel. Many minutes later Roger said, 'I am a coward. But I know myself. Nothing I do can really be a surprise to me.'

And when they got to their station there was no one on the platform to meet them. The man (in a suit, but not with a cap) was in an ordinary-sized car in the station car park, waiting to be found. But by this time Roger's mood had lightened, and he was able to deal, in a slightly exaggerated stylish way, with the driver.

Their host was waiting for them at the foot of the steps of the big house. He was in sporty style, and in one hand was playing with what looked to Willie (who knew nothing of golf and golf tees) like a very large and white extracted molar. He was a hard, dry, well-exercised man, and at the moment of meeting all his energy, and Roger's, and Willie's, and the energy of the plump-legged striped-trousered servant coming down the steps, went into pretending that this kind of reception in front of this kind of house was perfectly ordinary for everyone.

For Willie a kind of unreality, or a reality hard to grasp, veiled the moment. It was like what he had felt in the forest and in the jail, the detachment from what was about him. In a manner he couldn't reconstruct he became separated from Roger, and docilely, as in the jail, not looking too hard at anything, he followed a servant up to a room. The window had a view of many acres. Willie wondered whether he should go down and walk in the grounds or whether he should stay in the room and hide. The thought of going down and asking his way about the grounds was oppressive. He decided to hide. On the protective glass on the dressing table was an old, solidly bound book. It was an old edition of *The Origin of Species*. The cramped Victorian typography (the letters seemingly rusty with age) was daunting, as was the smell of the crinkled old paper and the old printing ink (calling up gloomy ideas of the printing shops and the printing workers of the time) that might have caused the paper to crinkle.

The man in the striped trousers (perhaps someone from eastern Europe) began doing the famous unpacking. But since the man was from eastern Europe Willie was not as disturbed as Roger had thought he might be.

Sitting at the dressing table, turning the pages of *The Origin of Species* while the man unpacked, unfolding the illustrations, Willie saw a little wicker vase or container with sharpened cedar-coloured pencils. It was like the one in his room in Roger's house. Then he saw a small crystal sphere, solid and heavy, ringed from top to bottom with scored parallel lines, and with a little well at the top with long pink-tipped matches. That, too, was like something in his room in Roger's house. It was from here – where Roger, behaving in an unexpected way, had brought her to awe her with a grandeur that wasn't his, the way a poor local person might take a visitor to see the grand houses of his town – it was from here (and perhaps from other places as well, perhaps even from places she had seen or known as a girl) that Perdita had taken some of her ideas of room decoration, focusing on what was small and incidental and attainable. Willie felt an immense surge of sympathy for her, and (surrendering to things within him) he felt oppressed at the same time by the intimation that came to him just then of the darkness in which everybody walked.

After some time he went to the bathroom. It had been constructed within the older room and the partitions were thin. The wallpaper was of a bold design, widely spaced green vines suggesting a great openness. But on one wall there was no wallpaper, no feeling of openness, only pages from an old illustrated magazine called *The Graphic*, closely printed grey columns in the Victorian way, broken up by line drawings of events and places all over the world. The pages were from the 1860s and the 1870s. The artist or reporter (possibly one and the same person) would have sent his copy or sketches by ship; in the office of the magazine a professional artist would have straightened out the drawings, probably adding things according to his fancy; and week by week these drawings, the products of advanced journalistic enterprise, illustrating events in the empire and elsewhere for an interested public, were reproduced according to the best methods of the day.

For Willie it was a revelation. The past in these pasted pages seemed to be just there, something he could reach out and touch. He read about India after the Mutiny, about the opening up of Africa, about warlord China, about the United States after the civil war, about the troubles of Jamaica and Ireland; he read about the discovery of the source of the Nile; he read about Queen Victoria as though she was still alive. He read until the light faded. It was hard to read the small print by dull electric light.

There was a knock at the door. It was Roger. He had been discussing business with the banker and he looked drawn.

He saw the book on the dressing table and said, 'What book do you have?' He took it up and said, 'It's a first edition, you know. He likes leaving them about casually for his guests. They are gathered up very carefully afterwards. This time I have a Jane Austen.'

Willie said, 'I've been reading *The Graphic*. It's in the bathroom.'

Roger said, 'It's in my bathroom, too. I will tell you about that. I have an interest, as they say. There was a time when I used to go to the Charing Cross Road to look at the bookshops. It's not something you can do today, not in the same way. One day I saw a set of *The Graphic* on the pavement outside one of the shops. They were quite cheap, a couple of pounds a volume. I couldn't believe my luck. *The Graphic* was a famous thing, one of the precursors of the *Illustrated London News*. They were in beautifully bound volumes. It was the way things were done at that time. I don't know whether the magazine did the binding, or the libraries, or the people who subscribed. I could only take home two of the *Graphic* volumes, and I had to take a taxi. They were very bulky things, as I told you, and very heavy. It was about this time that I was getting involved with our banker. I was beginning to understand the immense power of the true egomaniac on people around him. In fact, I was yielding to that power without knowing it. To the intelligent person, like myself, the egomaniac is in some ways pathetic, a man who doesn't see like the rest of us that the paths of glory lead but to the grave. And that is how the intelligent man is caught. He begins by patronising and ends by being a minion. Anyway. Just after I had seen the *Graphic* set I came here. The great man was still courting me, and in fact I had already been caught. I'm not punning. He showed me some of his pictures. He told me how he had picked them up. And, not to be outdone, I told him how I had recently picked up the two bound volumes of *The Graphic*. I was boasting. He of course didn't know about *The Graphic*, and I was telling him how much I knew. Having boasted to him about *The Graphic*, I thought, when I went back to London, that I should go and get a few more of the volumes. I found nothing. Our friend had sent his big car and carried away the lot. This was his wife's idea, pasting the pages on the lavatories. When the place is done up again, or sold, and becomes a hotel or whatever, all those pages will go to the builder's rubbish dump.'

'You think it will become a hotel?'

'Something like that. Ordinary people can't live in places like this. You would need a lot of servants. These places were built in the days of many servants. Fifteen gardeners, umpteen chambermaids. Those people don't exist nowadays. People in service, as they used to say. At one time they were a big part of the population.'

Willie asked, 'What happened to them?'

'It's a wonderful question. I suppose one answer would be that they died out. But that's not the question you asked. I know what you are asking. If we asked it more often we might begin to understand the kind of country we're living in. I realise now I haven't heard anyone ask the question.'

Willie said, 'In many parts of India it's the big issue nowadays. What they call the churning of the castes. I think it's more important than the religious question. Certain middle groups rising, certain top groups being sucked under. The guerrilla war I went to fight in was a reflection of this movement. A reflection, no more. India will soon be presenting an untouchable face to the world. It won't be nice. People won't like it.'

They went down later to drinks and dinner. It was not a formal affair. The banker's wife was not there. The only other guest was a picture-gallery owner. The banker was a painter, in addition to everything else, and wished to have an exhibition in London. He had told Willie and Roger, when telling them about their fellow dinner guest, 'Thought it would be better to ask him down to talk things over. These people like a little style.' Using that last sentence both to flatter Willie and Roger and to rope them into his conspiracy against the gallery man.

He, the gallery man, was dressed as stiffly as Roger. He had big red hands, as though he had been carrying about big framed pictures in his gallery all day.

Spotlights in the ceiling of the very big room played on three of the paintings the banker had done. Willie began to understand what Roger had said about the power of the true egomaniac. It was open to Willie and Roger and the gallery man to say that the paintings the banker had chosen to light up were second-rate work, Sunday painting, no more. It was open to them to be quite brutal. But the man had exposed himself in too innocent a way, and no one wished to wound him.

The gallery owner was suffering. Whatever excitement he might have felt about being a guest in the grand house (and having his elegant clothes unpacked and noted) was going.

The banker said, 'Money is of no moment to me. You understand that. I am sure you do.'

And the gallery owner struggled, and failed, to say that he was in the gallery business to make money and the last person he was interested in professionally was a painter who didn't need money. He spoke two or three disconnected ideas and then gave up.

The subject was then left alone. But enough ego and power had been displayed (the ceiling spotlights continuing to play on the banker's paintings) for Willie to understand that, after the artistic grand charge, whatever arrangements were going to be made with the gallery man were going to be made privately, without witnesses.

The banker said to Willie, 'Do you know the maharaja of Makkhinagar?' He gave Willie no chance to reply. 'He came to stay. It was just after Mrs Gandhi had de-recognised the princes and abolished their privy purses. This would have been in 1971.

He was very young, uncertain in London, very much pulled down by the loss of his privy purse. I thought I should do something for him. My father knew his grandfather. Naturally enough, with all the changes in India, the young man was very much standing on his dignity when he came here. No one minded that, but I don't think he appreciated the people I had brought together for him. Many doors would have been open to him if he wanted, but he didn't appear interested. They do that, and then they go away and talk about a lack of regard over here. In London I invited him to the Corner Club for lunch. Do you know the Corner? It's smaller than the Turf Club, and even more exclusive, if such a thing can be imagined. The dining room is very small. The Corner isn't called the Corner for nothing. Eyebrows were raised when they saw young Makkhinagar, I don't mind telling you. But I never heard a word from him after that. About fifteen years later I went to Delhi. One of the many occasions when the rumour was that the economy was going to be liberalised. I looked up Makkhinagar in the telephone book. He was a member of the Indian upper house now, and he had a house in Delhi. He invited me over one evening. Such a panoply of security at the house, watchmen and soldiers and sandbags at the gate, and men with guns inside. Makkhinagar was much more relaxed, in spite of it all. He said, "Peter, that was an amusing little lunch place we went to the last time." That's what I mean about the Indians. "Amusing little lunch place." The Corner! You put yourself out, and that's what you get.'

Willie said nothing. The gallery man gave a little laugh, already like a man pleased to be admitted to this kind of converse about the great; but Roger was silent and looked suffering.

More people were going to come the next day. Willie wasn't looking forward to it. He wondered why. He thought, 'It's vanity. I can only be easy with people who have some idea of what I am. Or probably it's just the house. It makes too many demands on people. I am sure it alters them. It has certainly altered the banker. It altered me. It prevented me from seeing things clearly when I arrived.'

In the morning after breakfast (which he went down for) he met the banker's wife. She greeted him before he greeted her, striding towards him and stretching out her hand as if in the completest welcome, a still-young woman with long bouncing hair and a big bouncing bottom. She gave her name and said, in a fine tinkling voice, 'I'm Peter's wife.' She was narrow-shouldered, narrow-chested, attractive: a very physical person, Willie thought. Nothing about her afterwards was as fine as that first moment. She was only her smile and her voice.

Willie thought, 'I must work out why, like the maharaja in the Corner Club, I am not at ease with these people. The maharaja felt the lack of welcome and settled the score fifteen years later. I don't feel like that. I don't feel the lack of a welcome. On the contrary, I feel anyone who comes here would be more than ready to meet the banker's guest. What I feel is that for me there is no point in going through with the occasion. I don't wish to cultivate anybody or to be cultivated by them. It isn't that I think they are materialist. No one in the world is more crudely materialist than the Indian well-to-do. But in the forest and in the jail I changed. You can't go through that kind of life without changing. I have shed my materialist self. I had to, to survive. I feel that these people don't know the other side of things.' The words came to him just like that. He thought, 'The words would have meant something. I must work out what the words mean. The people here don't understand nullity. The physical nullity of what I saw in the forest. The spiritual nullity that went with that, and was very much like what my poor father lived with all his life. I have felt this nullity in my bones and can go back to it at any time. Unless we understand people's other side, Indian, Japanese, African, we cannot truly understand them.'

The banker had been talking business with Roger, playing with his golf tee as with a rosary. When they came out from where they had been the banker took Roger and Willie and the gallery man and someone who had just arrived on a little tour of some of his things. He had come back from a world trip visiting business associates and (like a visiting head of state) getting presents from people. Some of these he now displayed. Many of them he mocked. He especially mocked a tall blue semi-transparent porcelain vase, crudely painted with local flowers. The banker said, 'It was probably done by the local manager's wife. Nothing to do in the long nights at those latitudes.' The vase was very narrow at the base, too wide at the top, unsteady, rocking at the touch of a finger. It had already taken a few tumbles and had a long diagonal crack; a piece of the porcelain had broken off.

Roger, speaking with an unusual irritation, possibly as a result of something that had happened during his business conversation, said provocatively, 'I think it's rather nice.'

The banker said, 'It's yours. I'll give it to you.'

Roger said, 'It will be too much trouble.'

'No trouble at all. I'll get them to wrap it up and see it into the train with you. I am sure Perdita will find some use for it.'

That was what happened the next afternoon. So the first-class tickets that Roger had bought at last had the witness for whom they had been intended, and Roger was spared the most horrible kind of shame. But again, at tipping time, he lost his nerve and tipped the servant ten pounds.

He said to Willie, 'All the way in the car I was trying to work out the tip. For everything extra connected with that odious vase. I settled on five pounds, but at the last minute I changed my mind. It's all the effect of that man's ego. I allow him to insult me, as he did with that cracked vase, and then I try to find excuses for him. I think, "He's like a child. He doesn't know about the real world." One day someone with nothing to lose will insult him in the profoundest way, and then the magic will be broken. But until then for people like me there's an electric charge around the man.'

Willie said, 'Do you think you will be the one to insult him in that profound way when the moment comes?'

'Not now. I have too much to lose. I am too dependent on him. But at the end, yes. When my father was dying in hospital his character completely changed. This very gentlemanly man began to insult everybody who came to see him. My mother, my brother. He insulted all his business associates. Really vile language. He said everything he thought about everybody. He kept nothing back. The nearness of death gave him that licence. I suppose you would say that for my father death was his truest and happiest moment. But I didn't want to die like that. I wanted to die the other way. Like Van Gogh, according to what I've read. Peacefully smoking a pipe, reconciled to everybody and everything, hating no one. But Van Gogh could afford to be romantic. He had his art and vocation. My father didn't, and I don't, and very few of us have, and now that I am within sight of the end I find myself thinking that my father had something. It makes death something to look forward to.'

When they got back to the house in St John's Wood Roger said to Perdita, 'Peter has sent you a gift.'

She was excited, and immediately began undoing the servant's unskilled and perfunctory wrapping (a lot of sticky tape) of the awkwardly shaped, tall vase.

She said, 'It's a lovely craft piece. I must write to Peter. I have a place for it. The crack needn't show.'

For a few days the vase was where she put it, but then it disappeared and wasn't spoken of again.

* * *

A WEEK OR SO later Roger said to Willie, 'You made a great hit with Peter. Did you know?'

Willie said, 'I wonder why. I hardly said anything to him. I just listened.'

'That's probably why. Peter has a story about Indira Gandhi. He never thought much of her. He didn't think she was educated or knew much about people in the wider world. He thought she was a bluffer. In 1971, at the time of the Bangladesh business, he went to Delhi and tried to see her. He had some project on hand. She ignored him. He twiddled his thumbs in his hotel for a whole week. He was furious. At last he met someone from the inner Indira Gandhi circle. He asked this person, "How does the lady judge people?" The person said, "Her method is simple. All the time she is waiting to see what her visitor wants." Peter no doubt took the tip. He was waiting all the time to find out what you wanted from him, and you said nothing.'

Willie said, 'I didn't want anything from him.'

'It brought out the best in him. He talked to me about you afterwards, and I told him some of your story. The result is he's made you an offer. He's involved with some big construction companies. They do a quality magazine about modern buildings. It's high-class public relations. They don't overtly sell any company or product. He thinks you might want to work for them. Part-time or full-time. It depends on you. The offer is perfectly genuine, I should tell you. It's Peter at his best. He's very proud of his magazine.'

Willie said, 'I know nothing about architecture.'

And Roger knew that Willie was interested.

He said, 'They do courses for people like you. It's like the courses the auction houses do in art history.'

* * *

So Willie at last found a job in London. Or found something to go to in the mornings. Or, to make it still smaller, something to leave the St John's Wood house for.

The magazine's offices were in a narrow, flat-fronted old building in Bloomsbury.

Roger said, 'It's like something out of central casting.'

Willie didn't know the meaning of the words.

Roger said, 'In the old days in Hollywood the studios had departments that did exaggerated sets of foreign places. Exaggerated and full of cliché so that people would know where they were. If somebody – doing *A Christmas Carol*, say – had gone to them and asked for a Dickensian office in a Dickensian building they would have built something like your building and enveloped it in fog.'

It was not far from the British Museum – pediment and columns, big front court and tall, pointed, black iron rails. And it wasn't far from the Trades Union Congress building, tight against the street, modern, three or four storeys high, glass and concrete in rectangular segments, with a strange cantilevered flying figure in bronze above the entrance, representing labour threatening or labour triumphant, or perhaps only labour or the idea of work, or perhaps again representing mainly the sculptor's struggle with his socialist subject.

Willie walked past that sculpture every day. For the first few weeks, until he ceased to see it, he felt rebuked: his work on the magazine was really very soft, and for a large part of every day was hardly work at all.

It was a part of London that Willie knew from twenty-seven or twenty-eight years before. Once the associations would have been shameful; now it didn't matter. The publisher who had done his book was in one of the big black squares. Willie had thought the building undistinguished. But then he was surprised, as he went up the front steps, to find that the building appeared to be growing bigger; and then the interior, behind the old black brick, was lighter and finer than anything he might have expected. Upstairs, in what would have been the main room in the old days, as the publisher told him, he was made to stand in front of the high window of what had been the drawing room and to look down into the square, and the publisher made him imagine the carriages and servants and footmen of *Vanity Fair*. Why did he do that? Was it just, in the grand first-floor room, to create the picture of the wealth of merchants and traders in the high days of slavery? He did that, of course; but he wished to make another point as well. It was that, in such a room in *Vanity Fair*, the rich merchant wished to compel his son to marry a black or mulatto heiress from St Kitts. Was the publisher saying that for those rich men money overrode everything else, overrode even a man's duty to his race? Was he saying, then, to take the other slant, that their attitude to money gave them, in racial matters, a kind of purity? No, he was saying no such thing. He was speaking critically. He was speaking like a man letting Willie into a national secret. What did he mean? Was he saying that a mulatto heiress should be shunned by all right-minded men? Willie (whenever, in Africa, he thought of his poor little book) had also gone on to ponder the publisher's gloss on *Vanity Fair*. And he had decided that the publisher meant nothing at all, that he was only trying in Willie's presence to give himself a point of view, was trying to work up a little anger about the rich and the treatment of blacks and mulattos at one and the same time, something he would forget when his next visitor came into the room.

And often, perhaps every day for a second or two, Willie thought, walking to the magazine from the Underground station, 'When I first came to this area I saw nothing. Now the place is full of detail. It's as though I've pulled a switch. And yet I can easily think myself back to that other way of not seeing.'

The building Willie went to work in, which was like something out of central casting, was old only on the outside. Inside, it had been so often renovated and restored and then, without a pang, ravaged again, partitions going up and then being taken down, that it had the appearance, on the ground floor, of being like a shop with no particular character, fitted out only for the moment, frail and brittle, fresh paint lying thin over the sharp lines of new soft wood. It seemed that the shopfitters could at any moment be called in to cart away what they had put up and do a fresh design. Only the walls and (perhaps because of some restraining heritage by-law) the narrow staircases with their slender mahogany banisters lived on from change to change. The small waiting room downstairs had a front partition of glass, just behind the receptionist's cubicle. On one wall was an old black-and-white photograph of Peter and two other directors of a building company welcoming the queen. On a small kidney-shaped table were copies of the modern building magazine. It was impressive, expensive-looking, with beautiful photographs.

The editor's office was upstairs, in the front room, in a much reduced version of the grandeur of Willie's publisher twenty-eight years before. The editor was a woman of about forty or fifty with a ravaged face and big pop eyes behind black-rimmed glasses. She seemed to Willie to be eaten up with every kind of family grief and sexual pain, and it was as though she had four or five or six times a day to climb out of that hole before she could deal with other matters. She was gracious to Willie, treating him as a friend of Peter's, and this made the pain in her face harder to witness.

She said, 'We'll see how you settle down. And then we'll be sending you to Barnet.'

Barnet was where the company's architecture courses were given.

When Willie gave Roger an account of his meeting with the editor, Roger said, 'Whenever I've met her I've always had a distinct whiff of gin. She is one of Peter's lame ducks. But she does her job well.'

The magazine came out once a quarter. The articles were written by professionals, and the payment was good. The editor's job was to commission the articles; it was the job of the photo editor to hunt out photographs; and it was the job of the staff to edit and check and proof-read the articles. Layout was done professionally. There was an architectural library on an upper floor. The books were big and forbidding, but Willie soon began to find his way about them. He spent much time in the library and in his third week he learned to say to the editor, when he was idle and she asked what he was doing, 'I'm checking.' The words always calmed her down.

One lunch hour, when he was walking in one of the quieter squares, a big car stopped beside him. A woman got out. She had a stamped letter which she wanted to drop in the letter box near by. When she had done that she greeted Willie. He had thought nothing until then about the woman. But her tinkling, happy, rhythmic voice was at once recognisable, that voice that went with her bouncing hair and bouncing bottom. It was Peter's wife. She said in a quick ripple of speech, 'I hear you're working for Peter.' He was flattered to be remembered, but she gave him no time to say anything. She tinkled away, 'Peter's having his exhibition. It's in all the papers. We hope you will want to come.' In that same ripple of speech she introduced Willie to the half hidden driver of the car, and, not waiting for either man to speak, got into the car and was driven off.

When Willie told Roger about the meeting Roger said, 'That's her lover. She could have gone on to another post box, but she wanted to show herself to you with her lover. She wants everyone who has seen her with Peter to see her with this other man. It torments Peter. It undoes everything for him. His head must be full of painful sexual pictures. And the man she showed to you is quite ordinary. A small-scale property dealer, not too educated. That's how Peter met him. Peter's ventures into property haven't been too successful, to put it mildly. And now nothing he does can win his wife back. I met her at the house many years ago, shortly after she married Peter. She began to tell me about her earlier marriage and why it had failed. She said it had oppressed her. I didn't know what she meant. She said, "Tim would say, just before he went to work, 'I've run out of toothpaste. Buy me a tube.' I am just giving an example. And all day I would be thinking of that tube of toothpaste I had to buy. Tim would be in his office, doing all his exciting deals, and having his exciting lunches, and I would be in the house thinking of the toothpaste I had to buy for him. Do you see what I mean? It oppressed me. You do understand, don't you?" She spoke this in her lovely voice and she fixed her lovely eyes on me and I tried very hard to understand her oppression. I felt she wanted me to do battle with her oppressor. I felt, to tell the truth, that she was making a pass at me. I could feel her wrapping me in her special brand of gossamer. And then, of course, I realised that I couldn't understand what she was saying because there was nothing to understand. She was only listening to herself speak. I became worried for Peter. He would give up many things if he could be sure of her. This is where big men can be overthrown. I haven't been the same man since I married Perdita. Now the whole world knows about her lover with the big London house. No one would believe that for years she pestered me to marry her. Now she becomes the one hard done by, the woman I let down.'

Now that on weekdays Willie had the building magazine and Bloomsbury to go to, he no longer had his mornings with Perdita. She would come up to his little room only occasionally, usually in the evening, perhaps once a week, when Roger (as she liked to say) was with his tart, and when she didn't have her big house to go to and was otherwise free. These meetings now had to fit into everybody's movements, and for the first time in the house Willie consciously became a deceiver. He wished it didn't have to be so, but he preferred the new arrangement. It was less burdensome; it made him like Perdita more.

They talked more than before. He never tried to find out more about the man with the big house or about Roger's other woman. Partly this was because of the reserve he had learned in the guerrilla movement (where in the strict early days it was forbidden, for reasons of doctrine and security, to ask other people in the movement too many questions about their family and background). This reserve had become part of Willie's nature. And he genuinely didn't want to know more about Roger's other life or Perdita's. He wanted to stay with what he knew; he didn't want greater knowledge to spoil the little life he had lighted upon in the St John's Wood house, in his little room, in the middle of the unknown.

Perdita let drop some details of her early life in the north. Willie encouraged her. He thought his own family life had been bizarre, his childhood blighted. To imagine Perdita's happy early life, to recreate it with the details she let drop, was to walk vicariously in a field of glory. It made her much more than he had thought her at the very start. She felt his new regard and she blossomed when she was with him. She developed, became less passive.

One Saturday morning she said, 'Roger may not want to talk about his caper with Peter' – 'caper': it was Roger's word – 'but I am sure he will soon now. His career is on the line.' And then she went on, in a more reflective way, 'I feel sorry for Roger. With Peter he has always been pathetic. Bringing home that awful broken vase as a gift for me. There are many ways of saying no, and he should have found at least one. All Roger's energy, or much of it, has gone into sounding and appearing. It's the great trap of men of Roger's class. They have a readymade style they can adopt, and once they've adopted it they don't feel they have to do too much more.'

Willie said, 'But you pestered him to marry you. In 1957 and 1958. I remember it very well.'

She said, 'I was attracted by his great show. I was young. I knew little of the world. He was a phantom. The best side of him is in his business, his law.'

Willie wondered for some time afterwards where Perdita would have picked up those words, and a day or two later it came to him: Perdita was using the words of her lover, the man with the big house, Roger's colleague. Roger was enmeshed in betrayal on every side.

* * *

AFTER SIX WEEKS in the Bloomsbury office Willie went to the company's training centre at Barnet. The editor would say, 'They'll be wanting you at Barnet pretty soon.' The layout man would say, 'Haven't you gone to Barnet yet?' Barnet, Barnet: it ceased to be only a place name. It appeared to stand for luxury and rest, a place where people lived for two or three or four weeks without supervision, getting their salary all the while, a blessing that came to the fortunate. There were stories about its beauty, about the food at the training centre, about the local pubs.

There was a leaflet about the place, with a map and directions. Roger decided to drive Willie down. They started early one Sunday afternoon. The London orbital motorway was very crowded. Roger turned off to the older roads, and the names of some of the places they had to drive through were touched with romance for Willie.

Cricklewood: twenty-eight years ago it was a mysterious place for Willie, somewhere far to the north of Marble Arch, where in his imagination people lived regulated and full and secure lives. It was where June, the girl from the Debenhams perfume counter, lived with her family (and also had a boy friend since childhood), and it was the place to which she had to catch a bus after Willie's miserable sexual moment with her in a Notting Hill tenement. Cricklewood, Willie learned later, was where a big bus garage was; it was also (Willie looking out at this time for news about Cricklewood) where the lovely young actress Jean Simmons was born and grew up: the fact threw an unbearable extra glamour on June at her perfume counter.

Seen now from the clogged Sunday-afternoon roads Cricklewood (or what Willie assumed to be Cricklewood) was an unending level red line of two-storey houses, brick and rendered concrete, with little local shopping areas in between, shops as small and as low as the houses they served: London here, as created by the builders and developers of sixty or seventy years before, a kind of toyland, cosy and confined: this is the house where Jack and his wife will live and love and have their litter, this is the shop where Jack's wife will shop, this is the public house at the corner where Jack and his friends and his wife's friends will sometimes get drunk. Nothing like a town, no park or gardens, no building apart from houses and shops. It all seemed to have been built at the same time, and Cricklewood (if it was Cricklewood) ran without change into Hendon, and Hendon into what came after, and it went on and on, with sometimes only a rise in the road over the mainline railway tracks below.

Willie said, 'I never knew London was like this. It's not out of central casting.'

Roger, who had been abstracted for much of the slow, demanding drive, said, 'It's like this east, west, north and south. You understand why they had to create the green belt. Otherwise half of the country would have been gobbled up.'

Willie said, 'I wouldn't want to live here. Imagine coming back here day after day. What would be the point of anything?'

Roger said, as if going against what he had said earlier, 'People do the best they can.'

Willie thought it a feeble thing to say, but then his mouth was stopped. Increasingly on the winding main road there were Indians; and Pakistanis; and Bangladeshis dressed as they might have been at home, the men with layers of gowns or shirts and with the white cap of submission to the Arab faith, their low-statured women even more bundled up and covered and with fearful black masks. Willie knew about the great immigration from the subcontinent; but (since ideas often exist in compartments) he hadn't imagined that London (still in his mind something from central casting) could have been so repeopled in thirty years.

So this Sunday-afternoon drive through north London was a double revelation. It did away with the fantasy Willie had had for more than thirty years of June going by bus from Marble Arch to the security and glories of her home. And perhaps it was right for the fantasy to be erased, since June herself, as Roger had said, would by now have been much battered (in every sense) by the years, was almost certainly fat and boastful (counting her lovers), changed in other ways too, adapting whatever ancient genteel perfume-counter yearnings she might have had to some new plebeian television pattern. It was more than right for the fantasy to go. And it was for Willie a relief, enabling him to shed the humiliation connected with the fantasy, to put it in its place.

The level red line of repeopled houses and shops went on and on. At last they turned off the main road. And then, quite suddenly, while Willie was still thinking of what he had seen, the red line of buildings and the costumes of the subcontinent, they were at the training centre. A brick wall, iron gates, a paved drive, and a few low white buildings in a large garden. When the car stopped and he got out he thought he could hear the traffic from the main road. It couldn't have been very far away. At one time the park would have been in real country. Then London had grown up and met it; bits of the park would have been sold; and roads had been opened up all around to serve the population. Now the park, much reduced, was in immigrant territory.

Roger said, with a kind of irony, 'It's one of Peter's property deals.'

The traffic sound was always there. But the green of the little park was wonderful after the roads and the level line of red houses and the clutter and signboards of little shops. It was far enough away from London to set people dreaming of adventure. And Willie could understand why it was much loved in the office.

Roger saw Willie settled into his little room in the hostel or residence building. He seemed to be in no hurry to leave. They went to the main lounge. It was in another building. At a table or sideboard they helped themselves to mineral water and tea. Roger knew his way about the training centre. There were other people in the lounge, in suits, a little stiff all of them at the start of their courses. There was an African or West Indian; and an Indian or Pakistani in white leather shoes.

Roger said, 'It's so strange. I've had to help you. And now I myself am in deep trouble. I have no idea what my situation will be when you finish your course here. You must have had some idea, since you've been with me, that there were problems.'

Willie said, 'You told me something the first day, when you were driving me in from the airport. Perdita dropped a word, but I know nothing else.'

'It's one of those things that begin quite legitimately. And then it develops into something else. I am sure when Peter started the caper it was nothing more than a wish to keep it all in the family, so to speak. Think of Peter's bank, then, with a property portfolio. Think of a very reputable firm of surveyors. Think of a very reputable firm of lawyers. That's where I come in. Think of a couple of perfectly sound property companies. When Peter wishes to divest himself of certain properties, the surveying firm does the valuation, the law firm does the papers, and the properties pass to the property companies, who might then after a couple of years sell at a huge profit. We are talking about city properties. They are not easy to value. It is always possible to be a couple of million out. We are also in a time of rising property values. Something bought for ten million today might in three years sell for fifteen, and no one will raise an eyebrow. That is why this property caper could pass for a long time unnoticed. It passed unnoticed for twelve years. But then somebody noticed and began to make trouble. Peter was able to smooth things out, pay millions in compensation. But some people have been awkward. And if they have their way my firm will be in trouble, and I am likely to be in a court. It will be the end for me. And yet I feel that when it started Peter wanted no more than to keep all the business in the family, so to say. To extend patronage, to win regard. He can't have enough regard. You know Peter. He's a raging egomaniac, but he has his generous side. And he has ideas. This training centre, for example. For years I have been going over this business in my head, trying to present it to myself and my imaginary court in the best possible light. It's driving me crazy. And just at this time my private life is about to blow up. It's always like that, two or three things at a time. All my life I have believed they come three at a time. It's my only superstition. When you see a magpie look for the second. I am waiting for the third blow.'

'Perdita?'

'Not Perdita. That's as settled as it can be. I have given away everything I can. There is no more to give. No, not Perdita. It's my life outside the house. Away from Perdita. A kind of life. I say no more. I am sure Perdita could not have been silent about the matter.'

Willie said, 'She might have mentioned something. But I never asked for more.'

'She's a working-class woman. My business colleague, the man with the big house, took away Perdita from me. I thought I would have been safe with this woman friend. I presented her to some of my lawyer colleagues, to show them that I was doing quite well without Perdita. I was a fool. Perhaps in these matters I will always be a fool. My woman friend is at this moment about to kick me in the teeth. She is going away for a weekend with a friend of mine. I didn't know it was possible to suffer so much. I thought I was the patron. I do everything for her. All these years I thought the condescension was mine.'

Energy came to him as he spoke. He got up decisively, said, 'I mustn't leave it too late. I have to get back.'

He left Willie desolate in the training centre, wandering about the lounge and garden, and then going too early to his little room to court sleep. He could hear, faintly, the traffic on the main roads, and in his gradually distorting mind's eye the level line of red houses rolled on and on. He wished there was another place to go to.

TEN

An Axe to the Root

THE COURSE AT the training centre was richer and profounder than Willie expected, and he sank into it, keeping Roger's troubles at the edge of his mind.

In the morning they had lectures about modern building techniques, about concrete and water-cement ratios, and concrete and stressed steel, things that were not always easy for Willie to understand but which (especially when he didn't understand them) challenged his imagination. Would the tension in stressed steel, for instance, last forever? Did the lecturer really know? Was it absurd to imagine that at some point in the future stressed steel, or the bolts that kept a length of steel under tension, might fail? And perhaps then, in the twenty-first or twenty-fourth or twenty-fifth century, month by month, and year after year, in a kind of architectural terror, concrete and steel buildings all over the world might with no external prompting start collapsing in the order in which they had been put up.

In the afternoon there was a course in the history of architecture. The lecturer was a slender man in his forties. His suit was black or very dark, and his big feet were in black shoes held at an awkward angle one to the other. His face was smooth and very white, and his thin dark hair made a thin dark line above his waxen brow and small blinking eyes. He did his lecture in his shy but determined little voice, and showed photographs and answered questions, but he seemed very far away. Where were his true thoughts? Did he, the possessor of so much knowledge, have some little grief? Was this his only job? Did he travel in, or did he live locally, in one of the low red houses to the north, living out there some architect's or developer's 1930 fantasy of how people ought to live?

The architecture of the lecturer's subject was only of the western world, and even then he was in a hurry to get to those periods in which his patrons had an interest. So he raced through Gothic and Renaissance to settle on the architecture of the later industrial age, the late nineteenth and twentieth centuries, in Great Britain and the United States.

Willie was fascinated. The idea of learning for its own sake had always attracted him, and he had been frustrated by his mission school and the London teacher-training college. Because these places hadn't given him a proper grounding, he had always been defeated afterwards in his casual attempts to extend his range. But architecture, dealing with what was immediate and everywhere visible, was open to him, he now discovered, and many of the things he was learning about had the elements of a fairy story. He learned now about the window tax in England, and the tax on bricks which had lasted from about the time of the French revolution to about the time of the Indian Mutiny. Putting dates in this way to the tax on bricks in England, Willie had, without the help of the lecturer, called up an all but forgotten memory that in British India, too, there had been a tax on bricks: absurd but unfair, since it was not paid on baked and finished bricks but on unbaked batches, and made no allowance for the many bricks damaged or destroyed in the kiln. (He remembered those kilns in many places, the tall chimneys, oddly swollen at the bottom, beside the rectangular clay pits and the stacks of finished bricks: perhaps, then, the kilns and the chimneys moved about the countryside, being set up where there was suitable clay.) Willie had always felt oppressed by the red brick of England, so widespread, so ordinary. He learned now, from the mild but stubborn lecturer, that the London brick of 1880 would have been stimulated by the abolition of the brick tax. Industrial Victorian England had the machines to make all kinds of brick in prodigious number. That brick of 1880 would have been the remote ancestor of the endless low red houses of 1930 of north London, from Cricklewood to Barnet.

Willie thought, 'What I am learning in these few days casts a glow even on what is around me here. I didn't really know just a few days ago what I was seeing when we were driving here. Roger said, "People do the best they can do." I was disappointed by that, but he was right. It is terrible and heartbreaking that this way of seeing and understanding has come to me so late. I can't do anything with it now. A man of fifty cannot remake his life. I have heard it said that the only difference between the rich and the poor in a certain kind of economy is that the rich have money ten or fifteen or twenty years before the poor. I suppose the same is true about ways of seeing. Some people come to it too late, when their lives are already spoilt. I mustn't exaggerate. But I have a sense now that when I was in Africa, for all those eighteen years, when I was in the prime of life, I hardly knew where I was. And that time in the forest was as dark and confusing as it was at the time. I was so condemning of other people on the course. How vain and foolish. I am no different from them.'

He was not thinking of the people from South Africa or Australia or Egypt, men in their forties, natural suit-wearers, high up in their organisations, and perhaps connected in some way with one or the other of Peter's companies. It gave these people a certain amount of pleasure to sit at desks like schoolchildren. They were not much seen in the big low lounge after lectures; cars very often came to take them to central London. He was thinking of people like himself, as it seemed to him: the big black or mixed man from the West Indies, who had worked his way up and was immensely pleased to be in this cosmopolitan company; the very neat Malaysian Chinese, clearly a man of business, in a fawn-coloured suit, and white shirt and tie, who sat in the lounge with his delicate legs elegantly crossed and seemed self-contained, ready to go through the whole course without talking to anyone; the man from the Indian subcontinent in his absurd white shoes, who turned out to be from Pakistan and a religious fanatic, ready to spread the Arab faith in this training centre devoted to another kind of learning and glory, other prophets: the pioneering nineteenth and twentieth-century architects (some the champions of brick) holding fast, often against the odds, to their own vision, and adding in the end to the sum of architectural knowledge.

In the lounge one afternoon (wicker chairs, cushions in chintz covers, matching chintz curtains) they assembled for tea. The lecturer had just been asking them to contemplate the fact that the simplest and most modest house, even a house like those seen on the main roads around the training centre, held an immense history: the poor no longer living in huts in the shadow of the great houses of their lords, no longer the helots of the early industrial age living in airless courts or in back-to-back tenements, the poor now people with their own architectural needs, these needs developing as materials developed.

Willie was excited by this idea and wished, as the lecturer had asked, to think about it with the others: the common house, the house of the poor, as more than a dwelling or shelter, as something that expressed the essence of a culture. He thought of the forest villages he had been in, marching futilely in his flimsy olive uniform with the red star on his cap; he thought of Africa, where the houses of thatch or straw were in the end to overwhelm the foreign world of concrete.

The man in the white shoes thought the lecturer was talking only of England.

Willie thought, 'That tells me a lot about where you come from.'

The man from the West Indies said, 'It's true for everybody.'

The man in the white shoes said, 'It can't be true for everybody. He doesn't know everybody. You know people only if you eat the same kind of food. He doesn't know the kind of food I eat.'

Willie knew where this argument was going: for the man in the white shoes the world was divided, quite simply, into people who ate pigs and people who didn't, people who were of the faith of Arabia and people who were not. He thought it sly and shameful that this simple idea was being presented in this way. And in this way the idea of the lecturer, about the houses of the poor in every culture, which had so dazzled Willie, became dissipated in this bogus discussion about diet as the great divider. In this discussion, such as it was, the man in the white shoes held all the cards. He would have raised the subject often before. The other people fumbled for things to say, and then the man in the white shoes, experienced in dealing with objections, came down on them hard.

The Malaysian Chinese man would have some idea about the real point of the discussion, but he preferred to keep his knowledge to himself. He smiled and steered clear of debate. He, who in the beginning had appeared to be very Chinese, reserved, self-contained, needing no one, had turned out to be the most frivolous of the group. He seemed to take nothing seriously, seemed to have no politics, and was happy to say, almost as a joke, that in Malaysia, no longer a pastoral land, now a land of highways and skyscrapers, he was running an Ali Baba construction business. Nothing to do with the forty thieves: in Malaysia 'Baba' was the word for a local Chinese, and an Ali Baba business was one in which there was an Ali, a Malay Muslim, as a front man, to placate the Malay government, and a guiding Baba, a Chinese like the joker himself, in the background.

For some reason, perhaps because of Willie's first name, or because of Willie's unusual English accent, or simply because he found Willie approachable, the man in the white shoes made up to Willie for most of the first week.

On Saturday, in the quiet lounge after dinner (many of the trainees had gone out, some to local pubs, some to central London), he leaned towards Willie and said conspiratorially, 'I want you to look at something.'

He took out a stamped envelope from an inner breast pocket

(revealing, as he did so, the label of a tailor in a town called Multan). Lowering his head, as though what he was doing made him want to hide his face, he handed the envelope to Willie. He said, 'Go ahead. Open it.' The stamps on the envelope were American, and when Willie unfolded the letter he found some small colour photographs of a sturdy white woman on a street, in a room, in a square.

The man said, 'Boston. Go ahead. Read it.'

Willie began to read, slowly at first, out of interest, and then more and more quickly, out of tedium. The man in the white shoes let his head fall lower and lower, as though shyness was consuming him. His dark curly hair hung down from his forehead. When Willie looked at him the man fractionally raised his head and Willie saw a face suffused, blurred with pride.

'Go on. Read.'

. . . as you say what are the transient pleasures of alcohol and the dance floor compared with life everlasting —

Willie thought, 'Not to talk of the ever renewed pleasures of sex.'

. . . what luck to have found you without you my dear I would have been wandering in darkness it is my kismet as you would say in the beginning I found all these ways of talk very quaint but now I see the truth of it all If you hadn't told me about Gandee or Gander being like Hitler I would never have known I would have gone on believing the nonsense they told me you see the power of propaganda or public relations in our diseased western civilisation so called PS Ive been thinking about my face cover Ive talked with my girl friends What I think would be nice would be for me to wear the Jesse James holdup style below the eyes and over the nose in the daytime for everyday and the Zorro eye mask at night for formal occasions . . .

Willie came to the end. Not saying anything, not looking up, he held on to the letter for a little longer than he should have done, and the man in the white shoes reached out with some sharpness – as though he feared theft – to take back the letter and the photographs and the envelope with the American stamps. He put it all together with a practised hand, put the envelope back into his breast pocket, and stood up. The look of conspiracy and then of a pleasure so great it seemed to veil his eyes was now replaced by something like gracelessness. Abruptly, then, he left the lounge, in a manner that seemed to say to Willie, 'You didn't know, did you? Now let's have no more nonsense from you.'

A gloom fell on Willie in the desolate lounge. He understood now why the man had made up to him during the week: it was only to boast: he had judged Willie to be susceptible to this particular kind of boasting.

The afternoon lecturer had talked all week about the accretion in the industrial age of learning and new skills, of vision and experiment and success and failure. To the man from Multan (and to others on the course as well, as Willie had noticed during the week) little of that story mattered: they had been sent by their countries or companies to get at knowledge that was simply there, seemingly divinely provided, knowledge that had for a long time been unfairly denied them for racial or political reasons but was now, in a miraculously changed world, theirs to claim as their own. And this newly claimed knowledge confirmed each man in the rightness of his own racial or tribal or religious ways. Up the greasy pole and then letting go. The simplified rich world, of success and achievement, always itself; the world outside always in disturbance.

Willie thought, 'I've been here before. I mustn't start again. I must let the world run according to its bias.'

* * *

A LETTER CAME FROM Willie's sister Sarojini. It was redirected by Roger from the house in St John's Wood, and that educated handwriting, still radiating confidence and style, showing nothing of the tormented life of the writer, was for Willie now full of irony.

Dear Willie, What I have to say will come as no surprise to you. I have decided to close down the ashram. I cannot give people what they come to me for. I was never a spiritual or unworldly person, as you know, but I thought after what I had been through that there was going to be some virtue in the life of withdrawal and stillness. I am sorry to say that I now have grave doubts about our father's way of going about things. I don't think he was above giving people little powders and potions, and I find that this is what people expect of me. They don't give a damn, to use a polite word, for the life of meditation and repose, and I find it horrible to think of what our father must have been up to all those years. Though of course it doesn't surprise me. I wonder if it hasn't always been like this, even in the ancient days of sages in the forest that the television people here so dearly love. A lot of people here have been to the Gulf, working for the Arabs. Recently things have not been going so well there and now many of the Gulf workers have come back. They are desperate to maintain their life style, as they have learned to say, and they come to me to ask me to do prayers for them or to give them charms. The charms they really want are like those they got in the Gulf from African spiritualists or maraboos, witchdoctors to you and me. For many people here this African Mohammedan rubbish is the latest thing, would you believe, and I can't tell you how I have been pestered in the last few months. For cowry shells and things like that. I imagine our father was dealing in this kind of thing for years. Money for old rope, I suppose, if you don't mind doing it. The upshot of all of this is that I have decided to call it a day here. I have written to Wolf, and the dear old man without one word of rebuke has promised to do what he can for me in Berlin. It will be nice to make a few documentaries again.

Willie began a letter to Sarojini the same day. *Dear Sarojini, You must be careful not to swing from one extreme to the other. There is no one thing that is an answer to the ills of the world and the ills of men. It has always been your failing* — He broke off and thought, 'I must not lecture. I have nothing to offer her.' And he stopped writing.

* * *

WEEKENDS BECAME WRETCHED at the training centre for Willie. Nearly everyone else on the course seemed to know people outside and went away for the weekend. The training centre's kitchens slowed down; fewer rooms showed lights; and the traffic on the main roads to the north sounded louder. To Willie, who had no wish to go to pubs that were within walking distance, and no desire to make the involved journey to central London to be with the idling tourist crowds, it was like being lost in the middle of nowhere.

He had thought that it would be better to be away for a while from the house in St John's Wood. But he very soon began to be assailed by a loneliness that took him back to long days and weeks as a guerrilla; terrible unexplained periods of waiting in small towns, usually in a dingy room without sanitation, where when the sun went down an unfamiliar squalling life developed outside, not attractive, not tempting him to wander, making him question the point of what he was doing; back to some evenings in Africa when he felt far away from everything he knew, far from his own history and far from the ideas of himself that might have come to him with that history; back to his first time in London thirty years before; back to some evenings in his childhood when – understanding the strains in his family, between his melancholy father, a man of caste, cheated of the life his good looks and birth had entitled him to, and his mother, of no caste and no looks, aggressive in every way, whom he, Willie, yet loved deeply; understanding as a result with the deepest kind of ache that there was no true place in the world for him – back to that childhood when on some especially unhappy evenings there came, with the utmost clarity, a child's vision of the earth spinning in darkness, with everyone on it lost.

He telephoned the house in St John's Wood. He was relieved when Perdita answered. But he was half expecting her to answer. The weekend was when Roger went to his other life. From what Roger had said, this other life might not now be going on. But Willie, understanding Roger better now, thought that it might be.

When he knew that she was alone in the house he said, 'Perdita, I am missing you. I need to make love to you.'

'But you are coming back. And I'm not going away. You can come to the house.'

'I don't know the way.'

'That's just it. And by the time you get here you might feel quite differently.'

So he made love to her on the telephone. She yielded to him, as she did when they were together.

When there was nothing more to say she said, 'Roger's been kicked in the teeth.'

Roger's own words: so Willie understood that Roger kept nothing secret from her.

She said, 'Not just by his tart, but by everybody. The whole property caper is coming tumbling down, and Peter's thrown him to the wolves. Peter's been well protected all along, of course. I suppose if Roger is struck off we'll have to give up the house. Climb down the property beanstalk. I don't imagine it will be a hardship. The house feels empty most of the time.'

And Willie fancied he could hear Roger speaking.

He said, 'I suppose I'll have to find somewhere else to live.'

'We can't think of that now.'

'I'm sorry. It sounded crass, but I was only trying to say something after what you said. They were just words.'

'I don't know what you're talking about. Roger will tell you more.'

So, quite late in their relationship, Willie felt a new respect for Perdita. On numberless occasions she had exposed herself to him; but this aspect of herself – the firmness, the solidity, the sharpness, this capacity for loyalty to Roger at this time of crisis – she had held back.

She must have talked to Roger afterwards. He telephoned Willie, but it was only to say that he was coming to Barnet to drive him back at the end of the course. His voice on the telephone was light: a man without a care: not at all what Willie was expecting after what Perdita had said.

He said, 'Do you like weddings? We have one to go to, if you want. Do you remember Marcus? The West African diplomat. He's served every kind of wretched dictatorship in his country. He's kept his head down and been ambassador everywhere. As a result he's now highly respected, as they say. The highly polished African, the man to wheel out if you want to make a point about Africa. He came to the dinner we gave in the little Marble Arch house half a life ago. He was still only training to be a diplomat, but he already had five half-white children of various nationalities. You were there, at the dinner. There was also an editor from the north who read out his own obituary. Marcus lived for inter-racial sex, and wanted to have a white grandchild. He wanted when he was an old man to walk down the King's Road holding the hand of this white grandchild. People would stare, and the child would say to Marcus, "What are they staring at, grandfather?"'

Willie said, 'How could I not remember Marcus? The publisher who was doing my book talked of nothing else when I went to his office. He thought he was being very fine and socialist, praising Marcus and running down the bad old days of slavery.'

'Marcus has succeeded. His half-English son has given him two grandchildren, one absolutely white, one not so white. The parents of the two grandchildren are getting married. It's the modern fashion. Marriage after the children come. The children, I suppose, will act as pages. They usually do. Marcus's son is called Lyndhurst. Very English. Meaning 'the forest place', if I remember my Anglo-Saxon. That's the wedding we've been invited to. Marcus's triumph. It sounds almost Roman. The rest of us peeled off into different things, ran about in a hundred different directions, and some of us failed, but Marcus held fast to his simple ambition. The white woman, and the white grandchild. I suppose that's why he succeeded.'

His voice was light throughout. Perdita's voice, on the telephone, had been heavier, full of anxiety: almost as if Roger had shifted his cares to her.

Two weeks later, at the end of the course, he came as he had promised to the training centre to drive Willie back to St John's Wood. His high spirits seemed to have lasted. Only, his eyes were sunken and the pouches dark.

He said, 'Did they teach you anything here?'

Willie said, 'I don't know how much they taught me. All I know now is that if I had my time over again I would have gone in for architecture. It's the only true art. But I was born too early. Twenty or thirty years too early, a couple of generations. We were still a colonial economy, and the only professions ambitious boys could think of were medicine and law. I never heard anyone talk of architecture. I imagine it's different now.'

Roger said, 'Perhaps I fell too readily into old ways, the charted path. I never asked myself what I wanted to do. I still can't say whether I have enjoyed what I've done. And I suppose that has cast a blight on my life.'

They were driving beside the low red houses. The road seemed less oppressive this time, and not so long.

Willie said, 'Is the news as bad as Perdita suggested?'

'As bad as that. I consciously did nothing wrong or unprofessional. You could say this thing crept up on me from behind. I told you how my father died. He had looked forward to that moment of death, or that time of dying, to tell the world what he really thought of it. Some people would say that is the way to go, to save the hate up for that moment. But I thought otherwise. I thought I never wanted to die like that. I wanted to die the other way. Like Van Gogh. At peace with the world, smoking his pipe and hating no one. As I told you. All my life I have prepared for this moment. I am ready to run down the beanstalk and take an axe to the root.'

* * *

WILLIE TOOK UP the letter to Sarojini again.

. . . perhaps if you get to Berlin I might find some way of getting round the law and coming to be with you. What nice months they were. But this time I think it would be nice if I could do some architecture course, which is what I should have done in the beginning. I don't know what you will think of this. You might think I am talking like an old fool, and I probably am. But I cannot pretend at this age that I am making my way. In fact, every day I see more clearly that here though I am a man rescued and physically free and sound in mind and limb I am also like a man serving an endless prison sentence. I don't have the philosophy to cope. I daren't tell them here. It would be too ungrateful. This reminds me of something that happened at Peter's magazine about a month after I went there. Peter picks up lame ducks, as I think I told you. I was one, and it didn't worry me. It rather pleased me. One day, when I was in the library on the top floor, doing my eternal checking, to keep the editress quiet, a man in a brown suit came in. People here have a thing about brown suits – Roger told me. This man greeted me across the room. He had an exaggerated drawling accent. He said, 'As you see, I am in my

brown suit.' He meant that he was either a worthless person or a defier of convention, perhaps both. In fact, he was a damaged man. The brown suit spoke truly in his case. It was a very rich bitter-chocolate brown. A little while later that same morning he came and sat directly in front of me on my table and said, with the weariest drawl, 'Of course, I have been to prison.' He said prison instead of jail, as though it was smarter. And he spoke that 'of course' as though that fact about him was well known, and as though everybody should do a spell in prison. He was quite alarming to me. I wondered where Peter picked him up. I meant to ask Roger, but always forgot. It is terrible to think of these people who look all right carrying their hidden wounds and even more terrible to think that I am one of them, that that was what Peter saw in me.

He stopped writing and thought, 'I mustn't do this to her.' And he put off finishing the letter until things became clearer to him.

* * *

IT WAS THEN, when the property caper was beyond mending or glossing over, that Roger began to talk to Willie, not of that calamity, but of the other, that had befallen his outside life. He didn't do so all at once. He did it over many days, adding words and thoughts to what had gone before; what he said wasn't always in sequence. He began indirectly, led to his main subject by scattered observations that he might have kept to himself before.

He talked of socialism and high taxes, and the inflation that inevitably followed high taxes, destroying families and the idea of families. This idea of families (rather than the family) passed on values from one generation to the next. These shared values held a country together; the loss of those values broke a country up, hastened a general decline.

To Willie this talk of decline was a surprise. He had never heard Roger talk of politics or politicians (only sometimes of people with politics), and he had grown to think Roger was not interested in the passing political scene (being in this like Willie himself), was a man of inherited liberal ideas, a man rooted in this liberalism, concerned with human rights all over the world, and at the same time at ease with his country's recent history, going with the flow.

He saw now that he had misread Roger. Roger had the highest idea of his country; he expected much from its people; he was, in the profoundest way, a patriot. Decline grieved him. Talking now to Willie about decline, with the view at the end of the sitting room, of the late-summer garden, tears came to his eyes. And Willie thought that those tears were really for his situation, that that was what he had been talking about.

He talked, obsessively, of the wedding of Marcus's son, and did not appear to be linking this to what he had said about the idea of families. He said, 'Lyndhurst aimed well. He aimed at what the Italians call "a spent family". A family with nothing more to offer, but still a family of name. Marcus would be very particular about that kind of thing. I am trying to imagine Marcus walking around the tents and marquees holding his white grandchild's hand and acknowledging the scrutiny of the guests. Would it be scrutiny alone, or would it be applause? Times have changed, as you know. Would he be in a top hat, you think, and a grey morning coat? Like a black diplomat from some chaotic country going to the palace, in a rare moment of clarity, to present his credentials. He definitely would want to do the right thing, Marcus. Will he bow to the crowd, or will he just look preoccupied, chatting to his grandchild? I will tell you something. In the lunch interval during a cricket match at Lord's cricket ground – not far from here, I should tell you – I once saw the legendary Len Hutton. He wasn't playing. The great batsman was old, long retired. He was wearing a grey suit. He was walking around the ground, at the back of the stands, as if for exercise. He was really doing a lap of honour at Lord's, where he had so often opened the innings for England. Everyone in the ground knew who he was. We all stared. But he, Len Hutton, appeared not to notice. He was talking to another elderly man in a suit. What they were talking about seemed to be worrying them both. Hutton was actually frowning. And that was how he walked past, looking down with his famous broken nose and frowning. Would Marcus be like Hutton, preoccupied on his lap of honour? In his fantasy that was how he wanted it to be. On the King's Road, holding his white grandchild's hand and minding his own business while the crowd stared. But at the wedding of his son he wouldn't be on the King's Road. He would have to acknowledge the guests. I imagine the old folk of the once great family on one side, and Marcus's son and his buddies on the other. It would be like a carnival. But Marcus would manage it beautifully, would make it appear the most natural thing in the world, and it would be lovely to see.'

He said on another day, 'Weddings are such a carnival these days. I went to a wedding not long ago. At the other place I go to. We've pulled everything down, we've changed the rules on everything, but the ladies still want weddings. It's especially true on the council estates. Council estates are blocks of flats or houses built by a municipality for the poor of the parish, as they used to be called. Only, the people there are not poor now. Women there have three or four children by three or four men and they are all living on benefits. Sixty pounds a week a child, and that's just the beginning. You can't call that a dole. So we call them benefits. Women see themselves as money-making machines. It's like Dickens's England. Nothing's changed except that there's a lot of money about, and the Artful Dodger is doing very well indeed, though everything is very expensive and everyone's hopelessly in debt and wants the benefits increased. People there need to take one or two holidays a year. Not in Blackpool or Minehead or Mallorca now, but in the Maldives or Florida or the bad-sex spots of Mexico. They need hours in the sky. Otherwise it's not a proper holiday. "I haven't had a proper holiday all this year." So the planes are full of this trash flying about and drinking hard, and the airports are packed. And every week the papers have twenty pages of advertisements for holidays so cheap you wonder how anyone even in Mexico can make money out of them. The wedding we had to go to was for a woman who has had three children by a club cook she lives with off and on. Usually a cook, but also off and on, on especially festive nights, the club bouncer. The thing was the most horrible kind of socialist parody. The top hats and morning coats on the weekday scroungers. It's what the battered women want for their men on wedding Saturdays. For themselves they want the long white dresses and veils to hide the bruises and black eyes of the love that comes and goes, what they call relationships. On this particular wedding day the beaten-up children, fat or scrawny, normally fed on sandwiches and pizzas and crisps and chocolate bars, were dressed up and displayed and were to be fed on even richer foods. Like young bulls bred for slaughter in the bullring, these children are bred sacrificially and in great numbers for the socialist benefits they bring to a council house. They are not really looked after, and many are destined to be molested or abducted or murdered, providing then, like proper little gladiators, but for three or four long days, socialist excitement for the burgesses. I told you once that the only people here who were not common, in the way of being false and self-regarding, were the common people.'

Willie said, 'I remember that. I liked it. You said it as we were driving in from the airport. London was very new to me just at that moment, and what you said was part of the romance of that moment.'

Roger said, 'I was wrong. It sounded good and I said it. I fell into my own liberal trap. The common people are as confused and uncertain as everybody else. They are actors, like everybody else. Their accents are changing. They try to be like the people in the television soaps, and now they've lost touch with what they really might be. And there's no one to tell them. You can have no idea what it's like down there, unless you've been. The worst kind of addiction is when you get no pleasure from the vice but can't do without it. That's what it's been like for me. It began in the simplest way. I saw a woman in a certain kind of outfit when I went down one weekend to see my father. Women have no real idea of the little unconsidered things that make them attractive, and I suppose the same is true about what women like in men. You told me you fell for Perdita at the first lunch we had together. Chez Victor, in Wardour Street.'

Willie said, 'She was wearing striped gloves. She pulled them off and slapped them on the table. I was enchanted by the gesture.'

'My woman was wearing a black lycra outfit. Or so I was told later. The trousers or pants had slipped far down at the back, showing something more than her skin. Quite cheap, the material, but that was a further attraction for me. The pathos of the poor, the pathos of an attempt at style at that level. I had an idea who she was and what she might be. And that fact, the difference between us, gave me the encouragement to press my suit.'

And this, when all the pieces were put together, was the story that Roger told.

ELEVEN

Suckers

My father was ill (Roger said). Not yet close to dying. I used to go down at weekends to see him. I used to think how shabby the house was, more a cottage than a house, how dusty and smoky, how much in need of a coat of paint, and that was what my father thought too. He thought it was too little to be left with after a life of work and worry.

I felt my father was too romantic about himself. Especially when he started talking about his long life of work. There is work and work. To create a garden, to build a company, is one kind of work. It is to gamble with oneself. Work of that sort can be said to be its own reward. To do repetitive tasks on somebody else's estate or in some great enterprise is something else. There is no sacredness about that labour, whatever biblical quotations are thrown at one. My father discovered that in middle life, when it was too late for him to change. So the first half of his life was spent in pride, an overblown idea of his organisation and who he was, and the second half was spent in failure and shame and anger and worry. The house epitomised it. It was half and half in everything. Not cottage, not house, not poor, not well to do. A place that had been let go. It is strange now to think that I was determined that things should fall out differently for me.

I didn't like going to the house. But duty is duty, and one of my big worries was getting someone to look after the house for my father. There was a time when a substantial portion of the population was in domestic service. There was no problem then. A certain amount of coming and going, but no lasting problem. When you read books from before the last war you notice, if you have this particular worry on your mind, that people quite easily leave their houses and go away visiting for days and weeks. Servants gave them that freedom. They are always there in the background, and mentioned only indirectly. Except in old-fashioned thrillers and detective stories there doesn't seem to be much talk of thieves and break-ins. There might be a robbery in P. G. Wodehouse, but only as a bit of comic business, as in the modern cartoon, where eye-mask and swag-bag identify the comic neighbourhood burglar.

The servant class has vanished. No one knows what they have metamorphosed into. One thing we can be sure of is that we have not lost them, that they are still in varying ways with us, in culture and attitudes of dependence. In every town and large village we now have ancillary council estates, clusters of subsidised dwellings meant originally for the poor. These clusters are recognisable even from the train. They have a deliberate socialist ugliness, a conscious suppression of those ideas of beauty and humanity that rise naturally from the heart. The theories of socialist ugliness have to be taught. People have to be trained to think that what is ugly is really beautiful. *Ancilla* in Latin means a nurse, a slave girl, a maid, and these ancillary council estates, meant to give the poor a kind of independence, quickly developed into what they had to be: parasitic slave growths on the main body. They feed off general taxes. They give nothing back. They have, on the contrary, become centres of crime. You may not guess it when you see them from the train, but they are a standing assault on the larger community. There can be no absolute match of one age with another, but I wouldn't be surprised if the percentage of people at one time in domestic service isn't matched now by the numbers on the council estates.

And, of course, it is still to these places that we have to look for help with our houses. We put our pleading little cards in the local newsagent's window. In due course the cleaning people come. And in due course they go. And, since no one keeps an inventory in his mind of all that he has in his house, it is only after they have gone that we realise that this is missing and that has gone. Dickens set Fagin's thieves kitchen in the Seven Dials area of London, around what is now Tottenham Court Road, with the bookshops. From there Fagin sent out his little people to pick a pathetic little purse or lift a pretty handkerchief. Fearful to Dickens, these wanderers abroad, but to us so innocent, so daring. Today circumstances require us actually to invite the Artful Dodger and his crew into our house, and the insurance companies tell us, too late, that nothing lost in this way can ever be redeemed. Strange and various needs the modern Dodgers have: all the sugar in a house, perhaps; all the coffee; all the envelopes; half the underclothes; every piece of pornography.

Life in these circumstances becomes, in a small way, a constant gamble and an anxiety. We all learn to live with it. And, in fact, after much coming and going we at last found someone suitable for my father's house. She was a country girl, but very much up to the minute, single, with a couple of children, dually fathered, if that is grammatically possible, who brought her quite a tidy sum every week. She spoke of people being of 'good stock' and she seemed to suggest that after her early mistakes she was striving after higher things. This didn't impress me. I took it as a mark of criminality. I have known criminals all my professional life, and in my experience this is how criminals like to present themselves.

But I was wrong about this woman. She stayed, and was good and reliable. She was in her thirties, educated, able to write reasonably well, an elegant dresser (buying stylish things cheap from mail order firms), and her manners were good. She stayed for six, seven, eight years. She became a fixture. I began – almost – to take her for granted.

I took good care all this time to show no interest in her private life. I am sure that it was quite complicated, with her looks, but I never wanted to know. I feared being dragged down into the details. I didn't want to know the names of the men in her life. I didn't want to know that Simon, a builder, was like this, or Michael, a taxi-driver, was like that.

I used to go down to the cottage on Friday evenings. One Saturday morning she told me, without any prompting, that she had had a hard week. So hard that one night she had come to the cottage, parked her little car in the little drive, and cried. I asked why she had come to the cottage to cry.

She said, 'I have nowhere else to go. I know that your father wouldn't mind. And after all these years I regard the cottage as my home.'

I understood what she meant; it tore at my heart; but even

then I genuinely didn't want to know the details. And of course in time she got over that crisis and was as serene and stylish and well mannered as ever.

Some time passed. And then again I began to understand that there was something new in Jo's life. Not a man, but a woman. Someone new on the council estate, or someone just discovered. These two women, Jo and the other woman, had been boasting to each other about the richness of their life, boasting in the way women boast. The other woman's name was Marian. She was artistic; she made curtains and painted earthenware plates; she infected Jo with a wish to do similar things. On weekends I began to hear about the expensiveness of kilns. Six or eight hundred pounds. I had the idea that I was being asked in the name of art and Jo's general social endeavour to spend some money on an electric home kiln. A business expense, which would apparently be recovered in no time. As it was, Jo was getting almost no return on her craft and art. By the time she had paid for the plain earthenware plates on which she did her painting, of flowers or a dog or a tiny kitten in a tea cup, and then the baking of her painted plates by a kiln-owner on the council estate, the renting of a stall at a craft fair, the travel to the fair, by the time she had done all that she was showing no profit at all. I imagined her sitting forlorn beside her craft goods at the fair, as an ancestor in long skirts and clogs might have sat in a simpler time beside her eggs in a village market, ready at the end of the weary day to exchange everything for a handful of magic seeds.

Sometimes in London a go-ahead young art dealer whom you have just got to know might invite you to dinner. And it seems at first that everything in his austerely laid out house or flat is exceptionally tasteful and well chosen, the enviable discoveries of an unusual eye. When at last you feel you must remark on the long and lovely old oak table on which you are dining, you hear that it is for sale, with everything else you have seen. You realise then that you have been invited not just to dinner but to an exhibition, the way a developer might ask you to a show house, for a little more than the pleasure of your company.

So now it was with Jo. She began on Saturday mornings to undo big, heavy bundles of her work, painted plates, enamel-and-wire work, very streaky landscapes and portraits in wax, charcoal drawings of animals, watercolours of rivers and willows. Everything that could be framed was framed, with very big mounts; that was why the bundles were so heavy.

These Saturday exhibitions put me on the spot. I actually was interested. It was moving to me to see these stirrings of the spirit where I had expected nothing. But to express interest was to encourage the display of another big bundle on the following Saturday. To say then to Jo that there was real talent there and that it might be a good idea for her to take drawing lessons or watercolour lessons drew no response from her. It was not what she wanted to hear.

Somehow the idea had been given to her that talent was natural and couldn't be forced or trained. When I said that one piece showed a big development she said, 'I guess it was all there.' She was speaking of the bubbling up of her talent, and she was not boasting. She might have been talking of something outside herself. I felt that these semi-political ideas about the naturalness of artistic talent – and its classlessness: there was more than a hint of that – had been given her by someone. I thought it might be her new friend Marian.

It took me a little time to understand that Jo had been presenting her work to me not for my criticism. She wanted me to buy her work; she wanted me to tell my London friends about her. I was a craft fair all on my own. And so was my father. The work Jo brought on Saturday mornings was not hers alone. There were many pieces by Marian, and she was generous about them. No jealousy there. I began to feel that these two women, one encouraging the other, had become awed by themselves. They were ordinary people; but their talent made them remarkable, above the common run of women. They liked every artistic thing they did. Each piece was to them a little miracle. I became nervous of these women. In some such way many working-class criminals, or people criminally inclined, present themselves to the middle classes. I became very much on my guard.

Sometimes they liked to leave work in the cottage. This was more for my father than for me. However fierce he was with outsiders, he was gentle with Jo. He liked to give the impression that he was in her hands. He actually never was. This little bit of acting pleased him: a little power play, still, letting the two women, suppliants in this matter of art work, think he was feebler than he was. The idea of Jo and her friend Marian was that after a week or so the beauty of a piece would be overwhelming, and my father would buy. You can't blame them; this is what some London dealers do.

An important craft fair was coming up. I heard about it weeks beforehand from Jo. It was to be on a Sunday, and on the morning of that Sunday a Volvo station wagon came in to the cottage drive. A woman I didn't know was driving. I took this to be Marian. Jo was sitting beside her. They had come to take away some of the art work they had left for my father to get used to. Jo came out first and, very much the woman who knew her way around, let herself into the cottage. She came out shortly afterwards with my father who, overdoing the dodderiness, leading Jo on (but only in this matter of art work), was helping ineffectually to bring various awkwardly shaped pieces (big frames, big mounts) out to the porch.

My room was at the other end of the cottage, near the entrance gateway, at the beginning of the small semi-circular drive. So when Marian came out, to greet my father, I saw her from the back. Her black, too loose, elastic pants, part of a black outfit, had slipped far down. And that energetic getting out of the Volvo, using the steering wheel to lever herself out, had pulled it askew and even lower.

She said to my father, 'I've been admiring your lovely house. I've heard so much about it from Jo.'

I had worked out a character for her, but, as had been happening more and more in my work in recent years, I had got it wrong. Such directness, such social grace wasn't at all what I was expecting. Nor was the big Volvo, handled with a matching grace as, sitting high, she eased it into the tight, awkward curve of our drive. For years afterwards I could recall that moment. She was tall, a further surprise, not plebeian or council-estate in figure, and exercised and slender. The glimpse of her lower body, the black coarse material contrasting with the lovely skin, fixed the moment in my mind. With a quick right hand she straightened the back of her pants, pulling it out and down a little more before pulling it up and straight. I doubt whether she knew what she had done. But the moment was ever with me.

When, later, we were together it could bring about immediate desire for her, or it could put life into a lagging performance.

I watched them put their pieces in the station wagon and drive away. I was too nervous to call out to Jo. And so it happened that for a week I was obsessed by a woman whose face I hadn't even seen. Ideas of comedy or crime fell away.

On Saturday I asked Jo how the fair had gone. She said it hadn't gone at all. She and Marian had sat all day at their stall (the rent was twenty-five pounds) and nothing had happened. Towards the end of the afternoon some men had appeared to be interested, but they were only trying to pick them up.

I said, 'I saw Marian last Sunday morning when she came here.'

I had tried to speak as neutrally as possible. But the look on Jo's face told me that I had given myself away. Women are sharp about sexual attraction, even when they themselves are not involved. All their senses are trained to detect the beginnings of interest and inclination, a man's loss of neutrality. Women may say that for them there is an important self beyond sexuality. We allow ourselves to see what they mean, but then we come across women's autobiographies that are boastful chronicles of screwing; and often in the biography of a dead woman writer, say, very sensitive and serious in her time, the life presented for our admiration (now that the books have faded) is principally the life of screwing.

Jo's bright eyes became shaded with roguishness and complicity. She herself was displaying a new character, as if to match what she had seen in me.

I asked, 'What does Marian do?'

'She is a swimmer. She works at the baths.' The municipal baths in our market town.

That explained the exercised body. I had never been to the municipal baths and I imagined myself in a biggish pool, with barefooted Marian in her swimsuit doing her round of the pool, walking a foot or two above the level of my head. (Though I knew it wouldn't be like that: she would more probably be in a synthetic shell suit of some sort, sitting in a chair beside the sun-bleached and water-stained plywood tea counter, having bad coffee or tea, and reading a magazine.)

Jo, as if reading my thoughts, said, 'She's lovely, isn't she?' Generous as always about her friend, but still with the new complicit look, as though she was ready for any adventure with me that might include her friend.

I thought of the exercised and relaxed body stretched out in her bed, clean body in clean sheets, smelling of chlorine and water and cleanliness, and I was deeply stirred.

Jo said, 'She's made a couple of mistakes. Like the rest of us.'

Jo's language was like that, with strange old-fashioned echoes: the mistakes were no doubt children by unsuitable men.

She said, 'She's been living with someone for ages.'

She began to tell me what this man did, but I stopped her. I didn't want to know any more. I didn't want to get a picture of him. It would have been unbearable.

* * *

My pursuit of Marian (Roger said) was the most humiliating thing I had ever exposed myself to. And at the end, to add to my humiliation, I discovered that council-estate women of

Marian's age thought of sex in the most matter-of-fact way, in the crudest way you might say, or the simplest, the most natural, almost as something they had to go shopping for, and in the same spirit of sport with which they went shopping for cut-price groceries (on certain evenings, when the supermarkets marked down certain perishable items).

Marian told me later (when my pursuit was done, and our weekend relationship was more or less established) that groups of young women in her area would make a party on Thursday or Friday or Saturday and go out to the pubs and clubs, trawling for sex with men they fancied on sight. Fancied: that was the word: 'I fancy him.' No woman wanted not to have a man she fancied. These occasions could turn very rough. The fancied men were also matter-of-fact about women and sex, and a woman could be easily knocked about. If a woman objected too loudly or with too many obscenities she could be given a 'beer shampoo': she could have a bottle of beer emptied over her head. It was all part of the sex game, part of the weekend clubbing. Almost every woman who did this kind of clubbing had at one time had her beer shampoo. At the end there was sex for everyone, however fat, however plain.

Marian was telling me one day about someone on her street, a young woman, who lived on crisps and very sweet chocolate bars and pizzas and burgers, and was immensely fat. This woman had three children, also very fat, by three different fathers. I thought this was a critical story from Marian, the swimmer, about bad diet and fatness. But I was wrong. Most of the women in Marian's area were fat. Fatness by itself wasn't a story. This was a story about the fat woman's sexual appetite and sexual success. The moral tone I thought I detected wasn't there. Marian was speaking in her gossipy way only of the presumption and absurdity of the fat woman. She said, 'It's like a Chinese laundry in that house, with men. In and out fast.'

That was Marian's language style. Sharp. It went with everything else about her. To me it all made a whole.

Even if I had all or some of this knowledge about Marian's background I don't think it would have helped me in my courtship, to use that inappropriate word. I couldn't have adopted the attitude of the fancied men of the pubs. I wouldn't have known how to knock a woman about in a pub or give her a beer shampoo. I could only be myself, and depend on such arts of seduction as I possessed. These arts hardly existed. Perdita and a few other women like Perdita had, as the saying was, thrown themselves at me. They didn't do so for flagrant sexual purposes. They did it only for marriage. Sex hardly entered into it. I was okay, as a partner or husband, and that was all. So I never had to seek women out or win them. They were simply there, and I discovered now that, in the winning of Marian, I had no talents of seduction at all.

Men are never more foolish or absurd than when they 'make a pass'. Women especially mock them, though these same women would be mortified if no pass were made at them. I felt this absurdity keenly, and I wouldn't have been able to pull it off, if Jo hadn't helped me. She prepared the ground for me, so to speak, so that when Marian and I finally met Marian knew that I was interested in her. We met in the lounge of the old coaching inn in the town. The idea, which was Jo's, was that she and Marian should be having coffee or tea on a Saturday afternoon, and I, coming into the town from the cottage, should happen upon them. It was simplicity itself, as Jo said, but it was easier for the women than for me. I was more than embarrassed. I could hardly bear to look at Marian.

Jo left. Marian stayed to have a lukewarm drink in the dark, low, almost empty bar. I presented my case. In fact, the legal analogy helped me to do so. Everything about her enchanted me, her narrowness above the waist, her voice, her accent, her language, her aloofness. Whenever I felt my courage failing I thought of her black, coarse elasticated pants slipping low when she got out of the Volvo station wagon. I thought it was important not to let things drag on for another week. I would lose momentum, perhaps lose courage altogether, and she might change her mind. She agreed to stay for dinner; in fact, she seemed to think that that had been already agreed. Jo had done her work well. Better than I had done mine. I had made no arrangements. For a minute or so I thought I might take her to the cottage, but I knew that would have been calamitous: my father, though decayed, had a strange canniness still. So dinner was only dinner. There was no working towards anything else afterwards. So you could say that Marian and I had a kind of courtship. We had the house wine; she loved that. We arranged to meet for lunch the next day. I felt I could shower Jo with treasure for all she had done for me.

I booked a room at the inn for the next day. I had an anxious night, and a desperate morning. I have searched myself to see whether I had ever spent such an anxious time, so full of yearning, so full of self-distrust, and I don't think I have. I felt that everything depended on seducing this woman, taking her to bed. In other crises one has more or less an idea of what one is worth and what work one has done and where things might be going. But in this business of seduction I had no experience. It was the completest gamble. Everything depended on the other person. Later, when I got to know more about the ways of Marian and her friends, this anxiety of mine appeared extraordinarily foolish and pathetic. But, as I have said before, even if I did know about those ways it would not have helped.

The long night ended. The lunch came. We went afterwards to the booked room with the strange dark and musty furniture. How terrible now to embrace a stranger, just like that. Marian seemed very slightly to repel me, and I was relieved. We undressed. I undressed as though I was at the doctor's, being examined for a rash. Jacket on a chair; then trousers, underpants and shirt, all very neatly.

Marian's armpits were dark with silky hair.

I said, 'So you don't shave.'

'Somebody asked me not to some time ago. Some people think it's disgusting. They make strange faces when they see it.'

'I love it.'

She allowed me to stroke it, to feel its silkiness. It over-excited me, and worked with the other pictures I had of her. I came a little before I should. She was cool. For a long time she remained on her left side, hip high, waist sunken, her right flank smooth and exercised and firm. Her left arm partly covered her small breasts. Her right arm was crooked above her head, revealing her underarm hair. On two or three fingers of the hand that covered her breasts she had rings: gifts, I thought, of previous worshippers, but I closed my mind to them now.

She said, in her cool way, looking down at me, 'Aren't you going to bugger me?'

I didn't know what to say.

She said, 'I thought that was where you were going.'

I still didn't know what to say.

She said, 'Did you go to Oxford or Cambridge?' And with a gesture of irritation reached across the bed for her bag. Easily, as though she knew where it was, she took out a tube of lip salve.

I hesitated. She passed the lip salve to me, saying, 'I am not doing this for you. You do it.'

I hadn't thought it possible for a naked, exposed woman to be so imperious.

She commanded. I obeyed. How well I did I didn't know. She didn't tell me.

When we were dressed again, she more or less fully, I only partly, there was a ring at the door. I remembered, too late, that in my agitation I had not put on the 'occupied' light.

She seemed to grow insane. She said, 'You, go to the bathroom.' She called out to the person outside to wait, and then she began pelting all my clothes into the bathroom, jacket, shoes, pelting everything she could see, as though she wished no sign of me to remain in the bedroom.

It was only a chambermaid, Spanish or Portuguese or Colombian, doing some kind of checking.

I was standing in the cramped bathroom like a man in a farce.

Yet afterwards I was more concerned to work out her behaviour. Perhaps it was some shred of shame or morality, something beyond her control. Perhaps it was because I was not one of the people who might have given the women of the estates a beer shampoo. So new rules, new manners, would apply, and perhaps even new feelings might be brought into play.

She never explained, and when I said that I hoped we could meet the next weekend when I came down from London she said yes and then said in her half-and-half, contrary way, 'Let's see.'

I bought her a pretty piece of jewellery, something with opals. It cost a few hundred pounds. I wanted something substantial because I knew she would show it to her friends, and one of them, Jo perhaps, would tell her to take it to Trethowans, the local jewellers, to have it valued. At the same time I wanted to be fair to myself: opals are not among the more expensive stones.

She was pleased when I gave it to her on Friday evening.

She held it in her hand and considered the blue flash and sparkle, the unending miniature storm in the stone, and though her own eyes were glinting, she said, 'They say that opals are unlucky.'

I had booked a room in the hotel for the weekend. The staff were Spanish and Portuguese and Colombian. Colombians, through some kind of network, had penetrated to our market town, meeting some local need beyond that of simple labour. They were Mediterranean in spirit, infinitely tolerant, and Marian and I were treated as old friends by them and the others. This did away with whatever awkwardness Marian and I might have felt about our new arrangement.

In fact, it was wonderful in the hotel. It was like being on a foreign holiday in one's own place, being an exotic in one's own place. Living the life of bar and dining room and bedroom, and foreign languages, just a few miles from my father's cottage-house and overgrown garden, which had for so long been for me a place of gloom, of tarnished ceilings and walls and foolish little pictures blurred below grimy glass, a place of a life lived out and now without possibility, steeped in my father's unassuageable rages against people I had known only in his stories, never in the flesh.

I had been anxious all week about meeting Marian again. Almost as anxious as about our first meeting. I got to the hotel early. And I sat in the low-ceilinged lounge ('a wealth of exposed beams', as the hotel brochure promised), and looked across the old market square to where, hidden round a corner, both the taxi rank and the bus station were. She was splendid when she appeared. It was the word that came to me. She was in pale primrose trousers, with the waist high up, so that her legs seemed very long. The flare on the trousers made them overwhelming. Her walk was brisk and athletic. I doubted that I had the capacity to deal with this splendour. But then it came to me, as I watched her stride towards the hotel, that the trousers were new, specially bought for this occasion. There was something like an ironing mark or a fold mark across the middle. It would have come from the shop: a garment folded and wrapped in tissue and placed in a box or a bag. I was very moved by this evidence of her care and preparation. It gave me a little comfort. At the same time it made me feel unworthy, wondering about the challenges ahead. So I was perhaps in a greater state of nerves than at the beginning.

There is no tragedy like that of the bedroom: I believe Tolstoy said that to a friend. No one knows what he meant. The recurring shameful need? Failure? Poor performance? Rejection? Silent condemnation? It was very much like that with me later that evening. I thought I had infected Marian with my feeling of the luxuriousness of the hotel in the market square, the strange feeling it gave, with all the foreign staff, of being somewhere abroad. The wine at dinner had strengthened that feeling, I thought. But her dark, distant mood returned at bedtime. It might have been another person who had accepted the opal piece and been pleased by it.

She undressed and offered herself, and then later exposed herself as before, the sunken exercised waist, the lovely high hip, the dark openness, showing me the hair in her armpits. This time I was better provided to do what she clearly wanted me to do.

But I never knew whether I was pleasing her. I thought that I must be, but she never let on. Perhaps she was acting; perhaps it was her style; perhaps it was something she had got from one of her too boastful friends; perhaps it was something that had been forced on her by her rough childhood on the estate, a little remnant of natural modesty, a way of dealing with that life.

And that – since the mind can deal with many things at the same time – was how I reasoned with myself while I was quite shaken with desire, hardly believing in what was being offered me, wishing at the same time to seize it all.

Later, when I had grown more into this fearful, undermining discovery of the senses, I would understand that in these early days I had not done very well. It would have destroyed me if I had known. But at the time, in the bedroom of the hotel, I didn't know.

Midway through the evening she said, 'I see you've come with your belt. Do you want to beat me?'

I had some idea what she meant. But it was too far away from me. I said nothing.

She said, 'Use the belt. Don't use anything else.'

When we had done with that she said, 'Is my bottom black and blue?'

It wasn't. Many weeks later that would be true, but not then.

She said, 'Did it give you a nice big fat come?'

It hadn't. But I didn't say.

She said, 'I had your number.' And she swung her strong legs off the bed.

So, after all that had occurred between us, she kept her distance. I thought that was the whole point of her attitude during this tragedy of the bedroom, and I admired her for it. I willingly granted her that distance. If I didn't it would have been another relationship, and that simply wasn't possible. Outside the bedroom, and that darkening of her mood, there was almost nothing between us. We had very little to talk about.

Something she had read, some saucy book or manual, or some conversation with a woman friend, had given her her own idea of my special need, my number, as she said. She was only a quarter right. I had always thought of myself as a man of low sexual energy. Just as your father, Willie, from what you told me, sank into melancholy and made it part of his character, part of his solace in a crisis, so this idea of my low sexual energy had become part of my character. It simplified things for me. The idea of sex with a woman, exposing myself to that kind of intimacy, was distasteful to me. Some people insist that if you're not one thing you're the other. They believe that I'm interested in men. The opposite is true. The fact is all sexual intimacy is distasteful to me. I've always considered my low sexual energy as a kind of freedom. I am sure that there have been many people like me. Ruskin, Henry James. They are strange examples, but they're the ones that come immediately to mind. We should be allowed to have our freedom.

I was in my forties when I first saw a modern magazine with sexual photographs. I was shocked and frightened. Those magazines had been in the newsagents' shops for years, all more or less with the same covers, and I had not thought of looking at them. This is absolutely true. Some time later I saw a variety of more specialist pornographic magazines. They made me ashamed. They made me feel that we could all be trained in these ghastly extensions of sexual feeling. Only a few basic sexual acts occur spontaneously. Everything else has to be taught. Flesh is flesh. We can all be made to learn. Without training we would know nothing of certain practices. I preferred not to be trained.

I believe Marian saw all of this ignorance in me. She wished to draw me out, of course within the limits of her own knowledge, within the limits of what she herself had been trained to, and to some extent she succeeded.

I saw her at a time in middle life when, rather like my father before me, I had begun to feel that the promise of my early years, my rather grand idea of myself, had gone sour. Perdita's infidelity – not the act itself, which I could visualise without any pain (and perhaps even with amusement), but the public humiliation the act exposed me to – had begun to eat me up. I couldn't make a scene with her, lay down the law, because I had nothing to offer her in return. I could only endure.

I have said that there was nothing between Marian and me outside the bedroom. But I wonder about that. Having got to know Marian, I wished to know no other woman in that special way, and I wonder whether that cannot be described as a kind of love: the sexual preference for one person above all others. About a year later, in our market town, I saw a young woman of plebeian aspect running on a cold Saturday morning from her place of work to the local baker's to join the queue for their famous apple pies. She was broader than Marian, heavier in front, loose-bellied. She was wearing black lycra pants and a black top. The elastication had gone slack top and bottom, and as she ran, hugging her charmless breasts in the cold, she was showing as much flesh and contour behind as Marian did when I first saw her getting out of the Volvo at my father's cottage. I had no wish at all to see any more of the woman running to the baker's.

And more than once, in the house in St John's Wood, I would consider Perdita's body and gait, which had its admirers, hear her stylish county voice, really quite nice, and wonder why it all left me cold, and why I willingly paid thousands for the sight and enjoyment of the other, in the other place.

* * *

I FELL INTO a new pattern of living. Weekdays in London, weekends in the country with Marian. In time I lost my anxiety with her, though there was always that darkness and distance in her bedroom mood. The more I got to know her, the more I pushed myself sexually with her. I never wanted during those weekends to waste her, so to speak; I never wanted to be idle with her. By Sunday morning I was close to enervation. I longed then to be free of her, to be on the road back to London. And, paradoxically, Sunday evenings were the best time of the week for me, a time of delicious rest and solitude and reflection, when sexual exhaustion and relief turned slowly to a general feeling of optimism, and I became ready for the week ahead. By Thursday I would be ground down again; my head would once more be full of pictures of Marian; and I would be more than eager on

Friday afternoon to get back to her. It was out of that weekday optimism, I should tell you, that I was able to work, and work hard, for my various good causes, including getting you out of your Indian jail. Those good causes mattered to me. They gave me an idea of myself which I could hold on to.

It was in its way a perfect relationship, with just enough separation to keep desire going. The pattern lasted until the time of Peter's property caper. Then, out of my wish to impress Perdita, and perhaps also more than a little to please myself, I spent a few weekends in Peter's big house. I should say I behaved very well with Perdita on those occasions. The optimism I drew from Marian served me well. Perdita loved visiting the big house and being waited on by the plump, spoilt men in striped trousers. Her lovely voice came into its own then, and it pleased me to play the perfect courtier with her. I tipped well: it pleased Perdita. And this extra time away from Marian sharpened my wish to get back to her as soon as I could. So everybody was served.

We changed hotels a few times, though staying in the general area: I wished always, while my father lived, to be within reach of the cottage. In the beginning this changing of hotels was to prevent Marian from being recognised by her friends or relations. Later it was mainly for the novelty: new rooms, new staff, new lounge and bar, new dining room. We thought for a time of buying a flat or house in an outlying small town, and the idea excited us for some months, but then as we began to go into the details the thought of housekeeping grew more and more oppressive to both of us.

A housekeeping weekend would have been not at all what I wanted. It would have brought out the family side of Marian which I closed my mind to. That family side was always there in the background; sometimes I could feel family problems pressing on Marian; but I wished to know nothing of them. To know more, to see Marian as a day-to-day council-estate housewife, would have done away with the enchantment I found in her rough ways and her deformed accent, things that went so strangely with her swimmer's clean-smelling, exercised body. But the idea of property had excited her; and in the end, in a kind of compensation, I bought her council-estate house for her. The law had recently been changed, to enable council-estate tenants to buy their houses. I could put no price on my weekends with Marian, and the price the council put on her house was more than reasonable.

Just as people – like my father, say – can gradually get used to a medical condition which, if presented to them all at once, would have been like an overturning of their world, something as calamitous as war or invasion, with every familiar routine undermined and some things destroyed, so I grew into my new social condition: living intensely at weekends with a woman with whom I could have no true conversation, whom I had no wish to 'take out' or to present to anyone.

And then, about nine or ten years ago, when you had just left the ruins of your Africa and were in West Berlin, minutes away from the ruins of the East, about that time I made a literary discovery. I read selections from the journals of a Victorian gentleman called A. J. Munby, and found a fellow.

Munby was born in 1828 and died in 1910. This makes him the exact contemporary of Tolstoy. He was a highly educated man, a fine and vivid writer in the effortless Victorian way, and he was deep in the intellectual and artistic life of his time. He knew many of the great names. Some, like Ruskin and William Morris, he knew by sight. When he was still a very young man he could greet Dickens in the street and then in a few words in his journal he could pin down the physical appearance of the fifty-two-year-old author: a dandy, a bit of an actor, vain of his slender figure, his hat tilted on his head.

But Munby – like Ruskin and like Dickens – had a sexual secret. Munby was passionately interested in working women. He liked women who did heavy work with their hands and literally got their hands dirty. He liked seeing servant women in their dirt, as he said, with their hands and faces black with soot and grime. And it is astonishing to us today how many dirty jobs of the time, cleaning fireplaces and so on, were done by women without tools, only with bare and uncovered hands. When these hands were washed they showed rough and thick and red. Ladies' hands were white and small. Munby's preference, away from drawing rooms, was for those red hands which, unless covered by the elbow-length gloves of fashion, could always give a working woman away.

Munby talked to any number of these women in the street. He sketched them. He had them photographed. He was an early amateur of photography. He posed women colliery workers in their coarse, heavily patched trousers, legs crossed sometimes, leaning on their man-sized shovels, looking hard and bemused at the photographer, one or two finding enough vanity for a smile. There is nothing pornographic in Munby's photographs and drawings, though for Munby the subject would doubtless have had some erotic charge.

For most of his life he had a secret liaison with a servant woman. She was tall and robust, a head above most people in the street. Munby liked women of size and strength. He liked the idea of this woman friend of his continuing to work as a servant in other houses; and though she sometimes complained about the inconsiderateness of her employers, he was not too eager to emancipate her. He liked to see the woman in her working dirt. She understood his fetish and didn't mind: before meeting Munby she had longed in a dreamy way to have a gentleman as a lover or husband. Sometimes, though rarely in the beginning, they lived together in the same house. Then, when people called, the woman had to get up from her drawing-room chair and pretend to be the maid. In the journal there is no hint of sex in the relationship, though this might only have been Victorian reticence.

For a man of Munby's tastes Victorian London would have been full of excitement. What pleasure, for instance, in a Bloomsbury square, to see, at six in the evening, every basement window lit up, each with its special treasure displayed as on a stage: a servant woman sitting on a chair, waiting to be called.

And just as in Munby's journal there is a sense of an encircling London servant life, full of pain and pleasure for him, so for me, with Marian, though I closed my mind to what she did when she wasn't with me, there came fragments, developing after a time into a full picture, of a frightening and brutal council-estate life I had never really known.

During the week Marian lived in her council house with the 'mistakes' Jo had mentioned to me right at the beginning. The mistakes were two: two children by different men. I gathered early on that the first of those men was a 'drifter'. It was one of Marian's words; she made it sound almost technical, almost an occupation that might be entered in social security or other government forms. *Occupation: Drifter*. The drifter was dark-haired. The hair was important: Marian mentioned it more than once, as if it explained everything.

And Marian herself had been one of four mistakes her mother had made with three different men. After these four mistakes Marian's mother, still only in her twenties, came upon a man she really fancied. It was what she had been waiting for all her life. Love: it was her destiny. She didn't hesitate. She left the four mistakes and went off with the man, to another house on the council estate. There was some trouble with the authorities then, because Marian's mother wanted to keep on claiming the benefits that the four mistakes had brought her. Somehow that matter was smoothed over, and Marian's mother lived with her man until he got tired of her and ran off somewhere with somebody else. It was the way of life down there.

This kind of thing happens elsewhere as well, but what is interesting to me is that at no stage was Marian's mother required by anyone in authority to live with the material or financial consequences of her decisions. There was always a council house available, and always a benefit of some sort. You might say that for Marian's mother every action brought an official reward. The people who paid were the children, the mistakes. And I suppose it can be said that they weren't being punished in any special way: they were only being trained for council-estate life, the way Marian's poor mother had been trained in her childhood, by other people and other events.

Marian and the other mistakes were taken into 'care'. A terrible technical word, and this was the most terrible part of Marian's childhood. It was a story of beatings and sexual abuse and repeated hopeless running away. Later Marian realised that other horrors might have befallen a young child on her own in the streets. Somehow the child endured and went through the government mill. She went to various correction schools. At one of them she learned to swim. It became the greatest thing in her life. And all this while there were days when Marian saw her mother driving by, living out her other life.

When that life of her mother's came to an end, her mother reappeared, and there was then something like a family life again, in another council house. As part of that life Marian and the others sometimes were taken by their mother on shoplifting excursions to supermarkets and local stores. They did very well. Sometimes they were caught, but then Marian and the other mistakes did what they had been told to do: they screamed the store down, and they were always let go. In time these excursions stopped.

Everyone Marian knew on the estate had a life that was like a version of her own.

Learning about this early life of Marian's, I began to understand her dark and withdrawn bedroom mood: the dead eyes, the shuttered mind. And then I wished I didn't know what I had got to know. I associated it with an awful and pathetic episode I came upon in Munby. A little paragraph, which I wished I hadn't read. Munby one day, either in a private house to which he had been admitted, or in a hotel, entered a room and saw a chambermaid standing with her back to him. He spoke to her and she turned. She was young and had a sweet face, with manners to match. She was holding a chamber pot with one hand and stirring the contents with her other uncovered hand: suggesting that there were solids in the chamber pot.

Something of this sorrow and disgust came to me when I

thought of Marian's past. It came upon me at our most intimate moments.

I knew the council estate where the bad drama of her childhood had been played out. To her at the time that drama would have seemed unending. I had passed many times the very ordinary place where she had been taken into care and from which she had tried to run away. It was as though, for her, but not for me, who drove by unseeing, unknowing, unthinking, existing almost in a separate age, an exact moral parallel of the Dickens world still existed. That parallel was concealed from the rest of us by the bright paint of the council houses, the parked motorcars, and our too easy ideas of social change.

Once, very slowly, over the period of a year or two, the council houses were refurbished. I had noticed it only with a quarter of my mind, wondering, with a little anxiety about builders, about the work that had to be done in the St John's Wood house.

One Friday evening a taxi-driver from the station rank said to me as we drove by, 'You can change the houses. You can't change the people.'

What he said was witty, but I was sure he had got it from somebody else. He was a council-estate man. He had told me that, and I knew that in his semi-criminal way he was speaking to me as to an outsider, telling me what he thought I wanted to hear.

Yet I feel, taking the taxi-driver's point now, as I am talking to you, that our ideas of doing good to other people, regardless of their need, are out of period, a foolish vanity in a changed world. And I have grown to feel, making that point much larger, that the nicer sides of our civilization, the compassion, the law, may have been used to overthrow that civilization.

But it may be that these oppressive thoughts have come only from my grief at the end of my affair with Marian, and the end of the optimism she brought me.

* * *

These things have to end, I suppose. Even Perdita's affair with the man with the big London house will end one day. But through a foolish remnant of social vanity I hastened the end of my affair with Marian. It happened like this.

Jo, Marian's friend, decided that she wanted to have a proper wedding with the cook she had been living with for some years, and by whom she had already had a profitable mistake or two. She wanted the works. Church, decorated big car, white ribbons running from roof to radiator, top hat and morning coats, shiny white wedding dress, bouquet, photographer, reception at the local pub where they do these council-estate receptions. The works. And Jo wanted me to come. She had looked after my father and his house while he lived, and he had left her a few thousand pounds. It was this relationship with my father, rather than her friendship with Marian, that she claimed as the stronger bond between us. It could be said that in the pettiest way she was a family retainer. It pleased her to make the point, and out of a most foolish kind of vanity and with every kind of misgiving – no one knows better than I that most class ideas are now out of period – I went.

It was as ghastly a parody as could be expected: Jo's brutish consort in top hat and all the rest, Jo's face glistening with make-up, eyelashes twinkling with glitter-dust. And yet the woman below all of that was trembling with real emotion.

I kept myself to myself, pretended not to see Marian and, more particularly, not to see who was with her. It was part of the deal with Marian and Jo. I got away as soon as I could, before the speeches, and the full merriment of the reception.

When I got to the car, some distance away, I found it dreadfully scratched up. On the front seats, in white paint or some sticky white pigment from a thick marker, there was, in a careful childish hand: *Piss off and stop scrooing my mother*, and *Piss off or else*.

It was a bad moment. That childish hand: I thought of the maid with the chamber pot in Munby.

I learned later from Marian that the child's father had been watching for me. Jo had told some people that I was coming to the wedding, never dreaming of the consequences.

The white paint the child had used had a special clinging quality. It was almost impossible to wipe away; it might have been devised for graffiti artists who wished to protect their work against smoke and weather and erasure. The white stuff filled every minute depression in the imitation leather of the car seats; on the smoother surface, even after it had been scrubbed off, it left a clear trace, like the drag of a snail, glinting when the light fell on it at a certain angle. It enabled Perdita, getting into the car soon after that wedding, to make one of her rare jokes. She said, 'Are those messages for me?'

The persecution that began that Saturday grew weekend by weekend. I was known; my car was known. I was followed. I was telephoned, and when I answered I was abused by the child. The feebleness of the man in the background, the father of the child, hiding behind the child, became more and more sinister to me.

I decided in the end to put a stop to our country weekends and to buy a flat for Marian in London. The idea delighted her, delighted her so much, the persecution could have been part of a plan: she had always wanted to live in London, to be near the shops instead of having to travel up to them.

But London is an enormous city. I had no idea where I might buy a modest but suitable flat. That was when I opened myself to one of the younger partners in our firm. I told him of my need, and told him a little more than I should. He lived in west London, in one of the smart Norman Shaw or Arts and Crafts houses near Turnham Green. He was friendly, even conspiratorial. He did not look down on me because of my relationship with Marian. He told me that Turnham Green was the place to look. Most of the Victorian or Edwardian houses in that area were being turned into flats; they were a quarter or a third of the price of flats nearer the centre.

And Turnham Green – a good journey south and west of St John's Wood – was where I bought. Marian relished the name; she spoke it again and again, as though it was a magical name in a fairy story. And when she learned that there was an Underground railway line that would take her from Turnham Green straight to Piccadilly Circus in twenty or twenty-five minutes it was almost more than she could bear. We decided to forget the council house in the country, to leave it to Marian's mistakes and the father of her second child. Because Marian, like her mother before her, wished now, with this vision of London before her, to be free of her mistakes.

This happened about eighteen months before you came. And, without wishing to frighten you, I think I should tell you that I fought your case with the very last of the optimism that came to me through Marian. Because, as anyone could have foreseen, that move to London was calamitous for me and for her. For me for many years Marian had been a weekend relationship. So intense on Friday and Saturday that on Sunday I was always glad to get away from her. Now she was, so to speak, always there. There was no longer that weekend intensity, and without that intensity she became banal. Even sexually, which I would never have thought possible. The whole pattern of my life was broken.

It was a failure of imagination on my part. So many calamities, big and small, are: the failure or inability to work out the day-to-day consequences, over a period, of our actions. A few years before you came to England I got to know a writer. He worked all week in the British Museum reading room and did his writing at the weekend. All week, sitting high in the reading room, he had a whole world under his direct gaze; all week his imagination was fed. The weekend fiction he did was immensely successful. People would go to the reading room only to have a glimpse of the famous man at his ordinary weekday duties: beaky-faced, making small, abrupt, nervous movements. In some such way, two centuries before, the ragged poor would go to the French royal palaces to see the king dine or get ready for bed. And, indeed, a little like the king, the writer took his position too much for granted, the celebrity, the talent. He began to feel cramped by his job in the British Museum. He gave it up and retired to the country and set himself up as a full-time writer. His writing changed. He no longer had a world under his gaze. His imagination became starved. His writing became overblown. The great books, which would have kept the good early books alive, never came. He died penniless. His books have vanished. I could see this writer's predicament very clearly. But I couldn't see my own.

And the same could be said of Marian. She had never seen the possibility of solitude in London. She had never seen that there was only so much of a day that could be spent looking at the shops. She had never imagined that Turnham Green, of the beautiful, verdant name, could become a prison. She began to long for what she had left behind. She became irritable. I was always glad now to get away from her, but now there was no intensity, no sexual fatigue. Our time together became pointless. We could see each other very clearly and we didn't like what we saw. So it wouldn't have mattered if I did as she endlessly asked and spent more time with her; that really wasn't what she wanted. She wanted to go back home. She wanted her old friends. She was like those people who retire to a place where they have holidayed, and in this holiday place become frantic with boredom and solitude.

It would have been better if, like Marian's mother or like many of Marian's friends, I had made a clean break. But I didn't have the courage or the brutality. It wasn't in my nature or upbringing. I hung on, attempting reconciliations that were empty, and in the process killing every last possibility of renewed passion, since the sexual delirium that altered the other person for me simply wasn't there now, and I saw the other person plain.

My life with Marian became almost like my life with Perdita. St John's Wood and Turnham Green: both these places with beautiful country names became hateful to me. It's been like that for all the time you've been here. That was why I was anxious for you to stay in the house in St John's Wood. It at least gave me something to come back to.

It was in this mood that I introduced Marian to the friend and legal colleague who lived in Turnham Green. I was hoping to be rid of her, and that was how it worked out. He dangled beautiful new names and old romantic ideas before her: Paris, France, the south of France. And – out of that social greed which I had known and loved for so long – she ran to him. So I was free of her, but at the same time I knew the most painful kind of jealousy. I did the work I had to do, I came home and talked to you, but my head was full of sexual pictures from the time of my passion, the passion which was now beyond me. I imagined her words. I never thought it was possible to suffer so much.

At about this time, too, the property caper took a bad turn. And now I am facing a challenge which I never thought I would have to face. I never wanted to die full of hate and rage, like my father. I wanted to go like Van Gogh, as I have told you. Smoking my pipe, or doing the equivalent of that. Contemplating my art, or my life, since I have no art, and feeling hatred for no one.

I wonder if I'll have the courage or the strength of the great man. Already I begin to feel, as yet in a small way, the great solace of hate. Perhaps my foolish little pictures will hang in another house somewhere and I will slowly see them blur below the grimy glass.

TWELVE

Magic Seeds

THAT WAS THE story Roger told, in bits, not in sequence, and over many weeks.

All this time Willie was doing his idle little job on the building magazine in Bloomsbury. Every morning he walked down to the Maida Vale main road and waited by preference for the number eight bus that took him very close to where he had to go. And all this time, sometimes in the office, sometimes in his room in the house in St John's Wood, he was trying to write a letter to his sister Sarojini. His mood changed as he heard Roger's story, and the letter changed.

Dear Sarojini, I am glad you are back in Berlin and doing your television work. I wish I could be with you. I wish I could turn the clock back nine or ten years. I have such memories of going to the KDW and having champagne and oysters —

He stopped writing and thought, 'I have no business to rebuke her, however indirectly, for going off to the guerrillas. The decision in the end was mine. I was responsible for all my actions. I got off remarkably cheaply, if Roger only knew. It would be awful if one day he found out. I think of that as the true betrayal.'

The next letter, perhaps a week or two later, began: *Things are changing here for me. I don't know how much longer I can keep on living as a guest of these nice people in this lovely house in this lovely area. When I arrived I was in a daze. I took everything for granted. I took the house for granted, though even on that first night I thought the picture-window view of the small green garden at the back was magical. But I thought of the house as a London house. Now I know London better and this St John's Wood house has spoiled me for living anywhere else. I don't know how I will buckle down to living somewhere else and doing a real job. The minute you start thinking like that London becomes another kind of city. It clutches at your heart.*

He put aside this letter. He thought, 'I mustn't write to her like this. I am no longer a child. I mustn't write like this to someone who can't change things for herself or for me.'

A long time later, perhaps a month later, he began another letter. This one occupied him for some weeks. *Because of my work I think I really should try to do something in the architecture line. It would take eight years or so (I imagine) to become qualified. This would take me up to sixty. This would still give me ten or twelve or fifteen active and satisfying years in the profession. The difficulty there is that to any logical mind it is absurd for a man of fifty to start learning a profession. The main difficulty is that to carry it out I would need an injection of optimism. My friend here used to get his optimism at weekends from a woman he adored but could hardly speak to. He survived on that optimism for years. I don't want to go down that road again, and these things cannot simply be ordered anyway.*

The only optimism I had was when I was a child and had a child's view of the world. I thought for two or three years with that child's view that I wanted to be a missionary. This was only a wish for escape. That was all my optimism amounted to. The day I understood the real world the optimism leaked out of me. I was born at the wrong time. If I was born now, in the same place, the world would have a different look. Too late for me, unfortunately. And with that pathetic little self that now exists inside me somewhere, the self that I recognise so easily, I put aside the architecture dream and think that I should get some undemanding little job somewhere and live in some little flat somewhere and hope that the neighbours are not too noisy. But I know enough now to understand that life can never be simplified like that, and that there would be some little trap or flaw in that dream of simplicity, of just letting one's life pass, of treating one's life only as a way of passing the time.

My friend here says that the happiest and most successful people are those who have very precise goals, limited and attainable. We know such a man. He is an African or a West Indian African, now a highly respected diplomat. His father or grandfather went to West Africa from the West Indies in the 1920s or 1930s as part of the Back to Africa movement. Our African friend at an early age (no doubt through some powerful feminine contact) developed one ambition (apart of course from making a lot of money), and this was to have sex only with white women and then one day to have a white grandchild. He has succeeded in both things. His half-English son, Lyndhurst, now a man of about thirty, has had two children by a pure-white aristocratic lady. One of these children is as white as white can be. The whole thing is being sealed this Saturday by the wedding of the half-English boy and his lady, mother of his white child. It is the fashion here, babies before wedding bells.

* * *

THE WEDDING WAS in a prettily named village a long way to the north of London. Perdita didn't go. Roger and Willie went by train, and booked into a hotel for the night.

Roger said, 'We are meant to dance through the night. No, not *through*. That sounds too much like hard labour. We are meant to *dance away* the night.'

They drove in their hired car through what would have looked like woodland if there hadn't been so many pubs and guest houses and small hotels with car parks beside the winding road.

Roger said, 'The founder of the girl's family was actually a great man, early in the nineteenth century. He was a supporter of the practical scientist Faraday, who was a kind of early Edison. Faraday was a poor London Oxford Street boy, and the aristocratic scientific figure to whom he attached himself in the early days treated him as a valet. Something happened to the family after this moment of glory. They produced no other great figure. Complacency perhaps, or genetic failure. In the great imperial period which followed, while so many other families came up, they went down, generation after generation. Some years ago they decided to let their big house rot. They couldn't afford to keep it up, and the heritage laws didn't allow them to pull it down. They took the roof off. In a short time the house was a ruin. They live in a cottage not far off.'

Friendly home-painted signs marked the turn-off to where the wedding was to take place. Not a church.

Roger said, 'The modern fashion. You don't go to them. You get them to come to you.'

Tall old neglected-looking trees, hung with vines and vegetable parasites, and with ragged broken-off branches, shaded the narrow road. More friendly hand-done signs directed them off the road and up a long-grassed meadow. They parked there – not far from a many-coloured painted bus marked *Aruba-Curaçao: the Band* in a comet-like arc, with a big red star at the top – and when they got out they could hear the roar from a motorway or main road two or three hundred yards away, below the meadow slope.

This was the view, once grand, that the big house looked over. The roofless house, an established ruin now, was strangely matter-of-fact, grey but not at all ghostly, more like a big piece of conceptual art set down with deliberation in clean, tall, vivid green grass. It could be taken in at a glance. And that was how the wedding guests appeared to deal with it, offering the ruin a glance, but not dawdling, moving on along the narrow rough road to the tented enclosure a little way ahead where people were assembling.

At this stage people were in two distinct streams, the dark and the fair. Soon, and nervously, they began to converge; and then in the full convergence, further on, Marcus could clearly be seen: very black, still slender, sharp-featured, grey-haired, benign, eager. Eagerness, enthusiasm: it had always been his style. He was shaking hands and at the same time throwing his head back in a way that Willie remembered.

Willie said, 'I was expecting to see him in a top hat and

morning coat. It's a bit of a letdown seeing him in a plain dark suit.'

Roger said, 'It's not a morning occasion.'

Willie said, 'Do you see any sign in him of the moral infirmity that shows with age?'

'I was looking for it. But I must confess I see no such thing. I see no intellectual strife. I see only a great happiness, a great benignity. And that's extraordinary, when you think that since you met him he has lived through any number of revolutions and civil wars. Small tribal affairs, of no consequence to the rest of us, but very nasty. Torture is torture, whether the cause is small or great. There would have been many occasions, I'm sure, when Marcus was within an inch of being hurried out at sunrise to some tropical beach of his childhood, stripped of his clothes, knocked about a little or a lot, shot or clubbed to death to the sound of the waves. He survived because he kept his eye on the ball. He had his own idea of what was important to him. It gave him an unusual balance in Africa. He didn't strike foolish postures. He always looked to mediate. He survived, and here he is.'

'Roger.'

'Marcus. You remember Willie?'

'Of course I remember him. Our author.'

Willie said, 'A great day for you.'

Marcus was gracious. 'They are a lovely family. Lyndhurst chose well.'

Other well-wishers pressed, and Willie and Roger left Marcus and went on to where a series of tents or canopies had been raised above the derelict gardens of the big house. From a distance these canopies created the effect of a camp. The first canopied enclosure they came to was the half-dead orchard. In one corner chain upon chain of ivy fattened the lower trunk of a dying old horse-chestnut tree. Often, where a branch had fallen off an old apple tree, a hole showed in the trunk: vegetable nature, at this stage of its cycle, seemingly human, disassembling itself. But the light below the canopy softened everything, gave every ruined tree an extra life, gave every spindly branch an extra importance, made the abandoned orchard look like a stage set, made it miraculous, a pleasure to be in.

Girls from the village appeared here with trays of cheap drink, and gave everyone something to do.

There was no sign as yet of Lyndhurst or his bride. Instead, as though they wished to steal the thunder of bride and groom, there was a startling black and white couple: like a 'human installation' of modern art, miming out the symbolism of the occasion. The white girl, in a blue skirt and red silk top, clung to the man around his waist, hiding her face against his bare chest. And everything about the man called for attention. He was slender, of the blackest black, in a black suit. His white shirt was expensive. It had a lifted collar, and was open almost down to the waist, showing a perfect inverted triangle of flawless black skin. He wore tinted glasses. His skin was oiled, with shea butter or some other African nut-derived cream, and this butter or cream seemed to be melting in the warmth of the afternoon, even in the shade of the canopy. This oiliness seemed to be threatening the crispness and snowiness of the white shirt, but that effect was clearly intended. His hair was done in an extraordinary way: reduced to little glistening balls, so widely separated you felt that the hair between might have been shaved off, down and across. The close-shaved scalp almost seemed to run with oil. He wore sandals without socks and appeared to stand on the russet outline of his soles and heels. This russet colour was the colour of the logo on the sandal strap. From head to toe he was a fantastic production. Every detail was considered. He drew all eyes. He outshone everyone, but he himself was lost behind his tinted glasses, concentrating on his burden. With the girl clinging on he appeared to be walking sideways and sometimes backwards because of her weight. People made room for them. They were like stars in the middle of a chorus on a stage.

Marcus had come up to where Roger and Willie were standing. He said, 'This is scandalous. It makes a mockery of a sacred occasion. I assure you they are not from Lyndhurst's side.'

But he too, when he passed the couple, gave them much room, as people do at an exhibition of disturbing human 'installations'.

There was a general gentle moving about in the various enclosures, people picking their way carefully on the uneven ground, women in high heels walking as on broken glass. Willie and Roger, who knew no one apart from Marcus, tried to distinguish the supporters of the dark and the fair. It was not easy. Things became clearer when it was time for the ceremony.

The ceremonial enclosure had a box hedge that had grown very high on all four sides. Many projecting branches had been roughly cut back. Chickens had recently been kept here, and there was a faint smell for those who could recognise it. In one box wall there was a gap, and in the facing wall was another gap; so the enclosure was perfect for its purpose on this afternoon. The main figures in the ceremonial came in formally through one gap. The guests entered by the other. A rectangle of green canvas resting on the grass marked the sacramental area. There were a few chairs here, in two separate sets, for the two sides. Marcus sat separated by the narrowest of aisles from his son's in-laws. His authority and pleasure, and the simple strength of his blackness, contrasted with the paleness of their remote, almost absent, dignity.

Roger said softly to Willie, 'They're confused. They're not too well educated. That was the smart thing at one time. But now they don't know who they are and what's expected of them. The world has changed much too quickly for them. Perhaps they don't feel a great deal about anything, and have been confused for the last hundred years.'

The priest's vestments, too ornate in the setting, sat stiffly on him. He seemed to be unused to them – they seemed to be heavy for him, to be threatening to slip off his shoulders: perhaps he hadn't put them on correctly – and he appeared to be fighting back a smile at the dignity of the garments even while struggling as quietly as he could to keep the extravagant things in place.

And after all this – the signs, the setting, the tents and canopies, the miraculous strained light – Lyndhurst, big-chested, thuggish-looking, with Africa more than half scrubbed off him, and his pale plain bride, in her simple silk frock, seemed curiously ordinary. Even with the theatre of the two pages, their children, one dark, one fair, the fair supporting the groom, the dark supporting the bride. Bride and groom had wished to have a simple occasion, and they had succeeded more than they knew.

The priest had a faraway plebeian accent, very difficult for many people in the enclosure, and he was as little used to reading aloud as he was to his fine vestments. He chewed up his words; their fineness seemed to embarrass him.

Someone from one side read a speech from Othello, and someone from the other side began to read a Shakespeare sonnet. Before the sonnet was through one of the pages farted, and no one knew whether it was the dark page or the fair one. But the guests lined up correctly on this matter: the dark people thought the dark child had farted; the fair people thought it was the fair child.

The fair child began to cry. She was in some distress. Marcus ran to her, took her little hand and began slowly to walk her out of the box enclosure to where the toilet facilities were. Someone, an old lady, seeing the old grey-haired black man running to the distressed white child, imagined old sentimentalities and involuntarily clapped, very delicately; then someone else clapped; and then Marcus and his grandchild were walking to general applause, and Marcus, understanding only after some seconds that the applause was meant for him, and meant kindly, began to smile, looking to left and right, bowing slightly, and leading the white child to where she wanted to go.

The Aruba-Curaçao band, when they began to play, were fierce. The black drummer sat at a drum as high as a dining table. At first, easing himself into his chair, and settling his wrists on the edge of the high drum, he looked only like a man about to eat or to write a letter. But then, while he held his upper body perfectly still, his big hinged hands began to work. He struck with the heel of the palm, the full palm, the palm immediately below the fingers, and the fingers, striking them flat and with the tips. He worked every part of the open hand separately. His fluttering palms showed red, creating a volume of sound that rocked and boomed below the tents and put an end to easy conversation. Other metallic instruments of the Dutch Antillean band then obliterated such patterns as the drum made, and over it all someone began to sing an amplified song in a Dutch Antillean patois that no one there could have understood. The din was fearful, but some of the fair women in new frocks were swinging their slender shanks, as if they were picking out a beat, and it was already too much to resist, though the dinner was still some time off, and the dancing away of the night was not to begin until after dinner.

Roger said, 'I'm getting a migraine.'

He and Willie walked back to their hired car. At this distance it was possible to hear something of the two or three patterns of the music.

Roger said, 'It's meant to stun you. I don't know what it tells you about the occasion we've just left. I imagine music like that being played on a Dutch slave plantation in Surinam in the seventeenth or eighteenth century. Played on a Saturday or Sunday evening, to reconcile the slaves to Monday morning, and giving some visiting Dutch artist an idea for a plantation night-piece. I've seen a painting like that.'

* * *

THEY DROVE BACK to the hotel, along the winding road, and they found, to their amazement, that the music was still with them. They could, if they had known, and if a path existed, have walked from the hotel up to the cliff where the abandoned big house was.

All night Willie heard the music. It invaded his sleep and mingled with other memories. Africa, with the conical grey stone hills and Africans walking on the red paths beside the asphalt road. The burnt-out concrete houses, smoke-stained around the windows. The forest and the men in olive uniforms with caps with the red satin star, and the endless marching. The strange jail where, as on a slave ship, the prisoners lay side by side on the floor in two rows separated by a central aisle. All night it seemed to him as well that he had found something good to write to Sarojini about. This thing eluded him. He looked for it, through all the slave music, and in the morning all he was left with was: 'It is wrong to have an ideal view of the world. That's where the mischief starts. That's where everything starts unravelling. But I can't write to Sarojini about that.'

September 2002–September 2003